GIRL ZERO

www.**penguin**.co.uk

Also by A. A. Dhand

STREETS OF DARKNESS

For more information on A. A. Dhand,
see his website at www.aadhand.com

GIRL ZERO

A. A. Dhand

BANTAM PRESS

LONDON • TORONTO • SYDNEY • AUCKLAND • JOHANNESBURG

TRANSWORLD PUBLISHERS
61–63 Uxbridge Road, London W5 5SA
www.penguin.co.uk

Transworld is part of the Penguin Random House group of companies
whose addresses can be found at global.penguinrandomhouse.com

First published in Great Britain in 2017 by Bantam Press
an imprint of Transworld Publishers

A CIP catalogue record for this book
is available from the British Library.

ISBNs 9780593076668 (hb)
9780593076675 (tpb)

Typeset in 11.5/14.5pt Aldus by Falcon Oast Graphic Art Ltd.
Printed and bound by Clays Ltd, Bungay, Suffolk.

Penguin Random House is committed to a sustainable
future for our business, our readers and our planet. This book
is made from Forest Stewardship Council® certified paper.

1 3 5 7 9 10 8 6 4 2

In memory of 'Dhand News' 1981–2016.
Gone but never forgotten.

PROLOGUE

THORNY BRAMBLES TORE AT the little girl's face as she ran desperately away.

She wiped blood from her temple and sprinted faster, shredding the skin from her bare feet on the bristly undergrowth of the forest floor. The ground beneath was solid, baked by an overwhelming heat that rose heavily from the earth. She had never experienced anything like it.

Where am I?

Where's Mum? I was with her yesterday.

He was gaining on her, this man. She could hear twigs snapping behind, her name being called. She didn't believe the concern in his voice.

He'd told her he owned her.

She cried out, shrieking for her mother until her voice cracked.

There must be someone who can hear?

She wasn't certain there was.

The smells were different here: exhaust fumes, manure and sweat.

The van had stopped abruptly, and when the back doors had been flung open she'd taken her chance, surprising them; lashing out and breaking free.

Her pursuer was relentless. She had caught a glimpse of him as she'd fled. Heavy-set, balding, with gleaming gold rings on his left hand.

She burst out of the forest, the darkness fading, and was confronted by a sight that evaporated any scrap of hope.

Open fields.

Stretching far into the distance. Green, brown and yellow.

Nowhere to hide.

The realization hit her like the heat had.

It was over. No escape.

She turned aggressively, determined not to be taken. She'd learned how to fight on the toughest estate in Bradford, but he gave her no chance. Before she'd locked eyes with her captor, he kicked her legs from underneath her. She hit the ground hard and a sack was thrown over her, overwhelming her with the smell of potatoes, rough fibres scratching her skin.

Unable to see, she lashed out, screaming wildly, but he grabbed the sack and began dragging her back the way she had come.

Then he stopped and she felt him straddle her, knees digging into her sides, his bulk pinning her to the forest floor. Jagged splinters pierced her skin, drawing blood.

Strong hands seized her neck through the rough fabric.

A sudden sharp scratch in her arm and it all came flooding back: she had felt this before.

A blackness invaded her vision and the world began to spin as the sound of her attacker's heavy breathing grew fainter. His words, in a language she didn't understand, floated away.

The grip around her neck relaxed, the coarse sensation of the sack across her face faded and a sudden warmth enveloped her.

A nightmare.

That was all.

She opened her eyes, her head heavy and spinning.

The darkness was absolute, the atmosphere thick, the air rancid and damp. She called out, her voice echoing, alien and frightened.

Not a nightmare.

She moved to stand but it made her feel more vulnerable, like she might somehow be seen, so she cowered, huddling her arms around her knees despite the heat.

She tried to scan the room – to make anything out in the dark. There was nothing; escape seemed impossible.

The dark had always terrorized her. At night her mother had left a bedside lamp on so she wouldn't be afraid.

A pernicious, crippling fear was making her breathless.

I'm going to die here.

She clamped her eyes shut and imagined she was at home, in the darkness of the cupboard below the stairs where her mother sometimes sent her when she was bad.

She started to cry – slowly at first, before hysterical sobs took over.

Then, everything changed.

A voice to her left. Young, like hers.

'Don't worry,' it whispered, 'you're not alone.'

ONE

Eleven years later

ANOTHER MURDER IN BRADFORD.

Another.

Detective Inspector Harry Virdee had taken the call an hour ago, a far from unusual event for a Monday morning.

Damn city was killing itself; killing him.

Why today?

Bad karma. No, the worst karma. Like disturbing a minute's silence for the dead.

Shit, he was getting more and more superstitious every day. He'd known this would happen when he married Saima.

What's next, Harry? Avoiding walking under ladders, fearing the number thirteen?

Bradford didn't appear to care for karma, Harry's or its own.

Gotham. That's still what the papers were calling it. It hadn't helped that the article had gone viral.

Pissed Harry right off.

He checked the time on the dashboard.

03:50.

He had left home shortly after receiving the call, but wasn't at the murder scene yet. Instead he was parked outside a house four miles away in Ravenscliffe, one of the most deprived areas of the city. Residents here were a third more likely to receive government benefits and crime was out of control.

Harry's team were regulars around here.

The occupants of number 19 Belle Avenue had never been interested in benefits.

Barry King had been a postman. His wife, Sheila, was a dinner lady. They'd both been signed off work.

Clinical depression, after losing their only son. Michael, nineteen at the time, had attempted to rob Harry's father's corner shop. The robbery had gone badly.

Wild arterial spray.

Harry had gone to his mother's defence and stabbed a pair of scissors into Michael's throat. Worse still, he'd got away with it. The guilt had been suffocating him for the last twenty years. One way or another it needed dealing with, and he knew the process started with the short journey through a rusted gate and up the footpath to a green door.

To tell Mr and Mrs King what? That he was sorry?

For which part?

That their son had joined a bad crowd?

Or that Harry had allowed someone else to take the blame for a murder he had committed?

He switched off the engine of his ageing BMW and removed the keys. His eyes lingered on his keyring, a picture of his one-year-old son, Aaron. He smiled at the image, then glanced at two unopened presents on the passenger seat.

Today was Diwali, the Indian New Year where gifts were exchanged and candles lit as a reminder that light would always overcome dark. Harry was no longer a practising Sikh but he entertained the tradition as his wife was determined to fuse their different backgrounds, which meant celebrating everything – as much for their son as to prove their families wrong about their marriage.

Harry glanced at the house.

You put the lights out in there for ever.

What if Aaron got involved with a bad crowd? And it cost him his life?

Is that fair? Is that reasonable?

'Fuck,' he whispered and ran his hand over his face, scratching at thick stubble. 'Argh,' he said and clamped his eyes shut. 'Why do you keep doing this? Let it go. Let it fucking go.'

It was no coincidence Harry had ended up working in HMET, the Homicide Major Enquiry Team, in Bradford.

Trying to correct his karma.

His colleagues thought he was just obsessive. They didn't know.

Only one person knew the truth: his brother Ronnie, who had taken the blame and gone to prison for Michael King's murder. It was a decision that had shaped the rest of his life.

Two decades on, Ronnie Virdee was the most powerful criminal in Bradford, the head of a cartel that controlled the supply of drugs on the city streets . . .

Harry focused on the door.

Maybe tomorrow?

Diwali. New beginnings.

New choices.

Harry started the car and pulled away from the house, heading towards the murder scene.

Wapping School had been built in 1877, on the fringes of the city centre. Like much of the city, the school had decayed into ruin.

Harry parked beside two patrol cars. He glanced towards the night sky, black like the soot soiling the once-impressive Victorian building.

A dead body here. It felt symbolic.

He got out of the car, opened the boot and pushed aside a fifty-shot firework. Bonfire night was two days away but he'd planned to surprise his wife and light the firecracker tonight. Saima might have been thirty-five, three years younger than Harry, but she still reverted to an excitable child at the mention of fireworks. More importantly, it was the perfect way to celebrate their first Diwali with Aaron.

He slipped on a raincoat, grabbed his SOCO suit and a torch. Beside them was a large black holdall that contained Harry's bulletproof vest and an illegal stun-gun – gifts from Harry's brother and permanent reminders that he was walking a glass tightrope, one apt to break at any moment.

You get him to stop, there is no other choice.

Harry closed the boot and leaned against the car. He saw the outline of a uniformed officer coming his way. A patrol bobby – first responder.

'Morning, Detective Inspector.'

Harry acknowledged him with a nod and got the headlines. DS Gemma Eccles was inside. She'd been the one to call him in.

He walked behind the PC, shining his torch up on to a building in woeful condition, the metal fencing around its perimeter breached in many places. The school had been derelict for years. Like so many heritage sites in Bradford, it had fallen into disrepair and simply been left to rot.

Harry focused on a white plaque by the entrance.

Wapping First School.

A vandal had spray-painted a red line through the first word and scrawled *Pakis First School.*

Harry stepped through a gaping hole where the entrance had once been, into a graveyard of broken dreams. The roof was missing, moonlight shining into the room. Dark, unsettling graffiti across the walls showed a veiled Islamic woman crying, her cowering body surrounded by what looked like skinheads. The school might once have been a refuge for vulnerable kids from the local area; now the place was infected by a dank misery.

Harry and the PC picked their way carefully across a floor strewn with old needles, used condoms and pornographic magazines. There were dead rats and the carcass of what might have been a cat.

Dust swirled, forcing the taste of abandonment down the men's throats.

With deep unease, Harry arrived at the far end of the building: a disused swimming pool. Now simply a pit in the ground, twenty metres by ten, one end filled with rubble from a partially collapsed ceiling.

In the centre, lying awkwardly across the bottom, was a body.

A murder case on the morning of Diwali.

Harry was briefed by his DS, listening as the ghoulish atmosphere of the place crept into his mind. An anonymous tip had led first responders to the body, but the caller hadn't stuck around. Harry moved away and lowered himself gingerly into the pit while Eccles finished her speech.

He approached the body, shining his torch on the floor, taking care where he placed his feet.

Realizing that he had been involuntarily holding his breath, he let it out slowly, watching it form a white mist in the chill as he squatted beside the remains.

He glanced once again around the room before his eyes settled on her and made a familiar silent promise.

I'll find out who did this.

For you.

And for me, to balance my karma.

Harry focused on the victim: Asian female, five-six, petite, maybe size eight; long black hair chaotically strewn across her face. It was hard to place her age.

She was on her back with a large kitchen knife sticking out of her chest.

Harry reached forward and shone his torch directly on the body.

Deep red stains on her white top.

A gold bangle on her left wrist; a Kara; a religious symbol of Sikhism.

Not stolen.

Harry had worn one for many years before he'd opted out of the Sikh faith.

He crouched beside the body, took a pen from his jacket pocket and used it to carefully move the girl's hair aside.

The blood drained from Harry's face and he felt unstable, as if the pool had suddenly begun to fill with water.

He knew that face.

A pain detonated hot and deep in his chest. He looked away, releasing a wounded cry. The victim was Harry's niece; daughter of the city's most dangerous man.

Bradford had been in perilous situations before, but it had seen nothing like the storm that was about to hit.

This murder would unleashed the wrath of two brothers.

One who enforced the rules.

And one who made his own.

TWO

A BATHTUB OF SKIN-WHITENING bleach swallowed Ali Kamran's body like a pill on the back of its tongue. The caustic burn on his skin brought relief from the nightmarish images that taunted him relentlessly.

Ali was breathing carefully through a wooden straw, an act he had rehearsed hundreds of times. But for the briefest of moments his lips twitched, breaking the seal and allowing the leaking liquid to burn on his tongue. The memory of his mother's voice always made him lose concentration.

Why did you curse my house?

Nobody will ever marry you looking like that.

You should have died in my womb.

Her words stung with an intensity the bleach never could.

After twenty minutes, Ali slowly raised his head, his face breaking through the sticky yellow surface. Keeping his eyes closed, he removed the straw from his mouth and reached for a towel to dry his face.

Once he could open his eyes, he stood up and systematically wiped bleach from his body. He'd used three towels by the time he stepped out of the tub.

Ali pulled on a pair of dirty white trainers and walked naked into his hallway, where the walls were covered in shattered mirrors and the floor glittered with razor-sharp pieces.

On the far side of the landing was an old Polaroid camera on a tripod. He sat on a chair in front of it and stared directly into the lens. He hit the timer switch and listened to the beeps, counting them until the camera flashed and took his picture. He remained seated until the photograph was processed and fell to the floor, coming to rest on shards of glass.

Ali took the photo into his bedroom. The room was sparsely furnished and the window boarded over, so light from the bare bulb overhead was reflected back unevenly at Ali from the hundreds of Polaroids that lined the walls. He added today's photo, minutely comparing it to the one from yesterday. Progress, he thought.

Inside the second bedroom, Ali's feet crunched on more glass as he took a seat on a rickety wooden stool. On the ageing desk in front of him were over seventy tubs and containers, all of them white plastic with neatly printed labels. He reached for the nearest one, unscrewing the lid and stroking his finger across the white unbroken surface of the contents.

One day.

After an hour's work, Ali lifted a jagged piece of mirror from the floor, paused nervously and turned it slowly until he saw a glimpse of his face. His hand tightened around it and there was the sudden warmth of blood across his fingers. He dropped the glass, grabbed a tissue and harshly, obsessively, rubbed at his skin.

Just short of two hours later, Ali's feet crunched their way downstairs, mirrors on both walls of the staircase also shattered, their remains coating each step.

In the living room, the far wall was covered in an enormous mirror that stretched from corner to corner, smashed in hundreds of different places. Ali scowled at distorted images of himself.

He slipped on a tight-fitting hoodie, as snug as a second skin, carefully drawing the hood secure across his face. Then he pulled a larger hoodie over the top, making sure its hood was tight over the first. He put on black combat pants; in each oversized pocket was a mirror, these ones intact. Finally, he walked back into the hallway, pausing outside the door to his cellar.

He smiled; it wasn't something he did often and it didn't suit him. Ali unlocked the first of three padlocks, feeling a surge of blood to his groin. His smile widened, make-up cracking around his lips.

Arriving at the bottom of the staircase, he turned on the light and looked towards the bed where a girl, *his girl*, lay peacefully, her back towards him, blonde peroxide curls falling down her shoulders.

He walked towards her, sat on the edge of the bed and put a hand on her naked body. Feeling its smoothness, Ali became more aroused, grabbing his crotch and slipping his hand inside his pants.

'You're so beautiful, Gori,' he whispered. 'So beautiful.'

He had renamed her 'Gori'; it was the Urdu word for 'white'.

Ali moved his hand from her body to her hair, feeling its silkiness.

'Look at me,' he said.

But she didn't. She remained perfectly still.

'We're nearly there, you know. Forty-eight hours from now? She'll be here.'

Ali leaned closer to her and ran his lips down her smooth, white body, momentarily allowing his rasping tongue to taste her.

'You are beautiful,' he whispered, paused, then added, 'but she's perfect.'

He walked to the other side of the room where a black silk scarf was covering a shelf which held a glass jar and an ageing bottle of chloroform. He slid his hand underneath the scarf, feeling the bottom of the hidden jar, and recoiled.

Not yet.

Not for another forty-eight hours.

He lifted an old Walkman from the shelf and slipped on the earphones but didn't press 'play'. He heard the faint memory of schoolgirls jeering and remembered them in a circle around his cowering body:

'Ring-a-ring-a-roses, Ali's face exploded.'

He walked back to the bed where Gori didn't resist, allowing him to turn her over and secure her wrists to the rickety metal bed frame. Ali undid his trousers and climbed on top of her, parting her legs, keeping his face to the side of hers so she couldn't clearly see it.

He pressed play on his Walkman and in the dim light of the cellar, Ali Kamran descended to the darkest of places, listening to the harrowing cries of a woman screaming.

THREE

WAPPING SCHOOL WAS BUSTLING with the sort of activity Harry was accustomed to as a DI, but not as one of the victim's family members.

Family? Could he even call himself that any more?

He hadn't seen Tara for four years. He remembered her laughing face as he crammed a large piece of cake into her mouth while Ronnie took pictures. Her sixteenth birthday: their last celebration as a family, before Harry's decision to marry Saima had put him on the outside.

Now Tara had been murdered on the streets of a city he was supposed to defend. A city Tara's father was supposed to run.

From a bench at the edge of the pool, Harry looked on as the area forensic manager liaised with the senior SOCO, their white suits in stark contrast to the surrounding gloom. A photographer was taking dozens of shots. Every time the flash went off, Harry saw Tara's bloodstained shirt. As he blinked the fluorescence from his eyes, he pictured Ronnie's face fracturing with an anger Harry knew he would be the one to counter.

Harry was squeezing his car keys, forcing them to bite into his skin as he watched the team erect a tent over Tara's body. The old school roof had more gaps than it did tiles and they needed to ensure the crime scene was protected.

He looked away as a dull anger started to set in.

That morning, when he'd received the call, he had thought about the family soon to be irretrievably damaged by the news.

His family. A family he was now a stranger to because he had chosen to marry a Muslim. The last time he'd seen his father, the old man had flown into a violent rage, forcing his mother to intervene. If she hadn't? Harry closed his eyes and tried to focus on the present.

He had always envisaged returning one day to open arms. Somehow. *Anyhow.*

Now he knew he would be returning to deliver the worst possible news.

Do your job like you've never done it before. For Tara. For them.

But his job had complications, and one of them was heading his way.

A slow, hesitant walk. Polished shoes. The hint of heels.

Smart grey suit. Blonde hair pulled into a tight ponytail.

'Harry.' It was Detective Superintendent Clare Conway.

'Clare,' replied Harry. Everyone else called her 'Ma'am'.

Harry was her best detective, closing more cases than all her other DIs put together.

He knew she wondered how he did it. They all did.

The truth was that he and his brother made a formidable team, controlling the streets of Bradford from opposite ends. Ronnie was the only member of Harry's family who hadn't disowned him.

It made for a tense partnership. There were rules. Both of them knew if one burned the other, he would ultimately burn himself.

How are you going to control Ronnie once this breaks?

How are you going to control yourself?

Conway took a seat on the bench next to Harry. They watched the SOCOs carry a body-bag into the tent, Harry clenching his teeth as he imagined them zipping Tara's body inside.

'Can't find the words?' he asked, pushing the image from his mind.

She put a hand on his arm and turned to face him. 'This isn't just another murder case. We'll get whoever did it.'

We.

'This is *my* case,' said Harry.

She squeezed his arm a little harder. 'Harry—'

'I'm not stepping aside.'

She sighed. Harry had known this would happen. It would be classed as a conflict of interest because the victim was family and Conway couldn't afford to have his judgement called into question.

'Don't make this any harder. You know—'

'I know I'm the best detective you've got. We both know that. Nothing's changed because it's Tara under that tent.'

'I wouldn't be doing my job if I didn't assign this away from you.'

'And I won't sleep at night until I get the bastard. Whether you like it or not, I'm working it.'

She removed her hand from his arm and they were momentarily blinded by a flash from the forensic photographer's camera. 'I'm giving it to Palmer,' she said, paused, then added, 'officially.'

Harry didn't reply. It was as good as a nod.

Palmer worshipped the ground Harry walked on, he wouldn't be a nuisance.

'I'll tell him to keep you updated,' she said, and stood up. Harry grabbed her arm.

'One thing.'

She turned to face him.

Harry got to his feet, towering above her. 'My family. Let me.'

She fixed him with intense blue eyes.

'Absolutely not. Not even the great Hardeep Virdee is immune from that kind of hurt.'

'I know.' Harry folded his arms across his chest. 'But he's my brother. Nobody knows better than I do how to handle this.'

'Are you two close?'

The answer was far from simple. He and Ronnie were danger-ously close, now more out of necessity than anything else. Harry knew that if his brother's underground activities were exposed, it would destroy what remained of his family.

'Close enough that I want to do this,' said Harry.

Conway hesitated. 'I'm sending someone with you.'

'I don't need—'

'I wasn't asking. Look, do you want to take some compassionate leave?'

'Yes,' said Harry, already starting to formulate his own investi-gation in his mind. Once he broke the news to Ronnie, his only hope would be to get to the killer first, before the whole thing exploded. 'I'll need to help with . . . arrangements.'

'Don't make life difficult for Palmer. He's a good guy. Give him space. I don't want to have to make this harder for you than it already is.' It was a warning that she'd be putting protocol first if push came to shove.

'Give me a week?' said Harry.

She nodded. 'I'm sorry, Harry. Truly I am.'

Harry left the crime scene in the early evening, after a long day overseeing the removal of Tara's body and ensuring that DI Palmer followed protocol to the last detail. He was en route to Ronnie's house in Thornton, a predominantly white middle-class village in Bradford West, isolated from the rest of the city by countryside. It was a different world out in the suburbs.

Harry turned into a winding gravel driveway but came to a halt ten metres short of Ronnie's Range Rover. Parked beside it was a Volvo Estate with a distinctive licence plate: R4 NJT.

Ranjit: Harry's father.

His parents had sold their corner shop a few months earlier and Ronnie had bought an enormous house so they could move in with him and his family. As the eldest child, it was expected of him, and he'd shouldered the cultural responsibility equably.

There were candles burning in every window and multicoloured lights hanging from the roof.

Diwali; the Indian festival of light.

A time for family celebrations.

A time when good overcomes evil.

Harry thought about his own home where his wife and son would be waiting for him to light their candles and open Diwali presents together.

He rubbed his hand across his temple, relieved he had ditched the family liaison officer Conway had appointed. This was a private affair.

The last thing he wanted was to see his father.

Or his mother. Harry didn't have the strength for that right now.

He gripped the steering wheel, resolve hardening his jawline. He had to go inside; it was the only way to ensure Ronnie wouldn't do anything stupid.

Like burn the damn city down.

There was a distinct possibility this was linked to Ronnie's business. But Harry was the only one in the family who knew that. Even Ronnie's wife, Mundeep, had no idea what he really did. Like everyone else, she thought he was a businessman; the boss of sixteen corner shops and a cash-and-carry.

Harry put the car in gear and crawled forward into the space beside the Volvo. Security lights flooded the area. No going back now.

He checked his mobile: five missed calls from Saima and a text showing a red, unhappy emoji.

Harry ignored it. He'd tell her everything when he got home.

God, he longed to hear her voice.

He got out of the car and leaned against it, staring at the front door. He had never been inside; Mundeep wouldn't allow it. Even though Harry and Mundeep – or Mandy, as he called her – had been close when they were younger, his decision to marry Saima had put an end to that instantly.

Harry now represented a dangerous message for her children; *marrying a Muslim was acceptable.* No responsible Sikh parent could afford to raise their children to believe that. On that score, Mandy was of the same opinion as Harry's father.

Looking up at the imposing farmhouse, it was as if the place was alive, breathing hostility.

He had done this so many times, broken the news, shown compassion, quietly speaking words no parent should ever have to hear. Keeping still and in control when everything around him fractured.

It was never easy, but tonight would pain both sides.

The only thing he could do was to show them that he too was hurting. That he wouldn't stop until they had justice. That this wasn't just 'the job'.

Harry turned back towards his car, afraid he would be tarnished with delivering toxic news every time he saw his family. *Dad, I've fallen in love with a Muslim girl and we're getting married.*

Mundeep, your daughter has been murdered.

He opened his car door, reached inside, and withdrew a plastic bottle, his hand shaking as he removed the top.

You're here to show them you won't sleep until the bastard is behind bars.

He took a mouthful of icy water.

You're here because you want to feel like you're their family again. Even if it is like this.

Harry took a deep breath, steadied himself, and marched towards the front door.

FOUR

HARRY STARED AT HIS feet, waiting for the front door to open, candles flickering in the windows either side of the entrance.

In spite of the bitter cold, sweat was trickling down his neck.

Twenty years ago, an officer did this for somebody you murdered.

Now it's come full circle and cost you one of your own.

He heard footsteps behind the door and a light came on in the hallway.

A glimpse of a face through the side-panel: greying hair, familiar glasses.

Harry's heart raced. He turned his face away and held up his badge.

'Police. CID,' he said, attempting to mask his voice.

A pause.

Hesitation before the door was opened.

For the briefest of moments, Harry forgot why he was here. Instead he remembered how, as a teenager, he'd come home late and try to slip inside without alerting his father, always helped by the woman now standing in front of him.

Harry's mother, Joyti, stared at him in disbelief. She spoke softly in Punjabi, almost a whisper. 'If I am dreaming, I hope never to wake up. If I am awake, this must be a nightmare because,' she said, shaking her head, eyes welling up, 'you *cannot* be here.'

Reflexively, Harry stooped and touched her feet; a sign of respect, something he had done throughout his childhood and continued to do now at his own home with an old pair of his mother's slippers; the last thing she had given him before he left.

Joyti instinctively acknowledged the gesture, touching his head gently before grabbing his shoulders, pulling him upright and embracing him, kissing Harry wherever she could.

Harry wrapped his arms around her slight body and inhaled the scent of her hair – the nostalgic fragrance of coconut oil – before glancing nervously down the hallway where dozens of tea-lights glowed a Diwali warmth.

He could smell the sweet aroma of halva, the traditional Indian semolina dessert made for special occasions. It brought him back to reality.

Today was not a special occasion.

Harry placed his hands on his mother's shoulders.

'Ma—'

Before he could say more, she gestured for him to stop and glanced nervously over her shoulder.

'Go,' she whispered, wiping tears from her face. 'Please, go.'

'I'm not here as your son,' he replied. 'I'm here to see Ronnie.'

'Why?' she asked, concerned.

'Ma, please. Get Ronnie. I need to speak to him.'

She kept her hands on his chest, unwilling to let go of a son she hadn't seen for four years.

Harry could tell it hadn't become easier.

Ronnie appeared suddenly in the hallway, dressed in a red sherwani, decorated with hundreds of sparkling sequins for the occasion. He stared disbelievingly at Harry, then he too glanced edgily down the hall for their father.

Harry stepped past his mother into the hallway.

'Are you crazy?' hissed Ronnie, storming towards Harry and gripping him hard. 'What's got into you?'

Ronnie was trying to push Harry back towards the front door, but he stood firm.

'I'm here on duty, Ronnie. I need you and Mandy to give me a few minutes.' Harry's tone made Ronnie back off.

'Where are the twins?' asked Harry.

'Upstairs,' replied Ronnie.

'Keep them there.'

'*Beta.*' Harry heard his mother's voice behind him. The word meant 'son' in Punjabi. He hadn't heard it for years and turned his face to the side. 'Ma, please. I need you to give us five minutes.'

Harry's father, Ranjit, strode across the end of the hallway, his bright orange turban and sparkling regal sherwani catching Harry's attention. The men locked eyes. As the smile on Ranjit's face faded, his hands balled into fists until the knuckles cracked.

Harry dropped his eyes to the floor.

'This morning, when I woke up, it was a good day. If I had known I would have to suffer seeing your face, in this house, on this day, I would have wished my own death.' His father's words cut as sharply as ever, like knives finding their target.

Harry exhaled slowly, keeping his eyes on the floor, his voice reduced to no more than a whisper. 'Ronnie. We need some privacy. Call Mandy.'

Ranjit marched towards them. 'Didn't you hear me?' he snapped, and swore a terrible curse in Punjabi upon Harry's marriage. It may have been Diwali, the night to make new wishes for the coming year, but for the Virdee family it simply meant carrying forward a familiar hurt.

Harry's mother stepped in front of Ranjit, putting herself between him and Harry with the resilience of a woman who had weathered this storm before.

'Not now,' she pleaded with her husband. 'Whatever it is, not today. I don't want to go back there. I cannot.'

Visions of the past. Harry's father lashing out with his fists after he had told him he was marrying Saima and finally drawing his kirpan, the sacred sword carried by devout Sikhs, and charging at Harry. He would have killed him if Joyti hadn't put herself in the way.

Harry couldn't look at his father. Not because he was afraid or ashamed, but because he wasn't; that would be the ultimate red flag to the raging bull. So he turned his back on him.

Behind him, Harry heard his mother cry out in alarm. As Ranjit went to move past her, Ronnie stepped forward.

'Not today,' said Ronnie to his father sternly. '*Not today.* I'll deal with this, Dad. Turn around and walk away.'

Ranjit didn't move.

'Now,' said Ronnie, raising his voice but not quite masking his nerves.

As Ranjit backed away, hissing spitefully, Joyti put her arms around him, apologizing for Harry's behaviour. She pulled him back down the hallway and they disappeared out of sight.

'Thanks,' whispered Harry.

'Shut up,' replied Ronnie. 'What the hell are you doing?'

'Ronnie, I'm here as a police officer and I need to speak with you and your wife.'

The living room was covered in rustic oak panels, a traditional wood burner in the corner, two big Chesterfield couches and a large, relatively recent picture on the wall of Ronnie with his family. For a few seconds, Harry's eyes didn't move from the sight of Ronnie's twins. He hadn't seen them in four years. They were thirteen years old now and had grown so much. Knowing they were in the house made Harry feel bitter that he couldn't see them, even if only a fleeting glimpse. He pushed aside memories of teaching them how to play cricket, Raj always wanting to bat whilst his sister, Kirin, tried to bowl him out. His eyes moved from them to Tara, standing behind her parents, next to Harry's mum and dad.

They look like your eyes, Harry; full of pain.

24

He forced himself to look away.

The incense burning on the mantelpiece reminded Harry of his own home; Saima also used it to ward away evil.

Harry was sitting opposite Ronnie and Mandy, next to the large bay window which looked out on to the driveway.

'It's Diwali,' said Mundeep. She placed her hands on the coffee table between them, sequins from her yellow sari tapping the wood. 'Really, Hardeep, you *had* to come today?'

She wouldn't call him Harry any more.

'Mandy—'

'Mundeep,' she said, correcting him.

'Sorry. I . . . I wish I weren't here.'

Mundeep had changed since Harry had last seen her. Her face had become thinner and she looked tired, with dark circles under her eyes.

'This better be important, Hardeep,' said Ronnie. In his wife's presence, even Ronnie wouldn't call him Harry.

Harry sighed, searching for the right opening.

This is the worst thing I've ever had to say.

It sounded so clichéd.

This is the hardest thing I've had to do.

Worse.

Candles on the windowsill flickered, making the shadows around them tremble. Harry had wanted the burden of breaking the worst possible news so it wouldn't be delivered in the formulaic terms dictated by protocol. Now that he found himself sitting with them, in a house where he wasn't welcome, Harry could think of no alternative to the official death-notification routine he had hoped to avoid.

He looked Ronnie square in the eyes. 'Tara's body was found this morning and we believe she was murdered.'

Silence.

The terrible, familiar stunned silence.

Ronnie searched Harry's face and found nothing but sickening honesty.

Then, as always, the cracking of the mother's face as she realized it was real.

Mundeep's lips creased, her eyes narrowed and she drew a long, shuddering breath before releasing a heart-rending wail.

FIVE

RIZ KHAN WAS STANDING in the penthouse apartment of the Gatehaus building. Unable to work, he could only look out over the centre of Bradford. In the distance, the newly opened Westfield shopping centre was reaching the lethargic end of a typically grey Monday evening. Riz rested his head against the floor-to-ceiling window, welcoming its icy touch on his clammy forehead.

What the fuck had happened?

Push the Virdee girl aside. No drama. No attention.

His instructions couldn't have been clearer.

But now he'd had a call from one of his pet officers. Thanks to Ali, they'd just launched a murder investigation.

Fucking Ali. Riz had never liked him. How could you trust a guy who wore two hoods? He should cut him out for this. What use was money to a loner like Ali, anyway? He couldn't even pay Bradford's hookers to fuck him with a face like that.

Unable to quieten the drumming in his mind, he closed his eyes and tapped his head against the window in time with the beat, leaving several grey strands of hair on the pane.

Only forty-eight hours to go before Riz was due to orchestrate the sale of a girl that he and his men had worked very hard to acquire.

Billy and Ali were the only ones who knew her location. Now they would have to go to ground. This was the first time a deal had reached seven figures – nothing could be allowed to jeopardize it.

Riz hit his forehead against the glass a little harder. He'd make it happen. Forty-eight hours and then the boss would oversee a swift handover, after which Riz would disappear someplace warm, this time with enough money to maybe never return.

Riz stepped away from the window, opened his desk drawer and pulled out a bottle of Glenfiddich. The forty-year-old whisky, a gift from the boss a year ago, came in at two thousand pounds and had been a fortieth birthday present. That and a weekend of debauchery in London, where the boss had an apartment overlooking the River Thames.

London was a rare treat, an opportunity to escape the darkness of Bradford, where poverty and destitution gave way to a very specific type of opportunism. Riz poured a generous measure of whisky into a crystal glass, picked up the articles he had printed that morning and sat down in his leather chair, overlooking the misery of a city where streets didn't have residents, they had owners.

He sipped the whisky and stared at the news items from the *Telegraph and Argus* website. They were all about detective Harry Virdee. Christ, how hadn't they known Tara's uncle was a cop?

False name.

False identity.

False age.

She'd played them.

But why?

Forty-eight hours before they completed and they had no clue how deep this thing ran.

If the boss got wind of this, he'd pull out.

Not an option.

Riz sipped more whisky, holding it in his mouth, allowing it to soak into his gums as he leafed through the articles. He paused at a black-and-white image of DI Virdee on the steps of Bradford

Crown Court. He examined the photo more closely, staring at the detective's face.

What could he possibly achieve in such a short time frame?

The intercom buzzed. Riz stared at a video-link monitor before pressing the button to open the outer door of the main building. A few minutes later, the door to the apartment was unlocked and his business partner, Billy Musa, strode inside, dressed in a sombre black shalwar kameez, heavy footsteps stomping towards the desk. He threw himself into a chair, looking like he had aged ten years since Riz had seen him the day before.

'Fuck,' he said, staring intensely at Riz. '*Fuck!*'

Riz took another crystal glass from his top drawer and slid it across the mahogany desk, nodding at the bottle of Glenfiddich. Billy snatched it, poured a clumsy measure into the glass and drank it like it was cheap wine. 'Yeah,' replied Riz. 'That about sums it up.'

Billy slammed the empty glass on the desk and leaned back. 'I called Ali. He ain't answering.'

Riz nodded and took a sip of whisky. 'What did you tell him on Friday?'

'What we agreed. Scare her. Make her disappear.'

'Disappear?'

'He knew what I meant – and it wasn't sticking a knife in her chest.'

'The problem with having a pit bull is being able to control it.'

Billy rolled his eyes. 'He knows we hand over on Wednesday night. He knows the stakes.'

'So why?'

'Maybe she caught him off guard?'

'Nobody is catching Ali off guard.'

Billy snatched the bottle of whisky again.

'Hey,' said Riz, shaking his head and pointing at the bottle, 'you're driving. Don't be careless today of all days.'

Billy put it back. 'You got a spliff? I've a bastard headache.'

Riz pointed to a cabinet to the side of the desk. 'Second drawer.'

He got off his chair, walked to a set of French doors and opened them to reveal a panoramic view of the city. Outside, the darkness was broken up by car headlights, bumper-to-bumper on Leeds Road.

'Bad, bad, headache,' said Billy, arriving by his side and lighting the spliff. 'Think we should call it off?'

'Don't be stupid. Boss knows we fucked up, you think he'll just let us walk away?' Riz replied.

'So what do we do? Move the girl?'

'She's where she is because there's no cameras in a two-mile radius. Anyway, we move her, he'll know there's a problem.'

'Damned if we do. Damned if we don't,' said Billy, inhaling deeply on the spliff.

'You think this guy Virdee is gonna give us a problem?' Riz asked, taking the joint from Billy.

'No. Unless . . . ' they looked at each other '. . . she was working with him,' Billy finished.

'Unlikely. Who uses their niece as bait?'

'Someone we don't wanna come up against.'

'Shit, Billy, how did you not see this? You've been chasing that bit of skirt for months,' Riz said bitterly.

Billy sighed, took the joint back for another drag. 'She . . . she . . . I don't know.'

'Here's the real concern. Who was she working for?'

'You sure we shouldn't shut it down?'

'Million quid's a lot,' replied Riz. 'And we'd still be left with the headache of telling the boss a year's worth of work is down the pan. Who knows what that'll bring.'

'He needs the girl. He's . . . got used to it.'

Billy took Riz's glass of whisky from him. 'We've done nothing that can't be undone,' he said.

'True,' said Riz. 'But . . . ' He paused, weighing the options in his mind as he stared out over Bradford, peak-hour traffic snaking as far as the eye could see.

'But?'

'We give them Ali. Then this all goes away.'

'Assuming he did it,' said Billy, turning to put the empty glass back on the desk.

'Course he did,' said Riz, shaking his head at the offer of a refill. 'You say you don't know where he lives?'

Billy sat in Riz's chair, dejected. 'You know how he is.'

'He won't pick up his phone? Sounds like he's running.'

'Not his style.'

'Style? That guy's got no style. He freaks me out.'

'Yeah, but he's useful.' Billy watched Riz stub out the joint on the metal railing across the French doors. 'Ali does the things we can't. Things we won't.'

Riz shook his head. 'The farmhouse,' he said, closing the doors. 'We all good there?'

'Perfect. I was there this morning. I'll head over again tomorrow for the final check . . .' Billy looked like he wanted to say something else.

'No choice but to complete.' Riz stood firm. 'What if Virdee comes our way?'

Billy took a moment to consider, then said, 'Get me his details. I'll pass them to Ali – just in case.' He stared out at the city beyond the windows. 'If Virdee becomes a problem, if he gets close? We'll do what we always do: give him to the streets – feed him to Bradford and let the city do what it does best.'

SIX

AN HOUR LATER, HARRY paused outside his front door. He could still hear Mandy's screams in his ears, raw and inconsolable.

Harry had been relieved when the family liaison officer had arrived, against his instructions. He'd been only too willing to leave her to break the news to his mother – he wasn't strong enough for that exchange. The momentary guilt at shirking the responsibility was quickly replaced with bitterness at not being able to share in their grief.

Harry looked down at the bag of candles in his hand.

Aaron's first Diwali.

How to light them now?

How to explain to Saima why he was late, why he hadn't called?

He had left the fireworks in his car. He wouldn't be lighting them tonight; this would be a sombre celebration. In the distance, he heard the crackle of happier people's fireworks in the night sky.

Harry focused on the door. His home was his world, safe and insulated from the memories of his past.

He found the key, waited a beat, before letting himself inside.

For the first time since he had moved in, Harry didn't touch his mother's slippers where they rested on the table by the front door. Tonight he'd done it for real. He could still smell coconut oil from his mother's hair on his skin and feel her embrace against his body.

In the hallway, Saima had lit a small red tea-light on each stair. Harry put his keys on the hallway table and stared at an Islamic painting above it which said 'welcome' – the first sign of Saima's Muslim world fusing with Harry's.

The heaviness in his chest increased. He removed his coat, then his shoes, and carried the bag into the living room.

Saima was sitting on the sofa holding Aaron, dressed in the elegant blue Indian suit with sparkling diamantés that Harry had bought for her. It was customary to wear new clothes on Diwali. His son was wearing a red and white traditional sherwani, waving his hands at the television where nineties Bollywood songs were playing.

Saima drove Harry mad with that shit.

'Look – it's Dada,' she said, pointing at Harry and not quite masking her annoyance with a smile. 'He's late. He didn't call. We had to decorate the house by ourselves, didn't we?'

Aaron flailed his arms at the sight of Harry, letting out a squeal of delight before shyly turning away. He had fair skin, a chubby round body, and Saima's hypnotic green eyes.

'Boo to Daddy,' said Saima, giving Harry a thumbs down and frowning. She pointed to the plastic bag in his hand: 'Our family candles?'

He nodded, and Saima saw the pain etched behind his smile. The kind she had seen before – the day Harry had left his family for her.

She stood up and walked quickly to him, putting Aaron into his arms.

Harry handed her the bag and lifted Aaron high, making him squeal. He brought him close and hugged him tightly – needily – before repeatedly kissing his chubby face and inhaling the pure scent of his skin.

'You OK?' she asked, placing her hand on his shoulder.

'Fine,' he whispered without looking at her.

'You aren't. What is it?'

'Not now.' He lifted Aaron high again, eliciting more gurgles of delight from his son. 'Let's light our candles,' Harry kept his voice soft and deceiving, focusing on Aaron, 'make some wishes and for the next . . .' he glanced at his watch, 'ninety minutes, pretend my day never happened.'

The living room was dark, lit only by streetlights shining through the window. In a cloudless sky, the crescent shape of the first new moon of winter was right above their home.

Harry was sitting at his dining table with his son on his lap, three red candles on a glass plate in front of him. Saima struck a match and lit hers.

'Don't forget your wish,' said Harry.

'Are you supposed to make one?'

Harry shrugged. 'Why not, let's invent it. We'll make our own traditions.'

She smiled, searching his face momentarily.

'Made it,' she said and handed him her match.

Harry held it carefully away from Aaron and lit his own candle with the same flame Saima had used, making a familiar wish: *Acceptance. Reconciliation.*

With the match burning quickly, Saima moved closer and took Aaron's hand. With all of their fingers touching it, they lit Aaron's candle, each kissing him on opposite cheeks.

'Shall we wish for him?' asked Saima.

'Confer a wish? Don't think that's allowed.'

'You make it then.'

Harry turned his son around so they were face to face. 'What shall we wish for? Something special, seeing as it's your first Diwali?'

Aaron blew a spit-bubble and wriggled to break free.

Harry made the wish, that much like the candle burning in

front of him, Aaron would one day light up the darkness that Harry had grown accustomed to since his family had disowned him. 'Done,' he whispered.

Saima smiled and touched his arm. 'I bought you a Diwali gift.' She reached under the table and removed a small silver parcel with a gold ribbon.

Harry handed her Aaron, who had started to rub his eyes.

'Guess first?' she suggested, trying to sound cheery.

'Don't know,' he said flatly.

Harry unwrapped the parcel and opened the box. He trailed his finger over a pendant of a candle within an Islamic crescent moon and a star; the perfect symbol to describe their shared celebration of Diwali and for the first time all evening his eyes softened.

'It's engraved,' whispered Saima. 'On the back.'

Harry took it from the box and turned it over to see 'Harry', 'Saima' and then 'Aaron' etched neatly on the back of the candle. He grasped it tightly in his hand, clenched his jaw to stop his bottom lip from trembling and smiled at his wife.

Harry was bathing Aaron. He always treasured this time alone with his son, but tonight his thoughts wouldn't settle.

He could hear Saima, verbally checking off her nightly to-do list: check that Aaron's room temperature was just right, that the blackout blind over the window was secure, and finally that his cot was pristine – all the usual jobs.

Harry was on his knees, watching Aaron attempt his daily escape from the bath seat, but his thoughts were of Tara.

The image of her alone on a cold slab in the mortuary was derailing his concentration.

Leaning forward, he put his arms along the side of the bath and rested his head on them, focusing on Aaron splashing his hands in the water.

When Tara was Aaron's age he used to help Ronnie and Mandy out all the time; the first baby in the Virdee household for three decades had been fussed over by everybody. Memories flooded his mind, and for a moment he closed his eyes and saw Tara giggling as she played with the bubbles in the bath.

He opened his eyes and smiled as Aaron broke into a wide grin, showing off two teeth.

What would he do if he lost Aaron?

This is the beginning. There's more pain to come.

Harry thought about the implications of Tara's murder. He imagined Bradford burning, Ronnie cutting loose and wreaking terrible vengeance on a city which had betrayed him.

Who are you going to save, Harry? Your city or your brother?

Harry lifted Aaron from the bath and put his lips to his son's head. 'I'll make it right,' he whispered. 'I swear I'll make it *all* right.'

Saima and Harry were back in their living room. It had taken longer than usual to settle Aaron; their little boy seemed to think sleep was optional.

'What is it?' asked Saima. 'It's been a while since you looked like you do tonight.'

'Wish it were longer,' he replied, his voice barely a whisper.

'You're scaring me.'

Harry stayed silent, standing by the bay window, his back to Saima, arms folded across his chest. His head was bowed, admiring the gift she had brought him, which was resting on the window ledge, gleaming silver in the candlelight.

'When that journalist wrote his article about Bradford being Gotham, it irritated me because I thought we were winning the war. I thought . . . I thought Bradford was starting to breathe again.'

'Harry, please, you're really frightening me. What is it?'

He closed his eyes and paused, leaving them in an eerie silence. Harry had already shattered one household with the truth tonight and loathed repeating the words.

'Harry?' whispered Saima, and he felt her hand on his arm.

Without opening his eyes, Harry told her everything: finding

Tara, meeting his family, not being able to see Ronnie's twins, and finally the guilt of not having been there to protect Tara or to share in his family's grieving.

'*Inna lillahi wa inna ilayhi raji'un,*' whispered Saima.

Harry turned to face her, arms still folded.

'Verily we belong to God and to God we return,' she said, her face wet with tears.

He turned away and Saima repeated the phrase.

'God?' whispered Harry mockingly.

'I believe enough for the both of us.'

Harry shook his head. 'Bradford's taken a bad step today, Saima. A really bad step.'

She moved to his side and slipped her arm around his waist. 'Forget Bradford,' she whispered. 'What can I do?'

'Nothing. Just . . . leave me to grieve.'

'I can't. I won't leave you to be in pain.'

'I'm always in pain,' he said, regretting it as soon as he'd said it.

'Don't say that.'

'I should be there.'

'Please don't do this to yourself—'

Harry turned to face her, eyes narrow, jaw clenched. 'I'll put this right. In my eyes. In theirs.'

Saima looked out at the crescent-shaped moon and didn't say anything.

'What?' said Harry.

'Nothing.'

'Tell me.'

'I married you knowing what you do. Last year – when . . . everything happened, you made me a promise; a kasam? Remember?'

Harry didn't reply.

'Do you remember?'

'Yes.'

'Good. We're parents now. We brought a little man into this world. Which means there are limits to what you can do out there.

Do your job. Find out what happened, but don't . . . do anything else.'

'You and Aaron are my priorities. Always will be, Saima.'

'I want to believe you. I know you want that to be true. But I can see it in your face. If you find the person who did this. If you get justice—'

'When.'

'When you get justice,' said Saima. 'It might mean the door to your family opens. It might mean it doesn't.'

'I know. This isn't about them. This is about a defenceless young girl.'

Harry thought about Ronnie and what he was capable of.

In just one year, Aaron had changed Harry's life. He knew there was nothing he wouldn't do for his son.

After two decades of fatherhood, he could only imagine what Ronnie must be feeling.

Bradford, for now, was sleeping peacefully under the watchful gaze of a new moon.

But in two houses at opposite ends of the city, peace was the last thing on the Virdee brothers' minds.

SEVEN

ALI HATED SUPERMARKETS. THE bright, hostile lights made him feel like everyone was looking. Two hoodies, face concealed; he looked like a thief. He could almost hear the CCTV cameras focusing their high-powered lenses, zooming in for a better look.

Tonight, he had no choice.

Ali loitered in the aisle by the pharmacy counter, waiting for the queue to die down. He could only clear his agitated mind by picking items from the shelves in front of him. A toothbrush, a hairbrush, nail varnish. All pink.

He handed the young blonde pharmacy assistant a slip. When she couldn't find a matching prescription, she returned.

When had he left it?

What was it for?

Under his hoods, Ali's face began to flush.

He mumbled, 'It's all on there, I was told it'd be ready today.'

As Ali spoke, the pharmacist emerged from a back room and tapped the girl on her shoulder.

'It's in the specials drawer, a carrier bag.'

Special? Is that how they referred to him?

Fucking *special*?

Sweat broke out across his brow. Ali's hands tightened around the handle of the trolley. They were mocking him.

The assistant returned with two carrier bags, the plastic handles stretching under the weight, and placed them on the counter.

'Do you want to pay for your shopping at this till?' she asked.

Ali hesitated. Was she pitying him now?

'Save you some time upstairs, and you're our last customer,' she continued. Her name badge said Deb, *happy to help*.

Ali's gloved hands started to remove the items from his trolley and place them on the counter for Deb to scan.

'Wow, someone's going to be a lucky girl,' she said.

Ali smiled to himself in agreement.

Back at home, Ali unpacked methodically.

He began in the cellar.

Pink towels by the sink.

Clothes hung carefully in the wardrobe.

Toys positioned neatly around the room, like Santa's grotto.

In the bed, Gori remained quiet, facing the wall.

'Just because these are not for you,' said Ali, ignoring her silence, 'does not mean I don't treat you well.'

Nothing.

Ali closed the door behind him, then carried the two heaviest bags upstairs to his bedroom and unpacked them.

Sitting at his desk, he pulled his hood back and glanced uneasily at a fragment of mirror. Ali rubbed at his face with his new cream, grimacing as his skin colour changed from a smooth heavy tan to a patchwork mess.

Why did you curse my house? Large sections of unpigmented skin appeared white, sometimes pink, and by contrast his smooth brown Asian skin seemed darker.

It looked like an infection, like the unpigmented patches were spreading, consuming everything in their path.

Vitiligo; it was seen as a curse in the Asian community.

Who will marry you, looking like that?

Ali glanced down at his torso. Many years of bleaching had lightened the skin colour, bringing it more in line with the unpigmented patches on his face. It was all he desired.

Ali leaned forward and stared closely into the mirror.

The bleach was working.

He smiled and rubbed the brown patches of skin on his face.

He sniggered; an uneasy, nightmarish sound.

It was working.

Ali stripped off the rest of his clothes and hurried into the bathroom.

So close.

As he immersed himself in the yellowish liquid, his mind was on only one thing.

Forty-eight hours.

Forty-eight hours until she was his.

EIGHT

HARRY WAS ALONE IN bed at one a.m. when his phone vibrated and woke him from a troubled sleep.

He picked it up from the bedside table and forced his eyes to focus on the illuminated screen.

Get moving. Black hole, 30 min.

Ronnie.

Much as Harry wanted to believe Ronnie was reaching out to him, the choice of location suggested otherwise.

He got out of bed. He hadn't drawn the curtains, hoping the hint of a new moon might assist his sleep – which it had, albeit only for a couple of hours. He had a vague recollection of strange dreams, images of Tara's face and a crescent moon covered in blood.

After dressing quickly he crept into Aaron's room. The orange glow-egg said twenty degrees and displayed a smiley face. Saima was lying in the bed next to the cot with Aaron asleep by her side. He must have woken in the night and cried until she had put him in bed next to her.

Harry crept towards them.

Aaron was almost nose-to-nose with Saima, breathing gently. Saima had told Harry it was the purest sensation – inhaling her baby's breath worked like a sedative, calming and peaceful.

He knelt by the bed and rested his hand on Aaron's body, feeling the gentle rise and fall of his chest. A few tranquil moments passed, each one steeling him for the difficult meeting ahead.

Harry drove through the city, cutting down Thornton Road, where hookers patrolled against the backdrop of abandoned textile mills towering on both sides of the road; looming demons providing shelter for a host of nefarious deeds.

Fifteen minutes later, Harry pulled into a lay-by in Queensbury and killed the engine. He stayed a moment, reluctant to leave. He hated this place.

Queensbury Tunnel was another abandoned part of the city. Passenger trains had long since ceased to pass through. The tunnel had decayed until the Highways Agency had announced plans to fill it with concrete, repairs being financially unviable. At the last minute, a private investor had stepped in to purchase it at a knock-down price.

Ronnie Virdee.

His bid had promised regeneration, but Ronnie had other plans.

Harry had brought a pair of boots and now slipped them on, together with his raincoat, in preparation for the tunnel's perpetually leaking roof. He armed himself with a powerful torch, and was about to close the boot when he remembered the key under the spare wheel, where he had hidden it last time.

He vaulted the steel barricade by the side of the road, sliding expertly down a steep embankment. At the bottom, he jumped the final few feet into a shadowy ravine. On his left was the vast cylindrical mouth of the tunnel, metal fencing blockading the entrance like bared teeth.

The padlock sealing the barricades accepted Harry's key without resistance. He slipped into the darkness and locked himself inside a portal connecting the world he knew with one he wished he didn't. Damp and decay hit him full in the face.

Ten men had died during the construction of the tunnel in the nineteenth century. Since Ronnie had acquired it, Harry couldn't be certain more hadn't joined them. Not on his watch.

He directed his torch beam to either side; a slick of green algae covered the walls like slime. The uneven ground stretched for a mile before it became unpassable due to flooding. On previous visits, Harry had been forced to dodge javelin-sized icicles hanging from the sixty-foot ceiling as they swayed precariously in a ferocious gale. Tonight, the only thing blocking Harry's path was the graffiti. He always stopped at the same line.

'Don't look behind you, ha, ha, ha . . . the dead are coming.'

After a while, he had to proceed with caution, picking his way through fallen bricks from the ceiling, pieces of twisted, broken track and razor-sharp rocks.

Beyond a ventilation shaft that leaked a constant stream of water, the railway track was intact and rusted a brilliant orange; deceptively colourful in the gloom.

'Have you seen the dead yet?'

The graffiti continued, right into the very depths of the tunnel.

Harry moved towards the far wall, where the ground was even. As the noise of the water fell away, he heard the sound he had been dreading.

A distant echo of screaming.

He closed his eyes, trying to remain calm.

'Have you seen the dead yet?'

Darkness was usually a comfort to Harry. But here, in a place where some of Bradford's worst secrets were buried, he wished the sun's rays would burn them away.

Harry's legs were heavy as he crossed the final hundred metres, arriving underneath a second ventilation shaft to see three shadows climbing up the curved walls from the harsh glow of a powerful light. The first was Ronnie's right-hand man, Enzo, who was blocking Harry's path.

Behind him, Ronnie was standing alongside a man holding what looked like a baseball bat, looping swings cracking bone every time they impacted.

Enzo put a firm hand on Harry's shoulder.

'We've spoken about this before, Elmo,' said Harry. 'Just because my brother has his hand so far up your ass it's affecting your brain, doesn't mean you can put your hands on me.'

Enzo cocked his head, eyes narrowing, and glared at him. Back in the day, he'd been an SAS operative. He hated Harry – not that Harry cared.

Pointedly directing his gaze at the hand on his shoulder, Harry said, 'If I wanted someone to touch me, I'd pick a better location with a better-looking whore.'

Enzo opened his mouth.

'Don't talk. You'll hurt yourself. Step aside.'

'If he wasn't your brother—'

'But he is.'

Harry swatted Enzo's hand away and pushed past, their shoulders colliding.

Ronnie had his back to Harry, and he was panting heavily.

'Ron.'

His brother hesitated, then raised the bat higher.

'You've got a 198 IQ and what you're doing is stupid. You know we don't do that,' said Harry.

The third man, now on his knees, was Nash, another senior member of Ronnie's organization. His nose was broken; there was blood everywhere.

Harry reached out and put his hand over his brother's. His skin was warm and sticky where it had been spattered with Nash's blood. Ronnie lowered the weapon but didn't let go, shrugging Harry's hand away.

Harry's voice dropped to a whisper. 'What happened?'

Nash was swaying precariously. He shook his head once.

'Silence? Really? I might be the only shot you've got,' said Harry.

'He won't do it now you're here,' spat Nash. 'Your rules? He knows what happens if he breaks them.'

Harry felt Ronnie tense beside him.

'Usually, that's true,' said Harry, stepping past Ronnie and snatching the bat from him. He crouched in front of Nash. 'But tonight isn't a usual type of night,' he said, tapping the bat on the ground. 'Shit that seemed important before? Not so much any more. You want to tell me? Or you want to see if Ron's going to break the rules on your skull?'

Nash looked away and spat blood on the ground. 'Do what the fuck you have to.'

Harry got to his feet and threw the bat on the floor.

'So?' he said.

'You want to save his life?' whispered Ronnie.

'Rule number one hasn't changed.'

'If I told you he was responsible for Tara?'

Harry turned his head halfway back towards Nash.

He waited.

An uncomfortable silence.

'I babysat her, like he asked,' spat Nash. 'If you wanted twenty-four-seven surveillance, you should've chipped her like a dog.'

Harry went to stop Ronnie, who had stepped forward ready to add another body to the tunnel's history. Enzo was already there.

'Outside,' said Harry to Ronnie, putting his hand firmly on his brother's shoulder, pulling him away from Enzo. 'Three's a crowd.'

NINE

THE BROTHERS WERE IN Ronnie's Range Rover in the lay-by above Queensbury Tunnel with a biblical rain hammering on the roof.

'Clean the blood from your hands, at least,' said Harry.

He grabbed a cloth from the floor, wound his window down and held it outside until it was saturated. 'Here,' he said.

When Ronnie didn't respond, Harry dropped it in his lap.

'I find out tonight from you that Tara had moved out. Why didn't you tell me?' Harry said.

Ronnie lifted the cloth and cleaned his hands, methodically wiping the blood away.

'Complicated.'

'No, Ronnie. *This* is complicated,' he gestured towards the entrance to the tunnel, 'teenage rebellion is not.'

'She wasn't a teenager any more. And it wasn't rebellion,' said Ronnie, and he looked at Harry in a way that pre-empted his next sentence. 'She knew.'

Harry's eyes widened. 'How much?'

'Enough.'

'About me?'

Ronnie ignored the question. 'Tara moved out because she was disgusted by what we do.'

There it was.

We.

'What *you* do,' Harry said quietly.

'It was all the same to her.'

'Does Mundeep know?'

Ronnie shook his head.

'*Shit*, Ronnie. How did Tara even find out?' spat Harry.

'Minor detail. Point is: she did. And she was pissed. But,' he smiled to himself, 'she wasn't stupid.'

Harry sighed. 'Blackmail?'

'Compensation, as she put it.'

'Christ, Ronnie, you were buying off your own daughter?'

'I was keeping her close the only way I knew how. She was a kid. An idealistic rebel – just like her goddamn uncle,' said Ronnie, throwing the bloodstained cloth on the floor.

'What's that supposed to mean?'

The heat from the brother's voices had caused the windows to steam over.

'Exactly what I said,' replied Ronnie.

'I'm forced to let you flood this city with drugs because of our past, but because I don't let you kill everyone you disagree with – I'm an *idealist*?' Harry spat the word.

'You've shackled me with these rules of yours. Bradford doesn't work with caveats.'

'Maybe it's time you quit.'

'Not an option,' said Ronnie.

'Then our agreement stands.'

Harry thought about the green door he couldn't knock on. Number 19 Belle Avenue.

'There's a line I won't let you cross.'

'Even now?'

'Even now.'

The brothers let the silence linger, looking out of opposite windows at the dull, black sky.

'Why am I here?' Harry asked eventually, turning back to Ronnie.

His brother ignored the question. 'Do you think I'm to blame?'

Harry didn't answer immediately.

'Got it,' said Ronnie.

'You're not to blame. But . . . if you were clean, none of this would have happened.'

Ronnie nodded. 'Can't change that.'

'You don't want to.'

'I didn't build an empire just to give it away.'

'The difference between an empire and a jail cell?'

Ronnie looked at him in silence, waiting.

'Physical bars. That's all.'

'Poetic.'

Harry's hand went to his jaw. 'What are we really doing here, Ron?'

For a while there was no sound but the hypnotic drumming of rain on the roof.

'I want to know which side you're on.'

'The one that gets my niece justice.'

'Your version of justice doesn't match mine.' Ronnie turned his body to face Harry. 'Before you left the house to come here tonight? What did you do?'

Harry's eyes narrowed as he thought of Aaron and Saima, sleeping nose-to-nose.

'How old is the little man now?' asked Ronnie. 'Eleven? Twelve months? Bet you walked into his room didn't you? Watched him sleep?'

'Ronnie,' said Harry quietly, 'don't.'

'You remember doing that with Tara?' Ronnie's face changed. 'What about when she was six and slept in your bed because she was scared of the dark? Or when she was ten and you carried her from the car after Jasbir's wedding? You put your jacket over her because it was raining. You got a chill so bad it put you in bed for two days.'

Harry was losing the battle to keep his emotions in check. 'Ronnie, this isn't—'

'I want the bastard who did this,' snapped Ronnie, slamming his hand against the dash. 'In a dark fucking room.' Ronnie almost hissed the next part: 'What happens after that is nobody's business but mine, and none of your shitty little schoolyard rules are going to stop me.' Ronnie hit the dash again.

Harry gritted his teeth. Not because of Ronnie but because he couldn't shake the image of carrying Tara from the car, his jacket wrapped around her, while the rain had soaked him. Her small body had been heavy as he carried her up the stairs.

'I don't know what you want me to say,' he whispered.

'Yes. You do.'

'You know I'll find him.'

'And what then?'

'I don't know,' said Harry truthfully.

Ronnie let out a long breath. 'Past four years – since you left Mum and Dad's shop,' said Ronnie, 'life's been about one thing? No?'

'We meet because you're my brother,' said Harry. Mention of the shop brought mixed memories.

Murderer.

'Getting back what you've lost,' said Ronnie. 'The family? Reconciliation? One day. Any day. Tell me I'm wrong?'

'It'll never happen while Dad's alive,' said Harry bitterly.

'You want to know how it is at home?'

'I know.'

'You have no idea. Mandy's lost. In shock. Old man's the same. We haven't told the twins yet. How do we even start to?'

Ronnie paused.

'And Mum—'

'Stop,' hissed Harry. 'Just. Stop.'

'Only in the darkest of nights, Harry, only then can you see the stars. Understand? Right now, in our grimmest hour – there's a way back for you.'

Harry turned away from Ronnie and massaged his temple, closing his eyes.

'The key to a reunion,' said Ronnie, 'is you knocking on my door late at night and handing me – handing us *all* the chance for justice. Put yourself on the line and prove you're still loyal to the family.'

Harry didn't want to hear it.

Could it be that simple?

'I'll find out who did this,' said Harry. He inched closer to Ronnie. 'What do I have from you?'

'Anything. You. Need.'

'I don't know what that is yet.' Harry stared down at his hands. 'Look, I can't promise this goes your way,' he said. 'I don't think I can live with more than we've already done on my conscience.'

Blood.

Murder.

19 Belle Avenue.

'Don't get in my way. Not on this.' For the first time, Ronnie was threatening his brother. 'Because if you do, I can't promise it goes your way. Understand?'

Harry banged his fists together, then jabbed Ronnie in the chest.

'I want revenge as badly as you do. I want my family back.' Harry's voice cracked: 'I want Tara back.'

Ronnie put his hand on Harry's shoulder, squeezing it tightly.

'Times like this make us realize there's nothing more important than family. I need this, Harry. I let her down. I wasn't there. I can't live with that.'

There was a moment's silence while the brothers looked at one another.

'Two things,' said Harry, removing Ronnie's hand from his shoulder. 'One – you might have issues with Nash, but the rule remains. You put him down, I put *you* down.'

Ronnie shook his head in disapproval. 'And two?'

'If I need your help, I'll ask. You look after the family.'

'I'll agree – if you agree to one of mine.'

'What is it?'

'This rule of yours – I'm going to break it when you hand me the guy who did this.'

'We'll cross that bridge when—'

'No. We won't.'

'Yes, Ronnie. I can't give you carte-blanche when I've no idea what I'm looking at.'

'Then when you leave this car, that's it,' spat Ronnie.

'This isn't the time to fall out.' Harry sighed and pushed his knuckle back into the side of his head again. 'This is messy.'

'An eye for an eye. That's my world,' said Ronnie. 'Your world too, if you'd stop obsessing about something that happened twenty years ago.'

'I'll make the decision once I've got him. If he turns out to be a deranged sociopath, he's all yours.'

Ronnie leaned back in his seat, resting his head on the window.

'When you have him. In front of you. Think about what he's taken from us. Think about Aaron.' Ronnie put his hand in his pocket and removed a single key and a wad of fifty-pound notes. 'Tara's house key. There must be something useful in there. Your team won't locate it until tomorrow. I told them we didn't know where she was staying and they won't find it easily.'

'How so?'

'She was staying there as a favour to me. It's owned by an affiliate of mine who can't be connected to me. Lives in Dubai. Owns sixty houses in Bradford. The house is in his company name.'

'Why there?'

'Easier for me to keep an eye on her – if Nash had done his fucking job right,' he added spitefully. 'The cash is for whatever you might need it for. Don't worry about CCTV.' Ronnie checked his watch. 'For the next three hours, Bradford has gone dark.'

'How—' Harry stopped. Truthfully, he didn't want to know. 'Nash was supposed to watch her twenty-four-seven?'

Ronnie opened his mouth to answer then closed it.

'The truth, Ron.'

'Just to make sure she was OK,' whispered Ronnie, looking away ashamedly.

'What's the address?'

'124 Killinghall Road. There's no alarm.'

Harry made to open the door.

'One more thing?' said Ronnie, grabbing his arm.

'Go on.'

'I want real-time updates, every step of the way.'

'Like I said,' Harry replied, 'you look after the family. I'll take care of this.'

TEN

THE FLUORESCENT LIGHTING FROM late-night takeaways provided a welcome contrast to the night sky and the wretchedness brewing inside Harry as he drove up Leeds Road. He stopped at a set of traffic lights, Ronnie's words at the forefront of his mind.

No loss of life. Was he still willing to enforce that rule? Did the fact that it was Tara's murder change anything?

The lights turned to green. As he pulled away, his thoughts shifted.

If he did help Ronnie avenge Tara's murder, would it open the door to his family's home?

He parked outside the address Ronnie had given him, killed the engine and sat in darkness staring at a nondescript end-of-terrace Victorian house.

Do what you do, fix it your way.

The dash blinked at Harry, minutes ticking by: 03:05.

Experience told him one of three things had happened to Tara.

One, her connection to Ronnie and the business he ran had made her a target. Two, she had been killed in a crime of passion. Or three, Tara had been involved in something that would lead Harry to discover his niece wasn't the innocent little girl he had always loved.

The location of the murder made the second theory less likely. He didn't want to entertain the third.

What would he find in the house?

Ronnie's words kept repeating in his mind.

This is your only way back to the family.

Harry pictured his own home, where Saima was sleeping next to Aaron. They were his family too, but as much as he wished they were all he needed, he knew he couldn't be content until his parents had taken him back. Until they let themselves see past all their religious bullshit.

With his boss's warning to leave the case alone fresh in his ears, Harry went to the boot and pulled out a SOCO suit and gloves. He couldn't afford to leave a trace of himself here.

Inside the hallway, Harry turned on the lights. A photo on the sideboard stopped him in his tracks. Tara wore a purple Ralph Lauren dress. It had been Harry's sixteenth birthday present to her; she'd begged him for months. He picked it up and traced a gloved finger across the glass. He swallowed the knots in his throat, opened the back of the frame and removed the photo, putting it in his pocket before getting to work and rifling through uncollected mail on the floor.

Tara K. Virdee.

Her middle initial stood for Kaur, given to all baptized Sikh girls, as Singh was to boys.

Kaur: princess.

A symbol that all Sikh girls were precious and to be protected.

There was no mail for anybody else and the envelopes in his hand all proved to be circulars.

Harry made a preliminary sweep of the house. This was no home, this felt more like a holding cell. Ronnie could have put Tara in one of the four penthouse apartments he owned in the centre of town. But Tara would have enjoyed that. This house was a way of letting her know: freedom had its limitations.

'There's monsters in the dark, Uncle Harry.'

'I know,' whispered Harry. 'Let's see if we can find them.'

His suspicions were confirmed.

No food in the kitchen.

Few clothes in the wardrobe.

Barely any personal belongings.

The bin outside the back door was empty. Collection day was tomorrow.

This house might have been where Tara was supposed to be living, but this wasn't where she'd spent her time.

'Tricksy little girl,' sighed Harry.

He thought about Nash, beaten and bruised in that tunnel, tasked with keeping an eye on Tara. Sentry duty was always dull; without specialist training, it was too easy to zone out. Still, Nash might know more than Ronnie had cared to ask.

Harry finished his sweep of the building, preoccupied by only one thing.

I need to find where she was actually living.

So much for Ronnie giving him a head start; this place was full of shadows, nothing more. Tara must have realized he'd have been keeping an eye on her here.

Harry was preparing to leave when his phone rang.

His first thought was Saima, but the number was withheld.

'Hello?' said Harry.

'Detective Virdee?' The voice was unfamiliar, female.

Harry looked at his watch. 'Who wants to know at half-three in the morning?'

A pause. He could hear her breathing, soft and rhythmic.

'I have some information about a case. Tara Virdee.'

Harry glanced at the staircase, as if whoever was calling might suddenly appear at the top.

'There's monsters under my bed, Uncle Harry . . .'

'I'm listening,' he said.

'Are you able to meet? Now?'

'Now? I'm at home. Like I said, it's half-three in the morning. What—'

'Telling me a lie isn't the best start.'

'Sorry?'

'You're lying. Because if you were at home right now, I wouldn't be looking at you.'

ELEVEN

HARRY STEPPED CLOSER TO the panes of glass either side of the front door and killed the lights, plunging the hallway into darkness. 'Where are you?' he said into his phone.

'Close enough.'

'Why the secrecy?'

'We don't have much time, but I can help you,' she said, ignoring his question.

'How did you get this number?'

'You're off the books, right? An uncle working his niece's case – that can't be protocol.'

Harry hesitated, unsure how to proceed. 'You called me, lady. What do you want?'

The line fell silent again.

Harry wasn't interested in her power games. He took the phone from his ear and looked at the screen, luminous in the dark hallway. When it hit thirty seconds and she still hadn't spoken, Harry hung up.

If this woman really wanted to help, she'd call back.

Harry's phone rang.

He let it ring six times. 'Yes?'

'Hanging up isn't—'

'This is really simple. If you want to help me, offer me something. Show me you're worth my time. Otherwise I—'

'Tomorrow night, something terrible is going to happen in Bradford.'

That got Harry's attention. 'Go on,' he said.

'I need you to trust me. And I need you to believe that Tara trusted me.'

Harry walked into the living room and across to the window. Peering through a gap in the curtains, he tried to get a wider-angled view of the street outside. 'Let's meet.'

'Later.'

'Why?'

'There's nothing in the house. You need to go where heads of state once met in secret. Stay free tomorrow, H. I'll call.'

'What?

'Hello? Hello?' he said, looking at his phone, but she had gone.

She had called him *H*.

Only Tara had ever called him H.

Harry tugged aside the curtain and scanned the street beyond, looking for a face in a window, a car pulling away, but there were no signs of life.

'*Where heads of state once met in secret?*' he whispered. A memory was shifting in his mind, trying to rise to the surface.

Harry's hand went to his pocket, pulling out the picture of Tara he had lifted from the hallway. 'What the hell did you get yourself caught up in, kid?' he whispered.

Where heads of state once met in secret.

'Shit,' said Harry, raising the photo so Tara's eyes were level with his.

It was something only they knew.

Who was that voice on the phone?

'Heads of state,' he whispered. 'Heads of fucking state.'

Fulneck School Foundation was in Pudsey, on the border of Bradford and Leeds; a private school where all the Virdee kids and grandkids had been educated. Harry had spent some of the happiest years of his life here. When he was feeling low or struggling with a case, Harry often came to the horseshoe car park he'd just pulled into. Staring down the long, straight path that led to the school gave him a sort of peace.

Not today.

Harry got out of the car and made his way to the south of the building. On his left was a gravelled terrace stretching the length of the school; to his right, the science building. Midway between was an overgrown path which led into the valley, a golf course on one side, the school on the other.

Leaving behind the streetlights of Fulneck, he followed the path as it descended into an abyss of darkness. He pulled a torch from his pocket and strode through dense nettles and overgrown grass until he reached a towering oak tree.

There it was.

Harry + Tara were here, heads of state forever

The memory lodged in his throat, his breath came shorter and shallower. He touched the bark where they had spent half an hour carving out their message; that had been the last time he'd seen Tara. He had wanted to tell her in person why he wouldn't be around any more, about the choice he had made.

Harry looked away.

Focus on why you are here.

Where heads of state once met in secret.

Harry had been head boy of Fulneck, and Tara had wanted to follow in his footsteps and become head girl. She'd succeeded, within months of that final meeting. Whenever Harry had visited the Great Hall, he'd sought out her name etched in gold writing on the honours board opposite the one that held his.

Whoever had sent Harry here knew Tara very well. That last meeting here had been their little secret.

An uncomfortable feeling crept over Harry, putting him on edge. The trees were a mass of shadows; he could hear the wind rustling through the overgrown brambles and bushes. In the sky the new crescent-shaped moon seemed to be looking down on him.

He shone the torch around, sweeping the area. There was something in the scrub not far from the tree. A leather satchel, well worn, buckle missing, top zip broken.

He picked up the bag and opened it to find a thick red diary inside.

Harry set off back to his car. Once inside, he turned on the interior light and started leafing through the diary, his progress getting slower and slower with each page he scanned.

'Christ, Tara,' he whispered, 'you've got to be kidding me.'

TWELVE

HARRY GOT HOME AT five a.m.

His mind was burdened with images of Ronnie beating Nash and the troublesome notes in Tara's diary.

What the hell had she been caught up in?

In the hallway, Harry touched his mother's slippers before making his way to the kitchen. Saima was sitting on a stool holding a cup of steaming hot chocolate, a baby-monitor at her side.

'Everything OK?' he asked.

'My husband comes home at five in the morning and asks if *I'm* OK?'

Saima looked at him expectantly.

'How's Aaron?' he asked, nodding at the monitor.

'Dreaming.'

'How come you're up?'

'Idiots setting off fireworks woke me. You weren't here.'

'Ronnie called.'

Harry saw Saima open her mouth to say something, then close it. Her dislike of Ronnie was well established. While he was the only member of the family who'd accepted Harry's decision to marry her, Saima despised the fact that he hadn't fought for his brother. He'd opted instead for a peaceful existence, refusing to upset his parents or his wife.

She saw him as gutless. But his daughter's murder had muted Saima's usual disdain.

'Is he all right?'

'He needed me.'

'And what about you?' she asked Harry softly. 'What do you need?'

'The guy who did it.'

Saima could see the tiredness in Harry's bloodshot eyes.

'You'll get him. You always do.'

'It's different this time.'

She nodded. 'Can I say something?'

'Shoot,' said Harry, taking a defensive step away from her concerned gaze.

'I don't want to sound like a bitch—'

'Hey, you're never—'

She raised her hands and continued: 'I don't want to sound spiteful. I never met Tara. I wasn't . . . allowed, so this isn't about that – what I've got to say.'

Harry leaned against the kitchen worktop. 'Sure.' He put on his detective face – open and receptive.

'I don't want you tearing into this blindly, consumed by guilt.'

'Guilt?'

'Because you weren't there. Because you feel somehow like you failed to protect her.'

'No guilt here.'

She smiled at him knowingly.

'You need to be careful. You're obsessive, Harry. You never give up. But the boss has told you: not this time, it's too personal. I agree with her. I'm worried you won't know when to leave it alone. That you'll make things worse.'

'Saima, this is my family.'

'*We* are your family. We need you to look after yourself.'

'Jesus, Saima, look at what—'

She put her hand up to stop him. 'I'm not finished.'

Harry sighed, then waited for her to continue.

'Your family has caused us unbearable pain.'

'So did yours,' he said, too quickly.

She glared at him.

'Go on.'

'I saw it in your face last night. You think this might give you a way back. You think that if you catch this guy, give them some sort of closure, they might welcome you back with open arms.' Saima paused. 'Harry, I'm telling you that won't *ever* happen.' Her voice cracked, but she kept it together. 'I'm not a bad person for saying that,' she added, almost pleadingly.

Harry shook his head. 'That's not why I'm doing it.'

'But you *are* going to work this case?'

'Yes.'

'Why? Why can't you leave it to your colleagues? You know they'll do all they can for you.'

Harry remained silent.

Saima put her arms on the table and rested her chin on them. 'Go on: say something.'

'Make us a cup of Indian tea,' he said finally. 'Then I'll tell you exactly why.'

'I . . . I can't not do this,' said Harry, taking a seat opposite Saima in their living room. 'It isn't right that in my family's critical hour, I'm not there.' He lifted the tea she had made from the table and sipped it, pushing a stray cardamom seed from his lips with his tongue. 'Might it open a door? It's possible, and yes, that is part of what's driving me. Awful as it sounds, Tara's death might be the opportunity for us all to reconcile and for them to finally get to know you and see that you're not the devil they think you are.'

Saima's eyes narrowed. 'You still don't get it, do you?'

'What?'

'They know I'm not a threat. That's the problem. If I was in a burka, praying five times a day and carrying around a ticking rucksack, their fears would be justified. It's because I am *not* like that, because I'm just a normal girl who happens to be a Muslim, that they're afraid.'

Harry hung his head.

'Even if you bring them justice, the door will remain closed. Your father has painted a picture of me, and people like me, as terrorists, religious fanatics, nutcases – all the usual nonsense. It doesn't match the reality. I'm dead normal. So what happens if they get to know me, like me, maybe even love me? They can't risk it, it goes against everything they've ever known.'

Saima was right; she was always bloody right.

'I know,' he mumbled, staring past his wife at the picture of Aaron on their mantelpiece.

He wanted his mother to meet her grandson. How could she keep this up if she held him in her arms?

She'd never betray her husband. He knew that.

'So you'll stand down?'

No lies, Harry. Not in this house.

'No,' he said flatly.

'How am I supposed to watch you suffer that heartache again?' Her face was drawn.

Harry put his tea on the table and went to the window; dawn was yet to break.

'When Mandy went into labour with Tara,' he said, 'I drove her and Ronnie to the hospital. Shit – we were so excited and scared; first baby in the house for decades. At the hospital, I was with them both for hours before everything kicked off, and I had to leave them to it – I'll never forget how excited I was.'

'You never told me this,' Saima said, making her way towards him.

He shrugged.

'Go on,' she said, arriving by his side, the streetlight outside throwing a golden ray across them, their shadows reaching towards the sofa.

'I heard a baby crying. Tara's loud, cranky entrance into the world. When Ronnie let me into the room, he went to call Mum and Dad. Mandy was ill from the gas and air and that just left me to hold Tara. For almost twenty minutes. I'll never forget her eyes. Wide. Inquisitive. She was so calm in my arms.'

Saima slipped her arms around Harry's waist and rested her head on his shoulder.

'Near enough the first twenty minutes of Tara's life were spent in my arms. Ever since I found her body, I haven't been able to shake those images from my mind.' Harry's voice started to waver. He turned and embraced Saima, kissing the top of her head.

'I have to do this,' he said. 'If I don't, the image of that baby girl will haunt me for ever.'

THIRTEEN

ALI KAMRAN HAD PULLED up outside the Bradford Hotel.

His phone vibrated in his hand, Billy Musa's name flashing on his screen. It might have only been ten o'clock but it was Billy's eighth call of the morning. Like the previous seven, Ali allowed it to ring out. It wasn't a call he wanted to answer with guests in his taxi.

The three young women sitting in the back of his cab were a traffic light of extravagant Asian suits: yellow, red and green, glittering with silver sequins. The fabric of their outfits rustled as they moved. They had asked Ali to wait at the hotel until the coach transporting the groom and his guests arrived. They were noisy, skittishly checking their jewellery and their make-up and giggling incessantly. One of them kept spraying perfume on her neck, the smell of citrus causing the throb in Ali's head to worsen.

Hood up as usual, Ali was safe from the gaze of his passengers. But the rear-view mirror gave him the opportunity to stare freely. The girl in the middle was fair for an Asian, her skin smooth and even like Tara's.

Tara.

Tara had had fair skin too. Beautiful.

The sight of rich, dark blood splattering Tara's pale face had forced Ali to crouch close to her. For the briefest of moments he had been mesmerized, reaching out his gloved hand to touch her, even though he knew he shouldn't stay.

The girls broke into laughter, high-pitched and boisterous, interrupting Ali's thoughts. If he turned around, reached back, would he catch them off guard? Just the thought of wrapping his hands around one of their long, bare necks was enough to start the familiar refrain screaming inside his head.

'Ring-a-ring-a-roses, Ali's face exploded!'

He shook his head slightly and closed his eyes.

'Aisha looked amazing, didn't she? Amazing!'

'I've never seen a bride look so perfect! Imran's a lucky man!'

As they carried on their chatter the doors to the main entrance of the hotel suddenly opened and dozens of girls in outfits of every colour of the rainbow spilled out on to the street.

'Shit, let's go, the boys must be close!'

There was a moment of turbulence from the back seat as the girls squealed and exited the cab. One of them threw a twenty-pound note on to the passenger seat.

Ali didn't pull away.

He forced himself to watch as the girls joined an exuberant mob of women blocking the hotel entrance, all of them waving as a Bentley arrived and a coach pulled up just behind it.

As the groom's side of the family disembarked and approached the bride's entourage on the pavement, there was a brief melee as everyone scrambled for the best vantage point, wanting to secure a view of the groom as he emerged from the Bentley.

Look at you. No father will ever give his daughter into this house! Why did you curse my home?

Ali's mother's voice was never silent for long.

He tugged at his hood. Beneath the mess of his skin, was he really so different to the groom in that Bentley?

Ali hated the delirium generated by ethnic weddings. He knew he'd never have one of his own.

The bride's guests started cheering as the door of the Bentley opened and the groom stepped out, dressed in a Mughal-style sherwani, a long silk jacket buttoned up the middle, with matching trousers and a red turban, a feather protruding from the centre. He raised his hands like a king greeting his subjects as several women from his side of the family surrounded him like guards. They moved towards the bride's guests, who barred the way, demanding money before they'd let him see his bride.

Ali sighed. These guys were honouring every tradition.

The groom removed a bulging wallet from his pocket, carefully selected what appeared to be a five-pound note and offered it to one of the bride's female guests. This was greeted by loud jeering from the crowd.

It was like watching a pantomime. Ali leaned forward, captivated in spite of himself.

Two women – the groom's sisters, he assumed – stepped forward, meaty arms folded to take over the tough negotiations. The crowd jostled for a better view and, right on cue, the dohl players appeared, pounding the ends of their cylindrical drums, keeping up a frenetic beat.

Ali had been unconsciously scratching at his hands. He felt the blood swell under his skin and a tackiness under his nails. He didn't stop scratching.

You will never get married, Ali.

Mirrors will crack when you look at them.

His mother had been so consumed with bitterness at her misfortune that instead of protecting Ali, she had mocked him at every opportunity. How was she to find him a bride when fair skin and good looks were priorities for any suitor in their community? It didn't stop her trying. But even the girls she found from Pakistan, so desperate to come to England, rejected Ali. It was the worst of insults.

As the groom made what looked like a final bid for his bride, Ali closed his window on the noise and pulled recklessly into the road. Another driver was forced to swerve and angrily blasted his horn.

The wedding party were momentarily distracted, eyes darting his way.

'Don't look at me,' he hissed, thoughts turning to tomorrow night. After almost twelve months of careful planning, tomorrow was the big night. Riz and Billy wouldn't know what'd hit them until it was all too late. Their reign over Bradford was nearing the end.

Ali was going to take what he deserved.

FOURTEEN

AT NINE A.M. HARRY was sitting at his desk in the spare bedroom with his laptop open and Tara's diary in his hands. The photograph he had taken from her house was on the desk, Tara's smiling face looking up at him.

With Saima and Aaron at a mother–baby playgroup, Harry had the house to himself. He'd promised Saima that he would use the time to sleep, but there was no way he could.

Tara's diary was written almost entirely in Punjabi, so Harry's progress was slow; he hadn't used the language in years. Relief spread through him when he found the occasional word in English. There were dozens of references to 'Olivia and Lexi Goodwin', long passages of Punjabi broken up by English names that couldn't be translated.

There was also a table, written entirely in English, under the heading: 'Why do girls go missing in Bradford?' Harry decided to start there.

The table was made up of four columns: mother's name and date of birth; daughter's name and date of birth; daughter's age when she went missing; and the date she went missing. There was an entry in the final column every year from 2007 to 2010, then nothing until the entry for Olivia Goodwin, where there was a question mark in place of a date.

Missing?

At the back of Tara's diary was a list of names: Billy, Riz, Omar, Ali and then a dash next to which she had written, *'Boss?'*

An anxious feeling in the pit of Harry's stomach caused it to spasm. He grabbed a handful of fennel seeds from a container he kept on the desk and shoved them into his mouth, an Indian herbal remedy his mother had given him as a child when exams had brought on a similar reaction.

Harry slipped a pair of headphones on and pulled up a playlist of heavy rock music on his phone to drown out the noise of other thoughts. He'd start with the names of the mothers and daughters – any prior convictions might help point him in the right direction.

It was the word 'missing' that had caught Harry's attention. The woman on the phone had promised, *Something terrible is going to happen in Bradford.* Was this notebook going to lead him to that terrible something?

While he waited for his searches on the police database to load, Harry removed his headphones and phoned one of his DCs for details of the coroner's report on Tara. It had been prioritized and completed yesterday evening, giving a probable time of death as Saturday night. No signs of sexual assault.

For that last piece of news, at least, he was grateful.

Harry asked the DC to raise an urgent enquiry with the Department for Work and Pensions and Bradford City Council to find out about any benefits claimed or registered addresses for the mothers and daughters listed in Tara's diary. He told the DC to stress it was of utmost importance; a potential danger to life. If Harry was lucky, the DWP would come through with the information before the end of the day.

A couple of hours later, Harry was finished with the diary. He powered down the computer, his stomach cramping again.

All the mothers on the list had lived in Bradford at some stage and all of them had misdemeanours for antisocial behaviour. Nothing new there.

Two had turned up dead, several years after the date in the 'daughter missing' column, in the Greater London area; one was found near the River Thames, the other in a known drug slum in Croydon.

No witnesses in either instance.

As isolated cases, they were not remarkable. Heroin overdose was not an unusual cause of death for women like these.

The files had been transferred down the line, eventually hitting Bradford CID – their last-known fixed abode.

Details on their children did not feature in the files. At first Harry thought it a glaring anomaly, but then he realized that by the time the women's bodies had been found, their children would have been over sixteen and legally adults, so they would not have been classified 'at risk'.

Harry turned off the lamp and closed his eyes. A picture was forming in his head, one he didn't like.

The fact that all the mothers on Tara's list had minor convictions was not in itself remarkable. That two had died of a drug overdose was, again, not unusual. But as he verified the dates of birth Tara had recorded in her diary, Harry was struck by something else the women on that list had in common: the daughters were all eleven when they went missing, and the mothers were twenty-six or thereabouts, having given birth when they were still in their teens. A sinister pattern was beginning to emerge.

Harry picked up the picture of Tara.

What were you doing?

For Tara to have stumbled on this, it had to have been connected to Ronnie's underworld activities. Drugs were bad enough, but this felt like something even worse. Harry didn't like it one bit.

The phone rang.

His DC had addresses for the women listed, going back ten years. Lexi Goodwin, the only mother with no missing date next to her daughter's name, had told the DWP she was moving to London a week ago. She hadn't supplied a forwarding address.

Her previous address was on the Thorpe Edge estate, notoriously bleak even by Bradford's standards.

If she'd moved on, the only way to get information about her would be by knocking on the neighbours' doors. That meant Harry had a problem: he wanted to keep this quiet, but that wasn't going to be possible at Thorpe Edge.

In some parts of Bradford, seeing a white face was the exception rather than the norm. Thorpe Edge was the opposite. The area boasted the only BNP councillor in England. Even Asian taxi drivers wouldn't go there. Harry would be spotted immediately and the enforcers on the estate who ensured unwelcome visitors didn't leave with their bones intact would come for him, detective or not.

Thorpe Edge was a no-go.

Harry turned the lamp back on and stared at the map of Bradford. He grabbed some pins from his desk and put one at each location his DC had provided for the four women on the list.

They were all in Bradford West except Lexi Goodwin. Her pin stood alone.

Even Ronnie didn't have a foothold at Thorpe Edge.

Which was too bad, because it seemed to be Harry's only option.

FIFTEEN

THORPE EDGE ESTATE WAS a lawless place.

Residents were mostly unemployed and all three local schools were under Ofsted improvement measures. Recent plans for redevelopment of the tower blocks had been fiercely contested by their occupants. The message came through loud and clear: Thorpe Edge wanted leaving well alone.

Harry had decided against his suit, opting instead for jeans and a hooded top.

He drove in from the south side, the towers rising steeply ahead of him, a hostile and intimidating view – four of them, forming a square, separated by a patchy area of grass.

Crime and drug use here were so ingrained that, short of demolishing the towers, there was little to be done. Government assistance in the city was weighted towards the Asian areas, where it was felt integration should be a priority.

Not Thorpe Edge.

Harry parked his car outside Gerard House. Two years ago, he'd come here to head up a morning drug raid which had gone disastrously wrong. Not quite a full-scale riot, but near enough. It didn't bring the warmest of memories.

For a few minutes, he sat in the car, mobile in hand, toying with the idea of sending Ronnie a message, deciding against it.

He peered up at the towers but still didn't get out.

What is it you always drum into your officers about this estate? Never go in there alone.

He had to fight the voice of reason, stronger since Aaron had been born. Nightfall was the risk – the camouflage of darkness released youths who acted like wild dogs, protecting their turf. Midday was surely the perfect time to go unnoticed.

He put his watch and wedding ring in the glove compartment, double-checked that he had locked the car, then walked briskly towards Gerard House. He passed cars with flat tyres, two bicycles with no wheels, and a vandalized waste-collection area, its door hanging by a solitary hinge. There were dozens of uncollected black bin-bags on the floor; the smell of decay nauseating.

A few metres from the entrance, Harry heard the first whistle.

He quickened his pace, stepping into a walkway smelling of urine.

More whistling. Louder.

There was no lighting, but he could see a staircase at the end. He bounded up the stairs two at a time, keeping to the sides where the darkness felt protective.

When he reached the fifth floor, the smell of marijuana and alcohol was overwhelming. There were empty cans of Skol Super, cigarette butts, and Harry spied at least one discarded syringe.

For now, he was alone. He marched to the end of the balcony, where it split left and right, then hesitated. Curtains were twitching, whistles bouncing around the towers with increasing frequency.

It was his BMW – a strange car attracting attention.

He should have parked it out of sight, but he'd wanted a fast exit strategy.

Don't take the tyres, you bastards.

Harry veered right, triggering a security light that illuminated the darkness – not ideal. He stopped in front of number fifty-two.

There was a small window to the left, glass cracked, curtains drawn.

Harry rapped lightly on the door. He waited impatiently.

He knocked again.

Nothing.

He looked through the letter box, assaulted by the smell of cigarette smoke, and saw nothing but darkness.

This time he hammered on the door, making it rattle on its hinges.

Still nothing.

Harry pressed his elbow to the cracked pane of glass and pushed, forcing it to crumble away.

His gloved hand just fitted through the hole. Harry felt for the latch, and after a couple of failed attempts, unlocked the door and stepped inside.

Abandoned.

Cupboards were open, empty. A pile of mail on the floor. He picked up a brown envelope with a Bradford City Council logo; it was addressed to Lexi Goodwin. Harry opened it. The letter was confirmation that, following her recent notification of an impending move, her housing benefit would be stopped in three days' time.

Harry quickly checked the rest of the flat.

Lexi had taken any personal items she possessed – clothes, jewellery, photos – but it looked as though all the furniture had been left behind.

The second smaller bedroom was plastered with posters of cartoon characters and Disney princesses.

Olivia's room?

In the kitchen, four black bags were leaking. He emptied them one at a time across the floor, sifting through the contents with his feet.

Schoolbooks, children's magazines and a girl's school uniform. He picked up a crumpled piece of paper filled with the awkward writing of a young child.

... when we gets to londen, uncle billy says we was goin to a big house with a big gardan and I cud get a dog. He says Mum will get better and we will get icecream ...

Harry put the note in his pocket.
Billy.
One of the names in Tara's diary.
He was starting to get nervous about Lexi and Olivia's move.
Why do girls go missing in Bradford?
Harry took a final sweep of the apartment and left with more urgency than he had arrived.
Outside, the corridor was empty but Thorpe Edge was still whistling.
Harry knocked on the doors of the flats either side, but no one answered.
Somebody must have seen them leaving.
He tried several more flats. He could hear the sound of a television in one, but nobody came to the door.
The noise of the whistles was intensifying; eyes on the stranger on level five. Harry heard shouting and yelling from the courtyard. The pack were gathering for the hunt.
You're pushing your luck.
The sudden appearance of an elderly man at the window next to him made Harry step back. Wrinkles. Silver hair. Thick black glasses. Harry put his hand in his pocket, removed his police identification, and held it against the glass, tapping on the door urgently.
Had it been a younger man, Harry wouldn't have revealed his position, but the old-timer was less likely to be a problem.
'Come on, come on, old man,' hissed Harry as the pensioner stared at his ID. The towers were closing in, he could hear kids racing up the stairs, yelling ethnic slurs.
He was starting to run out of options.
The old man disappeared from the window and, with him, so did Harry's chances.

'Shit,' he muttered, grabbing the door handle and turning it, but it was locked.

Harry retreated back to Lexi's flat, entering hurriedly and rushing through it.

The abusive threats grew louder as the voices reached level five.

Harry opened the back door and peered along an abandoned rear corridor. He stepped out. Below, kids were running wildly into the tower. They were children really, but here, kids were more dangerous than adults. They knew the law could only go so far in punishing minors. These bastards knew their rights better than Harry.

To his left, three doors down, the elderly man stepped out of his back door and waved him into his flat.

'Shhh,' he whispered, once they were both inside.

Harry froze, the voices were loud outside. The old man was glaring at Harry. Nothing friendly about it.

The tiny hallway was dimly lit with dark floral wallpaper and dull yellow blinds. It was claustrophobic, neither Harry nor the old man moved. Finally, the kids dispersed, their hunt moving further up the tower block. Harry was beckoned into the living room.

Dread hit Harry full in the gut. A St George's flag hung large on one wall and on the other – he'd never seen anything like it. The wall was an enormous map of Bradford. Areas were shaded in red, green and yellow. Harry stepped closer.

There were articles from the *Telegraph and Argus* pinned to the peripheries of the map. One in particular caught his attention: a petition to stop the pubs in Bradford being converted into Islamic religious centres.

'You stupid?' the old man finally spoke.

Harry nodded. 'Trying to change.'

'Funny man? That what you are?'

Harry put his hands up passively. 'Look, thanks—'

'Shut up.' The old man shook his head. 'I phoned the police – checked you were real. Otherwise?' He nodded outside to where the boys had been. 'Never thought they'd send a coloured fella about my complaints.'

'Complaints?' Harry ignored the word 'coloured'. The old fool had probably used it for half a century, wasn't his fault it was no longer acceptable.

'Complaints about coloureds dealing those damn drugs on my floor. The bottom three floors – that's where it's bad. But up here on the fifth? This is the best floor in Thorpe Edge. I'll be damned if I'm going to let it get like them below.'

'Absolutely,' Harry wasn't sure what else to say.

'You're not here about my complaints, are you? I've lodged one every week for the past three months, but nobody's bothered visiting me. You're here about the Goodwin girl. Seen you go in there. You broke the glass.'

Harry nodded. 'I'm looking for her. What do you know about it?'

'More than you, by the looks of it. What do *you* know?'

Harry backed off a step. The old man had made his way into Harry's personal space. He could smell his breath, stale tea. 'Can we start over? As you know, I'm Detective Inspector Virdee. You?'

'Wilson. Alfred Wilson.'

'Alfred—'

'Mr Wilson,' he snapped. 'Can't say I take too kindly to casualness in your job.'

'Sorry, Mr Wilson, why don't you tell me about your complaints?'

Thorpe Edge, it seemed, had become the site of a turf war and was no longer the white-only area Harry had always known it to be. Asians were now brazenly walking around the estate, clashing with the local hooligans.

Wilson told him there had been frequent late-night visitors to Lexi's house. The turf wars were her fault; she was a dirty whore, mixing with 'all sorts' and inviting the ethnics in.

'You're not going to write any of this down? I don't want that tramp moving back here. This is the fifth floor.'

Harry assured him she wouldn't be returning.

'They moved out a few days ago, right?' Harry's attention was split between the old man and the steady racket outside in the courtyard.

'Friday,' replied Wilson, taking a seat without extending the courtesy of inviting Harry to do the same.

There was another tirade of insults about Lexi before Harry could get a word in.

'Can you tell me anything else? What time they left? Who they were with?'

For the first time, the old man smiled, smug in his chair. 'I can tell you everything.' He moved a pair of binoculars from the armrest and pulled a notebook from the side of the couch. 'Most folk don't bother about what happens in these towers, but I'm not one of them. I keep notes about everything.'

'Mind if I have a look?'

'Damn right I do,' snapped Wilson. 'These notes are mine – I've got more in here than what that little tramp was up to.'

Harry nodded. 'It's people like you who really look after the community, Mr Wilson.' He cringed at his own bullshit.

The old man didn't reply but Harry could see him swelling with pride.

'Friday . . .' Wilson was leafing through the pages.

'Thank you,' Harry said. 'I want to make sure I find her so, firstly, she doesn't end up back here, and secondly,' Harry raised his hand when Wilson looked up alarmed at the prospect, 'to make sure she answers for all the disturbances you've reported.'

The old man went back to his book.

'How detailed are your notes?' Harry fought the urge to snatch the notepad and run. He needed to get out of here. 'Can you describe who she left with?'

'I can do better than that,' replied Wilson, and grabbed a pen from the side of the pad. He slid it down the page, then looked at Harry arrogantly. 'I can give you the make and model of the car she got into.'

SIXTEEN

HARRY LEFT WILSON'S APARTMENT via the back door, stepping quickly into shadow, relieved the rear corridors were deserted. The wild shrieks of earlier had dissipated to a low hum of activity.

On the ground floor, gangster-rap music sounded like a prelude to anarchy. Harry kept his head down, hood pulled up, and hurried past a group of teenagers smoking marijuana by the exit.

He almost got away with it. Four teenagers were hanging around his car, one of them sitting cross-legged on the bonnet, smoking a roll-up.

'Get off,' said Harry, removing his hoodie.

Three of them shuffled back awkwardly.

'What ya sellin'?' the one on the bonnet asked Harry. He hadn't moved.

Harry considered his position. At least two of them would scarper if it kicked off; they were already backing away, hands in pockets.

'Night in jail,' said Harry.

One of the nervier lads whispered to his mate to leave it alone. 'He's a cop, Craig.'

'I know the pigs. Fink I'm stupid? You ain't the first Paki I've run out of here.'

'Craig, is it?'

Craig clapped sarcastically. 'Pick up the language quick.'

Harry pushed his sleeves up, took his gloves off. 'Guess if I showed you my badge, it wouldn't make a difference.'

'What ya sellin'?' Craig asked again.

'I told you. You need me to write it down? You can read, can't you, Craig?'

The whistles had started up again, the sound of doors opening and closing, feet on the ground.

'What the fuck do you want?' Harry didn't have time to waste.

'Ya deal on my patch? I want ya stash and ya fucking money,' said Craig, leaping off the bonnet and removing a penknife from his pocket.

'I'm supposed to be afraid of that? My dick's bigger,' said Harry.

One of the hangers-on sniggered.

Craig's eyes were dancing and he was grinning stupidly, clearly off his face.

Harry stepped forward. 'Craig, some days guys pick fights with the wrong people. Today is one of those days. Do I look afraid of that needle-dick knife?'

Harry glanced past Craig, towards the towers. In a few seconds, there would be more of them, harder to predict.

The knife was loose in Craig's hand, blade pointing lazily to the floor.

'Just fuck off, yeah?' Harry said, glaring at him and shifting his feet ever so slightly, back foot on its toes, front foot turned inwards: fighting position.

Craig looked unsure; the knife had been his big move. Looking into his eyes, Harry saw a playground bully whose bluff had been called, but with his friends watching, he couldn't back down.

For a moment the stand-off teetered unstably.

Craig's eyes gave him away, widening slightly.

Before he could raise the knife, Harry grabbed the boy's wrist with his left hand and with his right jammed powerful fingers into Craig's throat. He collapsed theatrically to the ground and dropped the knife, clawing at his throat where his breath was trapped.

Harry turned aggressively to the others, who were momentarily caught in no-man's land, unsure whether to engage or retreat.

'Don't be stupid,' said Harry. 'You want to go home or you want to go to jail?'

They scarpered, leaving Craig writhing pathetically by Harry's feet.

'Relax.' He used his foot to roll Craig's body away from the car. 'You're not dying.'

Harry drove to the centre of the city and parked behind the *Telegraph and Argus* building. As he got out of his car, he saw an Asian man remonstrating with a delivery driver. The man would be a shopkeeper whose newspapers hadn't been delivered, forcing him to come down to the depot.

It was a familiar scene. Harry remembered his father having this argument regularly.

His thoughts were interrupted by his phone ringing. DS Conway. Had his DS ratted him out? He let it go to voicemail; if he was in the shit, she'd be sure to leave a message.

Opposite the newspaper building was Britannia House, home to Bradford council offices. In the basement, the entire city's CCTV surveillance was monitored. Armed with Wilson's information about Lexi and Olivia Goodwin getting into a white Audi A4 on Friday night, Harry entered via the main doors.

He made his way to the basement and stopped in front of a plain metal door. There was a short delay after he pressed a buzzer, then a crop of mad-scientist-like white hair appeared in the doorway. The CCTV manager, Charles.

'Charlie,' said Harry.

'How many times? It's Charles,' he replied with genuine contempt. 'It's been Charles for fifty-three years, ever since I was baptized. If my mother could hear you now, God rest her soul—'

Harry headed to the wall of screens at the end of the room. The entire city was being watched. 'It's the hair. If it was, you know, centre-parting, controlled, I'd give you Charles. But you look like you've been electrocuted; you nail a Charlie.'

'You make me sound like I should own a chocolate factory.'

Harry slapped him on the arm. 'That's the spirit. Christ, you're right, Willy might suit you better.'

'I take it you've come here to insult me before asking for a favour?'

'Much as I would love it to be a social call—'

'When? Where?' said Charles, reluctantly sitting at his desk and tapping keys on his computer.

'No guessing today?'

'All right, I'll say Holme Wood?'

'Nope.'

'Manningham?'

'Last guess.'

'Thorpe Estate?'

'Bingo. Friday night. Pull up seven thirty, eight o'clock?'

'Paperwork?'

'You'll get it.'

'You said that last time.'

'You wouldn't be able to read my handwriting.'

Charles pulled up the cameras and Gerard House appeared on screen.

'That one,' said Harry, pointing at the left-hand monitor. 'Car park, rear entrance.'

'What are we looking for?'

'White Audi. Asian lad.'

Charles played the video at four times its normal speed.

'There!' said Harry.

Charles paused the video. 'Got it. White Audi. You want the licence?'

Harry nodded, grabbing a pen and scrap of paper from the desk.

'GH12 YHG.'

'How much zoom can you get on the driver when he gets out?' asked Harry, writing it down.

Although the image distorted as Charles worked the software, it remained clear enough to show Harry a decent profile.

'Big lad,' said Charles.

'Probably all brawn, no brain.'

'Charming.'

Charles kept tapping keys on the computer and found him again. Forty minutes later the man returned, carrying two large suitcases and accompanied by a woman and a little girl. Olivia was younger than Harry had expected her to be. Her age had been missing from Tara's notebook, but he'd assumed she was eleven like the others. Now it appeared Olivia was much younger than that.

'Can you take a screenshot of that and send it to my phone?' Harry asked.

'You know I can't.'

'And copy the footage on to a USB stick,' Harry continued, ignoring him.

'Harry, there's—'

'You'll get the paperwork, Charlie, relax.'

'If the gaffer collars me, I'll—'

'You'll show him the footage of the many, many incidents you've got of his car parked on Lumb Lane while he gets blown.'

Charles looked awkward and glanced around nervously as if his boss might suddenly appear. 'He says he's taking the church to the streets to help them,' he said, dropping his voice.

'No gain for the girls then. Either way, they get screwed.'

Charles just rolled his eyes.

While the USB flash drive was being loaded, Harry sat in Charles' seat and used the controls to study the footage more closely. It looked as though Lexi and Olivia were leaving of their own free will with a man who looked like he had a lollipop in his mouth. At 20:33 the car pulled out of the car park. Harry clicked on another camera and tracked the car's exit from Gerard House.

When it hit the road outside the estate, Harry hit the pause button.

He leaned closer to the screen.

'What . . .' His eyes were fixed on the screen, his mouth open.

He let it play, stopped the clip and rewound it. He pressed play again.

'No fucking way,' he said, and rewound it a second time.

At the other side of the room, Charles hovered with the USB stick, nervous at Harry's sudden change in mood.

Harry played the clip a third time, the mystery caller's words from the night before loud in his ears.

Something terrible is going to happen in Bradford . . .

SEVENTEEN

ALI PULLED UP OUTSIDE Thornbury Primary School at quarter past three.

Billy had suggested they meet in town, but Ali knew that if he timed it with Billy's school run, it would force him to keep it brief.

The playground began to fill with noise as children emerged from the school and charged towards the gates. A few kids began playing a game that made Ali's mind scream; it was the game he thought of when he was in his cellar, in Gori's bed.

Kiss-chase.

He focused on the white girls, cheeks red, eyes watering as winter air hit their angelic faces. Skin so pure and smooth. Ali shifted in his seat.

As always, the Asian kids watched while the others played. They wouldn't join in, even if they were asked. Good Asian children didn't kiss other children, especially white ones.

Ali had been asked to play only once.

He wasn't a good child. He'd been told that enough.

The memory burned, forcing his breathing to quicken and hands to scratch at each other. Ali felt the slow, familiar trickle of blood.

It was the first time anyone had asked him to play.

Lily had approached Ali, her blonde plaits swinging, and taken him into the middle of the playground.

'Do you want to chase us?' she had asked, struggling not to giggle.

Ali had shaken his head, a little excited but at the same time terrified.

'But you get to kiss us if you catch us?'

Kiss them?

Ali hadn't been able to take his eyes from her hand on his coat.

'You're the only boy playing, so you should be able to catch one of us.'

Then she had giggled, unable to hold it in any longer.

The other boys weren't playing. He should have known.

'OK,' he had said.

Stupid.

'Go!' Lily had screamed.

Standing in the middle of the playground, he had felt instantly vulnerable.

'Come on! Come on!' the girls had screamed, scattering in all directions.

And he had chased them.

A tear leaked down Ali's face, clear at first and growing cloudy as it collected make-up on its way down his cheek.

Run! Run! The freak is coming!

If he kisses you, it'll turn your face like his!

They had laughed and pointed, but their fear had been real as they ran from him.

For the first time, seeing their fear, Ali had felt powerful.

'Come on! Come on!' the girls had screamed.

Ali had chased them, intent on catching Lily and showing them all how good he was at their game so they might ask him to play again.

Another tear rolled a haunted trail.

Ali wound the window up; he didn't need to hear the screams from the playground as the ones in his mind took over.

The white boys had watched, on their toes, ready to charge. Some of the girls ran towards them, knowing Ali would never dare follow.

Lily, however, had run for the corner. It was a corner Ali knew well, because it was where he spent all his break-times.

The other boys, realizing Lily was about to be caught, had charged protectively but they weren't fast enough. Ali had cornered Lily and, ignoring the look on her face, he had put his hands on her shoulders, pursed his lips and kissed her. To his amazement, a mixture of disgust and terror spread across her features, then she screamed and burst into tears. The boys had arrived then and started pummelling their fists into Ali's face.

'Ring-a-ring-a-roses, Ali's face exploded!'

Billy's seven-seater taxi pulled up outside the school gates, bringing Ali back to the present.

Not a lot had changed.

Riz and Billy thought they were better than Ali. They thought they were doing him a favour, using him to do their dirty work. But Ali knew what he wanted now. And they had no idea what he was prepared to do for it.

Tara had been an unexpected complication, Ali couldn't deny that.

But he was confident he could still find a way to turn it to his advantage.

He watched as Billy climbed out of his taxi and signalled for his son to keep playing with his friends before making his way over. Ali automatically checked that his hoodie was secure across his face.

Tomorrow night, Billy and Riz would be busy worrying about pulling off the biggest deal of their lives, selling the youngest girl they had ever secured.

They'd never see Ali coming.

Billy opened the passenger-side door and climbed in. Ali didn't look at him; he carried on watching the children in the playground.

'What happened?' Billy asked, getting straight to the point. 'Saturday night – what the fuck did you do?'

'You said she needed to disappear. She has.'

From the corner of his eye, Ali saw Billy's fingers twitch. He wasn't worried; Billy wouldn't lay a finger on him here, not with his kid in view.

'Why?' asked Billy. 'We complete tomorrow night. Why would you take such a dumb fucking risk? Christ, what the fuck is wrong with you, boy?'

What is wrong with you?

It wasn't a line Ali liked to hear.

'Her uncle is a detective. Did you know that?' spat Billy, eyes on his son wrestling in the playground.

'Detective?'

'Yeah, Ali. A detective. You see why Riz and I are fucking pissed!' he suddenly raised his voice, punching the dashboard and making Ali jump. 'Tell me – why? Give me something to go back to Riz with.'

'You talk to me like that again,' said Ali, finally turning to face Billy, 'and maybe you and me fall out.'

Billy was breathing hard as he locked eyes with Ali. He'd become accustomed to the way the boy shrouded himself under his hood. Any pity he felt didn't outweigh his anger.

He removed a crumpled takeaway menu from his pocket and threw it at Ali.

'ZeeZee's Kebab House,' he spat. 'Seven o'clock tonight. The parcel will be there.' Without waiting for a reply Billy grabbed the door handle to leave.

Ali stopped him before he could get out.

'This detective,' he said. 'Where does he live?'

EIGHTEEN

IN THE CORNER OF the basement of Britannia House, Harry was obsessively watching and re-watching the footage of the white Audi pulling away from Gerard House.

'Harry, are you all right?' asked Charles. 'You . . . don't look so well.'

Harry ignored him and played the clip again.

He scribbled a telephone number on a piece of paper and held it up to Charles without looking at him.

'Phone Val in Traffic and tell her to run a DVLA check on the licence of the Audi. Tell her Harry said it's life-or-death.'

Charles hadn't ever heard Harry speak so quietly.

'Why?' whispered Harry. The black-and-white of the CCTV gave everything a ghostly quality. As he watched the clip again, he saw the Audi pulling away from Gerard House. Behind it, maybe fifteen metres away, Tara Virdee was running across the estate manically waving her hands.

The Audi braked, as if the driver might have seen her in the rear-view mirror, but after only the slightest hesitation it accelerated away.

Tara kept running until the car was out of sight. Then she

stopped in the middle of the road, hands on her head, looking around desperately for help that wasn't there.

'Why?' he whispered again.

Why was Tara out at Thorpe Edge?

'Something terrible is going to happen in Bradford . . .'

Harry had immediately checked other cameras in the vicinity but lost Tara when she left the estate via a blind spot in the CCTV. He tasked Charles with finding her; if anyone could, it would be him.

What was she doing there?

He thought about the note in her diary: *Why do girls go missing in Bradford?*

Lexi and Olivia Goodwin were at risk; that much Harry was certain of.

He had nothing else.

If the woman on the phone was right, if something terrible was about to happen . . . Harry couldn't finish the thought.

It was four p.m., why hadn't she called again?

'Got it,' said Charles, rushing back to Harry. 'Car's registered to Manningham Lane Autos.'

Harry took the piece of paper from him, still warm from the printer: the registered owner's details, direct from the DVLA.

'Val says you owe her.'

'I do,' said Harry, removing the USB drive from the laptop. 'Charlie – email me this footage too.'

'You'll have it within the hour.'

'You're a good man.'

'Are you OK?'

Harry pulled out his phone and dismissed an incoming call from Ronnie.

'No,' he said. 'I'm far from fucking OK.'

Manningham, just a mile from Harry's house, was one of Bradford's bleakest areas. It had never recovered from the race riots of 2001.

Manningham Lane Autos was both a second-hand car

dealership and a repair garage. The main workshop was fifty metres to the rear of the showroom; you could hear the sound of engines from the street.

Harry pulled his car into a customer parking bay, waiting eleven minutes until the clock read 16:55, five minutes before closing. He wanted the owner impatient to go home; that usually meant they'd be more inclined to help. Harry totted up the value of the cars he could see – over two hundred grand. Business must be good.

Ronnie had texted Harry twice, asking for updates. Harry hadn't bothered to reply. This had to be somehow related to Ronnie. If Harry showed his brother the footage, Ronnie would surely be able to identify the man, feign ignorance and instead allow his rage to rule his head. Then there'd be no stopping him.

Parked directly in front of Harry, with a sign on the windscreen asking £8,999, was the white Audi that Lexi and Olivia Goodwin had got into on Friday night. The car Tara had been frantically chasing the night before she was murdered. Harry felt his anger rising.

He removed a small GPS tracking magnet from his glove compartment. He liked to use them to follow suspects – they weren't exactly legal, and definitely not admissible in court, but they were cheap on the Internet. He slipped it into his pocket and headed for reception.

Inside the office was a scruffy middle-aged Asian man with grey receding hair and a soft waistline. He wore blue overalls smeared with oil, his sleeves rolled back to reveal thick, strong forearms. He was tapping buttons on a calculator and flicking through invoices.

He greeted Harry with a nod.

'Looking for the gaffer,' said Harry.

'That's me.'

Harry slipped off his gloves and showed his identification.

'Inspector Virdee,' he said, no mention of a department.

'I'm Zed,' the man replied. He continued to tap the calculator, unfazed by the badge. 'Work car or personal?'

Harry shook his head. 'Got an enquiry.'

'Shoot.'

Harry looked around the makeshift cabin. 'How many staff do you employ?'

'Three.'

'Including you?'

'No. So four then.'

'White Audi parked outside. I'm looking for some information.'

Zed chewed his bottom lip and pushed the calculator aside. 'There a problem?'

'Not yet,' said Harry. 'You let staff borrow the cars for personal use?'

'If they ask nicely. What's happened? One of my boys got a speeding fine?'

'I just need to know if that white Audi was booked out last Friday.' Zed followed Harry's gaze towards the car.

'Hang on.'

Zed disappeared into the back and returned a few moments later with a black ledger. He leafed through a few pages before tapping twice on an entry about a third of the way down the last page. 'Got it.' He put the book on the counter, turning it so Harry could see. 'There: Omar checked it out Friday night.'

'Full name?'

'Omar Shah.'

'How old is he?'

'Twenty-two.'

'He doesn't have his own car?'

'Sure.'

'So why did he want this one?'

'Christ, I don't remember. He runs that shitty Ford outside,' said Zed, pointing behind Harry to a miserable-looking blue Fiesta, parked out of view of the customers. 'Usually they want a decent car to take a lady out.'

Harry took a good look at Omar's Fiesta before turning back to Zed.

'How long did he have the Audi?'

'All weekend.'

'Is he here?'

Zed checked his watch.

'In the garage – he should be closing up.'

'Can I have a word?'

Zed sighed and closed the file on the counter. 'You mind telling me what it's about? If there's a problem, I need to know.' He shrugged, palms up. 'I run this place clean – only way to survive in Manningham. It's taken me years to build the rep.'

Harry nodded. 'It shows. Nice set-up. He's not in trouble, I just need a minute.'

'I'll take you round. Couple of lights out. Don't want you falling over and putting a claim in,' he laughed. 'Let me grab a torch and lock this place down.'

Zed disappeared into the office. Harry opened the file on the counter again and scanned the entries in the logbook. There were three columns: name of the employee taking the car, address and mobile number. Harry quickly found his iPhone, checked Zed wasn't looking and took a photograph of the page. Omar hadn't bothered with his address, but he'd scrawled his phone number down.

Shouting to Zed that he would meet him outside, Harry walked to Omar's car and knelt down to untie and retie his shoelace. He checked that the CCTV cameras weren't pointing his way before discreetly attaching the GPS device to the underside of Omar's car.

The workshop entrance had been sealed by heavy steel shutters since Harry had arrived. He followed Zed through a side door.

Inside, the lights were dim, but Harry could make out three cars being worked on, their bonnets raised.

'Omar?' Zed's voice echoed around the workshop.

There was no reply.

Zed waited a few moments, then shouted again.

'Yo! Over here.' Omar emerged from the shadows in blue overalls identical to Zed's. He had a lollipop in his mouth. Harry thought of Tara, running after the car out front, the grainy video footage blurring her feet. He clenched his fists by his side until his knuckles cracked and discreetly exhaled his rage through the side of his mouth. Much as he would have liked to lock the garage doors, grab a steel wrench and get stuck into the guy, this was a time for patience, not recklessness. He wasn't Ronnie.

Omar was impressively built; every part of his body was taut with muscle. Harry hadn't noticed that on the footage. He had a neatly shaven head, sharp jawline and a broad welcoming smile.

'Last-minute emergency,' he said, pushing the lollipop into his cheek with his tongue. 'I'm almost finished and, to be honest, I'm done in.'

'Get rid of the lollipop,' said Zed. 'This detective wants a word.' Harry thought he'd probably forgotten his name.

Omar's smile fell.

'You look like you've seen a ghost,' said Harry. He didn't offer his hand.

'Nah, nah,' replied Omar. 'Just, er . . . you know . . . got a few parking fines I ain't seen to. You here to collect?' He forced a nervous laugh.

Harry turned his head towards Zed. 'Can you leave us for a minute?'

Zed faltered, then shook his head decisively. 'I'd like to stay.'

'I'd rather you didn't,' said Harry. 'Let's not make this all formal. Give me a few minutes and I'll be gone.'

Omar exchanged nervous glances with Zed before nodding at him. 'Go on, boss. Close up and I'll help . . .' He looked at Harry.

'Inspector Virdee.'

'Inspector Virdee with whatever he needs.'

There was another pause. An uncomfortable tension.

Reluctantly, Zed left them alone, saying he would wait in the office.

'So,' said Omar, shifting the lollipop to his other cheek. 'What's this about?' He was rubbing his hands together, bouncing on the balls of his feet. It was distracting.

'You mind?'

'Freezing, bro.'

When Omar didn't stop, Harry put a hand on his arm. Firmly. 'Seriously, "bro",' he said, squeezing a little, 'stop that. And like your boss said, get rid of the damn lolly.'

Omar took the little white stick from his mouth and threw it across the workshop.

'Better. Last Friday, did you take a car from here? To use over the weekend?' asked Harry.

'Er . . . maybe.'

'You want to think about it?'

'Sure,' said Omar, snapping his fingers. He seemed unable to stand still. 'I did.'

'Remember which one?'

'Shit, I can't remember what I had for breakfast!'

'Your boss checked the log. A white Audi . . . ?'

Omar was fidgeting like crazy.

'You OK, Omar? You seem nervous.'

'Nope. Just cold, you know. Us Asians don't like it, yeah? All right for you in the coat and gloves.' Another nervous laugh.

'The car? You remembered yet?'

'Sure. White Audi out front.'

Why was Tara chasing your car, Omar?

'So did you go anywhere Friday night?'

Omar shook his head. 'Skint. Waiting for payday, innit?'

'You left work and then what? Went home?'

'Can't remember. Probably. Yeah.'

'How about Saturday? Sunday? D'you use the car for anything?'

'Shopping. Maybe.' He paused, as if thinking about it, closing his eyes for emphasis. 'Yeah. Supermarket.'

'Thought you were skint?'

'The missus paid.'

'Married?'

Omar held up his hand, showing Harry a wedding ring.

Harry moved closer and dropped his voice. 'You guys happy?'

'What the fuck's that got to do with anything?' spat Omar, stepping back, keeping the distance to a few feet. 'Look, you want to tell me what this is about?'

'Easy there.' Harry raised his hands. 'Why the attitude?'

'Told you, bro. I'm fucking freezing.'

'You want my coat?'

'You taking the piss?' Omar's face creased in anger. "Cos, you know what? I don't need this aggro.' He made as if to move past Harry, who put a firm hand on his shoulder.

'Just a couple more minutes.'

Omar turned his face, looking at Harry side-on. 'If I say no?'

'I could take you down the nick. Do it there if you prefer?'

Omar hesitated a beat. 'OK, but hurry it up.'

'Anyone borrow the car from you Friday or Saturday night?'

Omar shrugged. 'Don't know.'

'Come on, Omar – you had the keys. Did you lend them to anyone?'

'Nope.'

Harry nodded. 'You know the Thorpe Edge estate?'

Omar's cheeks flushed red. Panic. He answered too quickly. 'Nope.'

Harry was closing in. 'Weird. Got the motor placed there Friday night. Helping Lexi Goodwin move house. You going to tell me you don't know Lexi now?'

Omar's eyes narrowed and he looked past Harry, at the closed garage door. He dropped his voice. 'Look, why're you busting my balls? You want to get me fired?'

Harry shook his head. *Let him talk.*

Omar's eyes lingered on the door before he looked back at Harry. 'Listen, the boss doesn't like us using the cars for favours. I know Lexi – not a lot, like, but we used to chill sometimes.'

Harry looked pointedly at Omar's wedding ring.

Omar shook his head. 'Just, you know, chillin'.'

'So you saw her Friday night?'

'She said she needed a lift to the station with some luggage. Last-minute holiday deal. You know how it is,' he said, shrugging his shoulders.

'Which station?'

'Bradford Interchange.'

'What time?'

'Seven?'

The Interchange was heavily monitored by CCTV.

'Where exactly did you drop her?'

Omar hesitated. Harry wondered whether he'd realized he'd picked an area that was well covered.

'Traffic was bad, I was rushing. Dropped her outside St George's Hall.'

'Just Lexi?'

'Her daughter as well.'

'What's her name again?'

Another pause.

Harry stared intensely at Omar, noticing all the usual signs of a lie. The hesitation. The shiftiness of his eyes. The involuntary twitch in his hands.

'Olivia.'

'How old is she?' asked Harry, thinking of the footage he had seen at Britannia House, how young Olivia had looked.

Omar couldn't meet Harry's gaze.

Harry let the silence linger. Then he asked again.

'Like, nine,' said Omar quietly, almost ashamedly.

'Tell me again?' said Harry stepping a little closer.

'What the fuck for?' snapped Omar. 'Listen, I'm done here, yeah? Maybe you got nothing better to do, but I got a home to get to.' The two men were almost toe to toe. 'You gonna move or—'

Harry stood his ground and Omar didn't like it. Not one bit.

'Olivia is nine?' Harry spoke quietly, his breath forming a white mist between the two men.

Omar brushed past Harry, opened the garage door and slammed it, making it bounce in the frame. Harry looked around at the emptiness of the garage. He thought about the way Tara had been frantically chasing the white Audi. He was certain of one thing: he'd be seeing Omar again soon.

Outside, Harry watched Omar speed out of the lot and on to Manningham Lane in the blue Fiesta. He pulled his phone from his coat pocket to check the tracking device was working. He was about to open the app when his phone rang – a withheld number.

'Yes?' said Harry.

'Find the diary?' the voice asked.

'I did.'

'Prove it.'

Harry hesitated before saying, 'Lexi and Olivia Goodwin.'

Now it was her turn to pause.

'The New Beehive Inn. You know it?'

'I'm not far from there.'

'Fifteen minutes?'

'How will I recognize you?'

'Trust me,' she said. 'When you see me, you'll know.'

NINETEEN

BILLY MUSA PULLED UP at the rear of the farmhouse just as the sun was starting to set.

Only twenty-four hours until he would be six-figures richer.

He rubbed his eyes hard.

What the fuck was Ali playing at?

Murder, so near to the handover. Madness.

'I'm out after this,' Billy whispered to himself.

He stood for a moment, struck as always by the enormity of Ilkley Moor with its foreboding nothingness. He had lived this life long enough.

The farmhouse sat half a mile from anywhere, surrounded by green fields, with the Cow and Calf Rocks towering in the distance – complete isolation. Their boss owned the place and Billy had got used to taking advantage of the empty, secluded house. Women and drugs – Billy was happy to pay for both and it was easy to get carried away out here in the dark moors.

Billy wasn't the only one using this house. For the past decade, once a year, the farmhouse became a prison for two carefully chosen people.

Chosen because, if they left Bradford, they wouldn't be missed.

Chosen because the mother would put her own happiness ahead of her daughter's and when Billy showered her with attention and enticed her into the unforgiving world of drug addiction, she'd be only too willing to follow.

This was getting easier. Only in Bradford, he thought.

Lexi Goodwin was a gift. Her own parents hadn't been interested when she fell pregnant at fifteen, sacrificing her youth for an ill-prepared parenthood. Now twenty-four, she was still a child. Exactly the type of woman Billy targeted.

It was always the same. He threw cash at her: nice hotels, restaurants, shopping sprees.

The younger the prize, the bigger the payday.

Six figures was the most they'd ever been offered . . .

Lexi might feel special in the glow of all that attention, but it was nine-year-old Olivia Goodwin who Billy had his eye on.

'Hey!' Olivia yelled, running towards Billy with outstretched arms. 'Big Bee's here!'

She charged towards him, excitement etched across her face, and threw her skinny arms around his towering body.

'Yo!' he said, holding the pizza box high above her head.

'Are you staying tonight?' she asked. 'We miss you!'

Billy ruffled her blonde hair.

'Big Bee brought you pizza and . . .' He handed her a new iPhone.

'For me!' she squealed.

'Don't tell your mother,' he said, lifting her up and carrying her into the living room. 'So, you like it here?'

'It's too big,' she said flatly. 'And Mum's phone doesn't get reception.'

'Who do you want to call?' he asked, laughing as he put her down on a leather couch.

'Cold,' she said, making a face at the leather.

'Leather couches are expensive.'

'Still cold.'

'So, who were you trying to call?' Billy asked again.

'Just you. I wanted pizza.'

Billy's shoulders relaxed.

'And I brought it? Hey, great minds!' he said, raising his hand for a high-five. 'Where's your mum?'

Olivia pulled a face. 'Sleeping. I thought you said the medicine would make her better?'

'It will when we go to London tomorrow.' He set the pizza box down on the coffee table.

'Are we definitely going tomorrow?' she asked excitedly.

'Of course. I told you, it's my last shift tonight.'

'And then we're going to that eye thing?'

Billy nodded and smiled, opening the box of pizza. 'The London Eye. Here,' he said, removing a slice of Margherita from the box. 'You want to eat with your hands?'

'Can I?'

'You're with Big Bee, we can do whatever we want.'

'You're the best,' she said, taking it from him.

'You've been very grown up, looking after your mum, you know.'

Olivia shrugged and took a bite from the pizza, strings of cheese hanging from her mouth. 'She's been sleeping most of the day,' she said through a mouthful of food.

'What time did she wake up?'

Olivia shrugged again. '*Judge Judy* was on TV.'

'Nearly lunchtime then?' he said.

'Suppose.'

Billy got up from the couch, heading towards the open-plan kitchen at the far side of the living room. 'You want a Coke?' he called out.

'Yeah.'

'Only got cherry,' he said, opening the fridge and looking back over his shoulder.

Olivia made a face.

'Water then?' he said jokingly.

She frowned.

'Let me ask you a question,' he said, removing a can of Cherry Coke from the fridge. 'How come you're so beautiful?'

Olivia frowned again and shrugged her shoulders. 'I told you, I'm not. Stop saying that.'

'Hey,' said Billy, opening the can and pouring its contents into a glass, 'when we get to London, I'm going to have to warn the boys to keep away from my princess.'

'I don't like boys,' she whined. 'Yuck!'

Billy laughed and from his pocket removed a small white pill, slipping it into Olivia's glass. The cherry flavouring in the Coke would mask the taste of the sleeping pill. Combined with a tummy full of pizza, Olivia would easily fall into a deep sleep.

'Olivia?' he called out.

'Yeah?' she said through another mouthful of pizza.

'Why don't you pick a film? I've got time for one before I start work,' said Billy, swirling the glass to ensure the pill had fully dissolved.

'Harry Potter!' she cried, taking the DVD from the shelf.

'Really?' Billy asked, bringing their drinks through. 'I'm sure we watched that last week.'

'No, this is the next one,' she replied, taking the glass from him.

'OK, magicians and wizards it is. Tell you what, let's see who can drink their Coke quickest? Like yesterday? If you win, we watch your DVD, but if I win, we watch football.'

Olivia grabbed the glass with both hands.

'No cheating,' said Billy, lifting his glass and pretending he hadn't seen her start.

'Oh, one thing?'

She scowled, impatient to get on with their game.

'Before I forget: tomorrow morning, my friend is coming to take a look at the boiler. I've given him a key, so when you see him, don't be scared. OK?'

She nodded, but wasn't really paying attention.

'Olivia, this is important,' he said. 'He's called Ali.'

*

Upstairs, Billy found the emaciated body of Lexi Goodwin in the master bed where he had left her. A potent smell of sweat and urine made Billy want to retch.

'Hey,' he said gently.

'You got me some?' she pleaded, her lips cracked and dry. 'I need some, Billy, I . . . I . . . just need a little.'

Billy nodded.

'We leave for London, tomorrow,' he said, gently wiping her mouth and pushing blonde hair back from her sweaty temple. 'We'll get you booked into that detox clinic my friend owns, yeah? Get you some real help?'

She nodded eagerly, looking at the syringe in his hands.

'No more after this,' she said, more out of habit than hope.

'You're going to do fine when we get there,' he said, wrapping a sleeve around her arm as a makeshift tourniquet. 'Just fine.'

'Are . . . are . . . you going to be here in the morning?' she pleaded.

'Last shift, baby,' he said. 'When you wake up tomorrow, we'll start our new life. You excited?'

Billy slipped the needle into her arm, watching as the blood entered the barrel.

'Yeah, babe,' she whispered. 'Dead excited.'

TWENTY

THE NEW BEEHIVE WAS in Westgate, on White Abbey Road. Harry drove through a side street, on to Lumb Lane. At six p.m. there were already several silhouettes lurking in doorways, waiting for a fee.

Skies which had earlier threatened rain now made good on their promise as Harry parked the car and climbed out, dismissing the woman who had come over to offer her services.

According to the plaque by the door, the New Beehive was the oldest public house in Bradford and the only gas-lit pub left in the country. He thought of Thorpe Edge and Wilson's living room wall with its long list of local pub closures.

Etched above the doorway, illuminated by a dim lamp, was a carved date: *1901*.

Bradford had been a thriving industrial centre back then.

Next to the pub was Rashid House. It used to be the place to buy car stereos, but it had been transformed into a vibrant Islamic shop selling hijabs, jubbas and other clothing, books and prayer beads.

The two buildings couldn't have been more different. One a decaying relic of days gone by when the local pub had been the heart of a hard-working community, the other a symbol of the new Bradford, a bold shopfront, smooth stone pillars and prayer mats in the windows.

And behind Harry, dominating the surrounding buildings was the dome of one the largest mosques in Bradford, the Jamiyat Tabligh-ul-Islam, one of over a hundred that had sprung up across the city.

From the outside, the pub looked decrepit. His first impression was of a tumbledown local where the BNP might have held meetings, but he was happy to be proven wrong. Inside, the pub was quiet. There were two elderly locals at the far end of the bar and what looked like a couple of students huddled in the corner, focusing on their mobile phones. The place looked like it had been recently refurbished.

The barman welcomed Harry warmly. His face was lined with wrinkles and his grey hair was receding. Harry couldn't help but notice his hands were the size of spades.

'Nice spot you got here,' said Harry, and ordered a Jack Daniels. 'Owner? Manager?'

'Both,' replied the man. 'Percy.'

Harry nodded. 'Outside could do with a spruce up.'

Percy smiled. 'Aye. You talking about my pub or the city?'

'Christ, like that, is it?'

Percy waved Harry's comment away. 'Tough trading all over.'

'Especially tough here?'

Percy grunted. 'Your words, friend. Not mine.' He poured a measure of Jack Daniels into a glass. 'Ice?'

'Please.' Harry took a seat on a barstool. 'Can't be many traditional boozers left in this city.'

'You really want to know?'

Harry nodded and accepted the drink, scanning the room for a woman he was supposed to recognize.

'Over the past twenty years, a hundred and seventy have closed.'

Harry whistled ruefully.

Percy nodded. 'You local?'

'Born and bred.'

'Different city nowadays.'

'But you're still here,' said Harry. 'When others have closed?'

'Students.' Percy nodded towards the couple in the corner, then pointed at the bar, where there were dozens of European ales. 'We try to keep them interested. Keeps us ticking over.'

Harry took another sip of his drink.

'You want to hear something funny?' asked Percy.

'Always.'

'These days, you want to open a betting shop, you need planning permission; all sorts of bureaucrats get involved. When a pub closes? Folk turn it into a restaurant or a mosque and nobody bats an eye. That sound fair to you?'

Harry shook his head.

'Anyways, friend, meeting someone or just fancied a change?'

'Meeting someone.'

Percy nodded. 'Sorta work you in?'

'The sort that tries to clean up this city.'

'Must be busy,' Percy said, raising his eyebrows.

Harry nodded, then smiled. 'I bet you remember when this place used to be something.'

Percy held up his hands, scarred, wrinkled and hardened. 'Used to be a foreman in Lister Mill. Long time ago, like.'

'I always thought a good barman should be steeped in local history.'

Percy clinked glasses with him. 'Kind of you to say.'

They both sipped their drinks.

Harry's phone beeped with a text message from an unknown number.

Downstairs.

'You got a downstairs?' he asked Percy.

'Aye. Function room.'

'Can I?' said Harry.

Percy nodded and pointed to the stairs at the side of the bar. 'There's a girl working down there. Wanted some quiet.'

'My date,' said Harry, smiling.

A narrow stone staircase descended into a darkness which was absolute. He made his way down, taking in the faint smell of damp.

The cellar was nothing like Harry could have imagined: neatly organized and inviting, despite the cold. There were disco lights hanging from a ceiling that looked like it had no right being so high when the entrance to the room was so low.

Harry heard a chair scrape against the floor.

He walked towards the noise and saw the silhouette of a girl sitting at a table in the far corner.

When he finally laid eyes on her, his grip on the bourbon wavered. Harry stared at the girl in disbelief.

TWENTY-ONE

ALI KAMRAN PULLED UP outside ZeeZee's Kebab House.

As usual, there were no customers inside, just one lone worker idly playing with his mobile phone.

Six cars parked outside. Probably more round the back.

There was more on the menu here than just food.

Ali glanced upstairs where curtains were drawn, only the faint glow from a lamp hinting it was business as usual.

The cars were all regulars; Ali recognized the makes and models. Their owners were takeaway delivery men and Asian taxi drivers who would both assist and abuse passengers in equal measure. This was how they dealt with their frustration at being confined to undesirable arranged marriages which fulfilled cultural demands but not carnal desires. They didn't want diseased street whores and couldn't afford high-class escorts, so instead they came here.

Ali hated them, these men who had been able to pick and choose from a cohort of potential wives.

But soon they would see.

Let them mock him after tomorrow.

Let them whisper.

Why did you curse my house?

Anger brought his mother's words to the surface.

'I cursed your home,' he whispered, thinking of her last few moments, her horrified expression as Ali had pushed a pillow over her face; legs thrashing weakly amidst muffled cries for a saviour who never arrived, 'because *you* cursed me.'

Ali entered the kebab house, pulled out the takeaway menu Billy had given him earlier with the number 'six' scrawled on the top and handed it to the guy behind the counter. Reluctantly he put his phone away and headed out back. Hidden, as usual, under his hoodie, Ali waited. The assistant returned with a small takeaway bag containing a closed plastic food-tray and handed it to Ali.

Ali headed upstairs. In the kitchen, a squalid room littered with empty vodka bottles and oily takeaway cartons, he took a seat at the table. Ali could relax here, listening to the familiar quiet whimpers of the girls as beds creaked. Three of the four rooms had their doors closed. Through the open door of the end room, Ali could hear a zip being fastened. Seconds later, a burly Asian man with sweat trickling down his face opened the door and stepped on to the landing.

He reached for the jacket that was hanging on the bannister, but stopped when he saw Ali. A grin split his face and he whispered in Urdu: 'Ali, brother, try her – she knows how to please.' Then he disappeared down the stairs, slamming the door at the bottom on the way out.

Ali didn't move. He sat there, listening to the headboard banging against the wall from the room next door, Urdu curses getting louder and louder.

Ali had never experienced what the men were doing. Forcing himself on young girls wasn't his idea of a good time – he wanted the real thing.

A girl of his own, not like Gori, who was as damaged as Ali. There'd been a time when that had bonded them tighter than he could ever have imagined. But then he'd seen Olivia and realized that she was the one he had been waiting his entire life to meet.

A wife, a life he could cherish.

Ali could hear the girl in the far room starting to cry. Leaving his seat, he inched closer, stopping at the threshold, where the door had been left wide open. He peered inside.

She was lying on the bed with her back to him, blonde hair a chaotic mess, knees huddled into her chest.

Blood on the bedsheet. A used condom hanging from the bin.

He wanted to pity her.

He opened the bag he had been given downstairs and pulled out the plastic takeaway container. Two loaded syringes. One for Lexi Goodwin, one for Olivia.

Only one day to go.

Ali closed his eyes and thought of his cellar.

After tomorrow, Olivia Goodwin would be his. His alone.

And there was nothing Billy or Riz could do to stop him.

TWENTY-TWO

'IS THIS SUPPOSED TO be a sick joke?' asked Harry, pointing at the girl.

'Nothing funny about it,' she replied, staring at Harry with intense silvery eyes.

She was a stranger to Harry, petite with peroxide blonde curls to her shoulders, fair skin and eyes that shimmered like bullets. While she was unfamiliar, the dark purple Ralph Lauren dress she was wearing awkwardly over her clothes wasn't.

Tara's sixteenth-birthday gift from Harry.

'Take it off,' said Harry, pointing at it. 'Before I make you.' He put his drink on the table, hard enough that bourbon sloshed from the glass.

Small and unthreatening, she pulled the dress over her head. Harry seized it, bunching it in his fists.

'Sit,' he said, noting she was now left wearing what appeared to be a burka, its hood lowered. 'Who the fuck are you?'

'Sarah,' she replied, sitting down.

'Sarah what?'

'Brewster.'

Harry examined the dress in his hands. It smelled unmistakably of Tara's perfume. He sat down opposite her.

The silence became awkward.

Sarah's eyes were unlike anything Harry had ever seen. He assumed they were contact lenses, shimmering silvery in the dimness of the room.

'Are you going to just sit there all night? I thought you might tell me what I'm doing here?' Harry said eventually. He held the dress up. 'This is all either very smart or very stupid.'

Sarah lifted a bottle of beer from the table and took a sip, her eyes never leaving Harry.

More silence. More staring. Harry's patience was starting to crack.

'If I wanted to stare into a strange girl's eyes all night, Sarah, I'd go back across the road and pay one of the hookers.'

'I've heard so much about you,' she said. 'You'll forgive me if I want to take a minute.'

'Are you trying to tell me I should be flattered?'

'Yes.'

'I'm not. I'm more interested in what the fuck you're doing with this dress and why you're acting more like somebody I should nick than somebody I should be working with. Where are you getting this information from? What aren't you telling me?'

Sarah replaced her beer on the table and pulled an iPhone from a bag on the floor. She swiped the screen and entered the passcode, tapping through to an app before sliding the phone to Harry.

'I want you to trust me,' she said.

Harry lifted the device, one hand still clutching Tara's dress.

There were over four hundred photos of the two of them.

'We were close,' said Sarah.

'Yeah,' Harry replied. The oldest photo was a selfie dated eighteen months ago; they were in City Park by the water fountain. Tara was sticking her tongue out, trying to conceal a smile that Harry longed to see again.

'This yours or Tara's?' he asked, handing back the phone.

'Mine.'

'So?' he said. 'Why all this secrecy?'

'Do you believe we were close?' she asked.

'I believe there are a lot of photos of you and her on your phone.'

'Where heads of state met in secret?' she replied, smiling for the first time. 'I liked that story.'

He looked away, exhaling deeply.

Play detective not uncle, Harry.

'I'd only know that story if we'd been close,' she said.

'Agreed.' He stared into the dark corners of the room, taking his time.

'That dress was her favourite. Said she badgered you for months about it.'

'OK, OK, OK,' Harry snapped, finally looking at her. 'I don't need a 101 of my history with my own niece.'

Sarah picked her phone off the table and put it away. 'You won't like what I'm going to say, Harry, which is why you need to know I'm credible.'

'What the fuck did you get her involved with?' he asked.

Sarah leaned back in her chair, slouched her shoulders resignedly and sighed. 'I know, if it weren't for me—'

'Did you get her killed?' Harry expelled his words bitterly.

She nodded and blinked away tears.

'Tell me,' he said, leaning forward until his body pressed against the table.

'She moved out of her parents' place. Did you know that?' asked Sarah.

'Yes.'

'Cultural crap, as she put it. Grandparents hassling her about marrying some Sikh guy they found for her in the community.' Sarah smiled ruefully. 'She said it was your phrase – "cultural crap"?'

'Yeah, something like that.'

Harry had coined the phrase when they'd all been living together, a throwaway comment when he'd had to endure bullshit that held no importance for him.

'Anyway, her parents hit the roof when she said she wasn't going to university after they'd spent all that money on a private education. All she wanted to do was be a journalist. She didn't need to spend three years at some fancy institution. So she moved out, got herself an internship at the *Telegraph and Argus*, but it just turned out to be making coffee and shredding paper.'

Sarah paused. 'So I gave her a story of her own, one she couldn't ignore.'

'What story?'

She sat there, studying him intently, offering no reply.

'What?'

'Are you here as part of your job? Or as "Uncle Harry"?'

'Both.'

'And if you had to choose?'

'I don't.'

'But if you—'

'I don't.'

Sarah took a deep breath. 'Fine. Promise me something before I start?'

'Go on.'

'You won't interrupt until I've finished.'

Sarah told Harry about a sophisticated child-trafficking gang operating in Bradford. They targeted young, vulnerable single mothers with younger, even more vulnerable daughters. Their front man was Billy Musa, a taxi driver who would strike up a relationship with the mother and, over the course of a year, ensure that she became addicted to heroin. The addiction would isolate her. The more dependent she became on Billy, the more dependent her daughter became. Billy would treat the daughter like a princess, and then one day he'd ask the mother to marry him, promising her a fresh start and a new life for them all in London.

Once they left Bradford, they were never seen or heard from again.

When she had finished, Sarah looked at Harry expectantly.

'And you know all this how?' asked Harry.

She sighed.

'I can't help if you withhold,' said Harry.

'As well as these targets, Billy and his mates also have a harem of young girls they like to . . . you know.'

'No. I don't.'

A scowl spread across Sarah's face. 'Have a "good time" with.'

He waited for the next part.

'For a while, I was one of those girls,' she said quietly.

Harry leaned back in his chair and nodded for Sarah to continue. It was clear she didn't want to go on.

'This is hard for me,' she said, glancing into the dark corners of the room. 'Would you mind . . . if I turned my chair around, so I don't have to look at you when I tell it?'

'Whatever makes you comfortable,' said Harry. He'd never been a fan of that tactic, but he needed Sarah onside at this point.

She turned her chair to face away and closed her eyes. She spoke for almost a quarter of an hour. There had been a few girls in the group. Billy would buy them takeaways and drive them around in his taxi. Before long, he wanted something in return.

'Stupid,' she hissed, 'not to have seen it coming.'

Harry wanted to tell her it was far from stupid. Her innocence had made her unaware how malicious the streets of Bradford could be. But he remained quiet.

'To start with, it was just a kiss,' said Sarah. 'I thought Billy was only fooling around. But as he gave me more and more alcohol and the days turned into weeks then months, eventually he did whatever he wanted to me and . . . and . . . I never realized just how badly I had let him abuse me.'

Sarah raised her head from her chest, dead eyes looking into the middle distance. 'I became dependent on him,' she whispered, then fell silent.

Harry got to his feet, placed Tara's dress on the table and made his way around to her, grabbing a chair and placing it in front of her.

'You're talking about eleven years ago? Correct?'

Sarah nodded, looking ashamedly at Harry.

'When did it stop?'

'In 2011. When I was sixteen. I was too . . . old.'

'You didn't go to the police?'

She sniggered, it was a cruel sound. 'You think it was just Billy who had a good time with us? There were so many – and he told us they were powerful people. Policemen, judges, prison officers . . .'

'Tell me how Tara fits into all this.'

'There's more. The names in Tara's diary – you looked into them?'

Harry nodded.

'Their junkie mothers all turned up dead a few years after they left Bradford. Did you realize that?'

Another nod from Harry.

'Nobody even wondered about the daughters though. Why would they? Do people give a shit about some random junkie's daughter?'

'What are you trying to say, Sarah? Give me the small print, not the headlines.'

Sarah told him she had known Melissa and Anna, the first two girls on the list. At the time, she'd been envious of how Billy cared for them. They were treated differently, like precious jewels. Sarah told Harry how one day Melissa had disappeared – moved to London, was what Billy had told her. A year later, Anna also moved away.

'I was twelve or thirteen. I didn't think anything of it. Billy got bored with me and I got out. Later, I tried to get the others to talk, but we were all too ashamed and too frightened. I spent almost a year trying to track down Melissa and Anna. Neither of them are on social media – no Facebook, Snapchat or Instagram. Do you know how rare it is for young girls to have no Internet presence?'

Harry nodded, he was starting to see the size of the shitstorm.

'I couldn't find anything on them *anywhere*. Tara searched the archives of the newspaper library and found out about their mothers. As individual cases they aren't remarkable; dead addicts turn up in gutters every day. But when you put it all together, you start to see a really frightening picture.'

'You think the girls are dead?'

'No,' she said. 'I think they've been sold.'

'What makes you think that?'

'If they were dead, one of them would have surfaced. And . . .' Sarah hesitated, then grabbed the neck of her burka and pulled it down to reveal livid scars on her neck. 'Three years ago, I confronted Billy with what I knew. I . . . I . . . was angry and stupid – I thought he'd be shocked or scared and maybe stop.'

Harry leaned closer and stared at her neck. In the dim light he could see where deep lacerations had formed angry-looking scars. They looked like knife-wounds.

'Billy did that?'

Sarah nodded. 'He thinks I'm dead.'

'How?'

She shook her head, looked away and wiped away a tear.

'I guess he panicked. Did this,' she said, touching her scars, 'then threw my body into the Leeds and Liverpool Canal.'

'How did you survive?'

'Just did.'

'Come on.' Harry wasn't about to accept that.

'Look,' Sarah said fiercely, glaring at Harry, 'they left me for dead and I stayed that way.' She grabbed hold of the burka. 'No easier place to disappear than Bradford.' She let it fall. 'We're dealing with the bottom end of this chain – Billy and others—'

'Others?'

'Omar, Riz and Ali. But they're not the endgame. There's someone higher up that they work for.'

'How do you know all this?'

'Because Billy told me, right before he came at me with a knife. He said, "Little girl, you don't know who you're fucking with . . ." And I believe him.'

'So why did you drag Tara into all this?' Harry asked, fixing her with a penetrating stare.

'I had nobody to trust until I met her.'

'Run me through it.'

'Cultural crap,' said Sarah. 'Remember?'

Harry nodded.

'I met her at a bar one Friday night. Two angry girls sharing war stories and getting drunk.'

'Thought you stayed off the grid?'

'I do,' she corrected herself quickly. 'But I'm smart with it.'

Harry nodded for her to continue.

'We became friends. She was bitter at her family situation, I was bitter at . . . everything.'

Harry went to speak but Sarah stopped him with a raised hand.

'Tara wanted to prove her decision to move out was the right one.'

Sarah leaned closer to Harry. 'She was driven, I mean *driven*. I could see it in her eyes, in every breath she took. She wanted to quit the internship, but I told her not to because I had a story worth investigating. I knew she'd be all-in, so I told her. Everything.'

'When?'

Sarah shrugged. 'Just over a year ago. I didn't realize how far she'd go, Harry. You have to believe me. Tara was so fair-skinned, she easily passed for white and looked girlish enough to pass for a teenager. The only way to find out which girl was Billy's next victim was to get close to him.'

Sarah struggled with her next sentence but forced it from her lips. 'She used herself as bait.'

Harry scratched his stubble wildly then swept his hand across his face and rubbed his eyes.

'Tara?' he said dismissively. 'She was just a kid.'

'You hadn't seen her in, what, four years? She was twenty years old, Harry. She wasn't a kid, and she knew exactly how to play Billy to make him think he had a shot.'

'Jesus,' said Harry, standing up and moving back to the table. He picked up the remainder of his drink and finished it, struggling to reconcile this version of Tara with the Tara he had helped raise.

'He *never* touched her,' said Sarah, standing up, reading his thoughts. 'But we realized Olivia Goodwin and her mother were next. I told Tara to back off, but the closer it got to the deadline—'

'Deadline?'

'Tomorrow night.'

'How do you know that?'

'I've watched Billy for years. The girls always disappear the day before Ramadan begins, which is tomorrow night.'

'Tell me about Olivia,' said Harry, unsure how much of this he could believe.

'You've been to her mother's flat, I assume?'

'Empty.'

'They took her on Friday and Tara panicked.'

'Panicked?'

'We'd been monitoring Billy. And since I *have* to remain invisible,' she said, pointing to the scars on her neck, 'Tara was the one who got close to Olivia.'

Harry didn't want to hear any more, struggling to believe Tara could be so bold, so brazen.

'Tomorrow night, Bradford loses another girl, Harry. We're almost out of time.'

She held his gaze.

'You *will* help me. You're more responsible for Tara's death than you realize.'

Harry registered the change in Sarah's tone. He didn't like being threatened.

They stared at each other, eyes dancing before she tried one last stab of the knife.

'You could have stopped her death, Harry,' she whispered, and stepped a little closer. 'We were out of our depth and we knew it. So she called the one person she was *sure* would help us.'

The penny dropped and suddenly Harry felt his heart sink. Sarah saw it in his face. She nodded.

'She called you three months ago, Harry. Left messages for you.'

Sarah stepped closer still, right into his personal space, as sickening, overwhelming guilt spread through his stomach.

'She needed you, Harry. And you let her down.'

TWENTY-THREE

OUTSIDE, HARRY LEANED AGAINST the wall of the New Beehive Inn, welcoming the sensation of drizzle on his face like an alcoholic might a drink. He had stepped outside for a moment of air. To be alone with his guilt.

Tara had called Harry three months ago, half a dozen calls at the office over the space of a week. She had left messages. Harry had not returned her calls. Ronnie had forced a promise on him, that he'd cut all ties with the family – the only way the brothers could keep their own relationship strong. Mundeep had threatened Ronnie with divorce if he allowed Harry to be part of their children's lives. She wanted to be clear that if the kids did what Harry had done, they'd receive the same treatment.

'Christ,' he whispered, raising his face towards a sombre, starless sky, moving his head left then right so the rain caught every inch of his face. 'Christ,' he said again.

Harry's mind was a mess, anger surfacing, his ability to reason fast disappearing.

How much more was his decision to marry Saima going to cost him?

He suspected that Sarah might have held back on some of the

details, but he'd heard enough to more than spike his interest in her story.

'That poor girl,' Harry whispered to himself. 'All of them, Christ.'

He pulled his phone from his pocket, ignoring several missed calls from Ronnie and an impatient text asking him again for an update. He scrolled through dozens of emails until he arrived at the one from Charles. The video file was attached – Tara chasing after Omar's Audi.

Why hadn't she called him then?

Because you'd ignored her, Harry, and she didn't trust you to help after that.

The realization cut deeply, forcing the breath out of his lungs. Harry leaned against the wall of the pub as the world started to spin.

He thought of Tara's diary, the names: Billy, Riz, Ali and Omar; Olivia and Lexi Goodwin. The question: *Why do girls go missing in Bradford?*

Harry focused across the street where hookers were approaching kerb-crawling cars. Everything Sarah had told him had changed his view. If these women disappeared off the streets, would anyone give a shit? Who would report them? People were so caught up in their own lives, it seemed easier than ever to simply forget about others, especially those on the fringes of society. Alienation of vulnerable young mothers wasn't a hard sell. Harry believed that part. He also bought into the possibility the real target was an innocent little girl.

Harry watched the footage again. Tara chasing Omar's car. Her desperation when it pulled away. The anger and guilt inside him reached boiling point.

He needed to put this right.

These bastards thought they were untouchable. They were wrong.

'Where do you live?' asked Harry, retaking his seat opposite Sarah, rainwater dripping from his hair.

'I move around a lot,' she replied. 'I don't know who in this city is involved in this mess and I'm afraid of staying in one place too long. At the moment, I'm staying here.'

'Here?'

She pointed upstairs. 'Room five. I . . . was too scared to go to Tara's place, but I knew you would. So I waited for you.'

'How did you get my number?'

'Tara got it from her father's phone. And I got it from hers,' she said, putting her hand in her pocket and bringing out another iPhone. 'This is the one Tara used with Billy and the others.'

She gave Harry the pin to unlock it.

'Real James Bond stuff you got going on here,' he said patronizingly, taking it from her. 'Anything useful on it?'

'No. Billy was really particular about people using phones around him.'

'Smart man.'

'Suspiciously smart, no?'

Harry looked at her.

'What about the others?' he asked, not revealing he'd already met one of them. 'Omar, Riz and Ali?'

'Omar works at a garage on Manningham Lane. Riz is the boss of the taxi firm Billy works for. And Ali . . .'

She trailed off, breath coming quicker, fear spreading across her face. 'He's the guy Billy sends if the girls won't do what he says. Wears a hoodie . . . I . . . I . . . met him once. His eyes . . . they don't look human.'

Sarah produced a card from her pocket and slid it across the table to Harry.

'Triple-B Taxis,' she said. 'Billy drives their only seven-seater.'

'You think he killed Tara?'

Sarah shook her head. 'He's too smart for that.'

'So?'

'Billy will know.'

'Which number was your room again?'

Sarah looked at him nervously. 'Five.'

'I want to see it.'

'Why?'

'Because I asked nicely,' he replied, standing up and beckoning for her to follow.

'You always in disguise like this?' asked Harry, pointing at her outfit.

She nodded. 'Since he tried to kill me.'

'What do you do for money?' he asked, staring at her so hard she looked away uncomfortably.

'Am I under investigation now?'

'Damn right,' said Harry. 'Your room. Let's go.'

'Why?'

'Because if we're going to work together, you have to earn my trust.'

The room was bigger than Harry had imagined. Two double beds, an oak dressing table, desk and wardrobe. The door to the en suite was open, the edge of a shower cubicle visible.

'What now?' said Sarah.

Harry closed the door, looking around the chaotic room, burkas and western clothing flung across the floor, a laptop on an unmade bed and a half-empty bottle of vodka on the bedside table.

'ID,' said Harry. 'Something official.'

'What?'

'You heard.'

As if prepared for it, Sarah put her hand in her pocket and brought out her driving licence. She handed it to Harry, who looked at her suspiciously.

'A flat on Leeds Road?' he said, noting the address.

'I rented it for a few months. Like I said, I move around.'

'Give me your hand.'

'My hand?'

'Are you right or left handed?'

'What?'

'Right or left handed?' he said impatiently.

'Right,' she replied.

'Give it to me.'

'No.'

'We haven't got a lot of time, have we?'

She puffed her cheeks out and thrust her hand at him.

'Under the light,' he said, moving near the bottom of the bed where a light fitting was hanging from the ceiling.

Sarah rolled her eyes and held out her right hand.

Harry slapped a pair of handcuffs on her, the other end on the metal bed frame at the foot of the bed.

'What are you doing?' she hissed, panic in her eyes.

'Due diligence,' he said. 'If what you've said checks out, we'll talk some more.'

'You can't do this,' she said.

Harry looked at his watch. 'Nine p.m.' he said. 'You should get some sleep. Might be a late one.'

'Seriously,' she said, rattling the handcuffs against the bed frame. 'This is ridiculous.'

'You make too much noise, that old barman downstairs will call the police. Either way, you end up with me. You choose,' he said, turning to leave.

Sarah sat down on the bed, shaking her head. 'If I need the bathroom?'

Harry pulled a drawer out of the dressing table and placed it by her feet. 'I'd hold it,' he said, 'but if needs must.'

'You're kidding me?'

'I lost my sense of humour when I found my niece's body,' he replied.

There was a half-eaten apple on top of the dresser with a small knife sticking out of it. Harry removed it, tapped his finger on the blade then put it in his jacket pocket.

'Give me your mobile number.' Harry thrust his phone into her left hand.

'What are you going to do?' Sarah asked as she saved her number.

Harry waved the business card she had given him earlier.

'Call myself a taxi,' he said, and picked up the key to her room from the table so he could let himself back in later. He picked up the half-empty bottle of vodka and threw it on the bed. 'Sleep aid.'

Before opening the door to leave, Harry paused with his hand on the doorknob. 'Your hand,' he said. 'The tattoo? What do the initials stand for?'

Sarah glanced at her handcuffed wrist, turning it to reveal the letters GZ.

'Nothing,' she said quietly. 'Nothing at all.'

TWENTY-FOUR

HARRY WAS ON WHITE Abbey Road heading towards Bradford Royal Infirmary. The roads were quiet; rain spraying across his windscreen. He parked in a side street adjacent to the hospital, slipped on a raincoat and grabbed another pair of handcuffs from his boot before setting off for the hospital's main entrance.

Saima worked as an A & E sister, so Harry knew the place better than most. At the reception desk, he showed a harassed-looking young Asian woman his identification and asked to urgently see Consultant Balraj Patel. He was an old friend whose father had also owned a corner shop in Bradford. They'd spent their childhood in each other's stores. Balraj was one of only a handful of friends Harry had.

Harry took the last seat in the busy, humid waiting area. He was about to join everybody else in staring down at his phone when Balraj appeared and beckoned for Harry to follow him along a corridor and into a consultation booth.

'Not a good time, mate,' he said, pulling off a pair of blue latex gloves which he threw into a yellow clinical waste bin. They shook hands quickly, pulling each other in for an embrace.

'One of these days we'll just meet up to chew the fat,' replied Harry. 'What's happening?'

'Night before Bonfire Night,' replied Balraj. 'Burns. Wish they'd ban the things.'

'I won't keep you long,' replied Harry.

'How's Saima?' asked Balraj. 'Christ, I can't wait to see her back here. No one else knows what they're doing.'

'She's great. Motherhood suits her.'

Harry fished Sarah's driving licence from his pocket and handed it to Balraj. 'I wouldn't ask if it wasn't critical,' he said.

'It's always *critical*, Harry.'

'Forms and protocol are the death of progress. You know that. Just tell me if she was ever admitted with lacerations to her neck, stab wounds? Anything, really.'

'I can only give you the A & E records.'

'Can't you request her file from Medical Records?'

'What are you looking for?'

'Anything.'

'Off the record?'

'Obviously.'

'It's mental in here tonight, Harry—'

'You remember Tara?'

'Your niece?'

Harry nodded. 'She was . . .' he sighed. 'Murdered. I need this, Balraj. As quick as you can get it.'

'Shit, I'm so sorry, had no idea,' he said, putting his hand on Harry's shoulder and squeezing it before falling silent, unsure what to say next. 'Corner-shop boys stick together,' he said after a beat. 'I'm on it.'

Inside the entrance of the hospital was a payphone. Harry called Triple-B and ordered their seven-seater taxi, telling them he needed to go to Liverpool – no cabbie would turn that fare down.

Dispatch told him what he already knew; they only had one seven-seater, Harry would have to wait half an hour. With time to kill, he walked along the ground floor to a vending machine and bought a couple of chocolate bars and a Lucozade. Hovering around the entrance, he couldn't stop himself thinking of Saima; how he had repeatedly visited her here at work until she had finally agreed to go out on a date with him.

Outside, Harry sat on a bench where a smoker was lighting up under a no-smoking sign. The rain continued to fall.

'You should have nailed him when you had the chance.' The smoker edged closer.

Harry faced the man, rainwater sliding inside his collar, and stared at the battered, bruised face of Nash, almost unrecognizable after what Ronnie had done to him early that morning.

'Fractured wrist. Two broken ribs. Might have been worse if you hadn't intervened,' he said, raising his left arm, which was plastered from knuckle to elbow. 'You want to sign it?' Nash grinned and took a deep pull on his cigarette.

'You're in good spirits for a man who almost didn't see sunrise today,' said Harry.

'I didn't see it.'

'Don't get smart.'

Nash grunted and dragged hard on his cigarette.

'At least his boy Enzo did the decent thing and dropped me off here,' Nash said, smiling again.

'What did you say to the doctor?'

'Fell off my bike.'

This time it was Harry's turn to smile.

'I can't think why you put yourself through this with him.'

Harry stared across the car park, dimly lit by lampposts. He wasn't prepared to talk about that with Nash. 'Tara,' he said. 'What can you tell me?'

Nash removed a blister of tablets from his pocket, dry-swallowing two white pills before continuing with his cigarette. 'She didn't like her old man,' he said.

'Which twenty-year-old girl does? I meant what can you tell me about what she was involved in?'

Nash shrugged.

An ambulance pulled up, sirens screaming. Blue lights bounced off the buildings as it flashed past the men.

'How long were you watching her?' asked Harry, his concentration unbroken by the drama.

'It wasn't like that. Sentry duty wasn't my thing. I just checked in on her a couple of times a week. Ronnie was taking his own shit out on me this morning. He knows I did my damn job.'

'Haven't seen him like that before.'

'He's getting worse.'

'Tell me.'

Nash shook his head. 'He's got a year, maybe eighteen months before Bradford becomes too much for him. And he's drinking again.'

'Fuck off,' said Harry, incredulous.

'You didn't smell it on him this morning? I thought you were supposed to be sharp.'

Harry cast his mind back eighteen hours. Doubt began to creep in.

'Don't be surprised. Never met an alkie who could fight the thirst.'

Nash finished his cigarette, stubbed it out on the bench and slipped the stub into his pocket.

'You know something about Tara,' said Harry. 'You might not think you do, but it's there.'

'In . . .' Nash looked at his watch '. . . three hours, I'm on a train out of here. Contractual obligation. This isn't my problem any more.'

'I could stop you—'

'No, you can't,' said Nash, laughing and turning to face Harry. 'You're as guilty as anyone. But unlike me, someone is foolish enough to trust you with safeguarding this city.' He spat on the floor.

'You want to tell me something,' said Harry, 'or you wouldn't have started talking. What is it? You owe me.'

A couple of doctors, stethoscopes bouncing around their necks, hurried out of the main entrance, running past them towards the ambulance bay.

'Seems the shit's hitting the fan everywhere tonight,' said Nash, looking after them. He struggled to his feet, yawning widely. 'Almost makes me feel lucky.'

'Come on, Nash.'

'Argh, it's probably nothing,' he said, searching his pockets for something. 'You got a tenner?' he asked.

'What?'

'You got any cash? Need a taxi to the station. No way I'm catching the bus like this.'

Harry found his wallet and withdrew a ten-pound note but didn't hand it over.

'Used to be a time information was paid at decent rates,' said Nash.

Harry removed another note. 'You don't need it, Nash. I know what Ronnie was paying you.'

'Yorkshireman always likes a good day's pay for a good day's work, you should know that.'

Harry put his wallet away but kept the notes in his hand.

'He tell you why she left home?' asked Nash.

Harry nodded.

'Which part?'

'She found out what he really does.'

Nash sniggered. 'Right.'

Harry stood up. 'She didn't know?'

'Oh, she knew,' said Nash. 'You ask the boy wonder how. But that's not why she wanted to leave home.'

'No?'

'No.'

'Come on, Nash,' said Harry.

'You know what? I think I will get that bus.'

Harry put his hand firmly on Nash's broken arm, just above the plaster, squeezing hard.

'That's low.' Nash winced. 'Even for you.'

'Why'd she leave?'

'You like to go out on Friday nights, Harry?' he asked, easing his arm free of Harry's grip.

'Not really.'

'Tara did.'

'OK,' said Harry, not seeing where this was headed.

'Can't be easy for a dad, or a granddad like hers, when the lady of the house wants to go to the Candy Club every Friday night.'

'Candy Club?'

'Don't know your city quite as well as you think, do you, Harry?'

Harry ran a search on his phone.

'Friday nights, Harry,' said Nash.

Harry brought the screen closer to his face.

'Question is,' said Nash, grinning shadily before walking away, 'who knew about it – and was it worth killing for?'

TWENTY-FIVE

HARRY WAVED DOWN THE seven-seater Peugeot as it arrived outside the entrance to A & E, his mind bursting with questions. The tinted window of the passenger side was lowered and Harry confirmed the booking name with the driver.

He climbed into the back and searched for the driver's ID on the dash.

Bilal Musa. *Billy*.

'Cheers, boss,' said Harry, keeping the hood of his raincoat over his head to conceal his face, 'pissing it down.' Harry felt for the knife he'd borrowed from Sarah's hotel room, tucking it up the sleeve of his jacket.

Billy glanced in the rear-view mirror with narrow eyes and nodded. His frame was packed into the seat, meaty, thunderous. 'Others?'

'Sorry,' said Harry, brushing water on to the floor from his coat, 'things changed inside with my grandma.' He pointed towards the hospital. 'My brother needs to get home to bring my mother here. He's got a car full of relatives and is waiting next to the M606 on the Euroway Trading Estate. Can we collect them from there? Saves time.'

Billy looked apprehensive.

Harry passed £140 over Billy's shoulder. 'They said this would cover it?'

That eased Billy, who took the money and pulled away.

Harry slouched into his seat, his mind overloaded with noise. The Candy Club was a notorious gay bar in Bradford.

Was that why she had been so desperate to leave home?

For now, he was forced to push Nash's new information from his mind and focus instead on what Sarah had said about Billy.

Harry engaged him in bullshit chat, the usual about his car and the taxi firm. He carefully established that this was Billy's personal car, one he had purposely bought because the seven-seater gave him a niche in the market.

Harry could see a simple tracker wired into the GPS and radio. As soon as they were unplugged, Billy would be all Harry's.

Billy looked a little older than Harry, maybe forty. He had a neatly shaven head, spoke with a Bradford accent, and was wearing a traditional black shalwar kameez and a jacket.

Harry's attention turned to a piece of string hanging from the rear-view mirror, a tiny cylindrical container swaying at the end.

A taweez; an Islamic necklace to ward away evil. It held a scroll on which protective Arabic words were written. Over the years, Saima had paid a holy man to create several; to protect her pregnancy, to watch over Aaron, to keep their home safe.

Billy, it seemed, was afraid of something.

An Asian radio station was playing Bollywood tracks from Harry's youth and his mind was briefly taken back to his parents' living room above the corner shop, aged twelve. A Saturday-night ritual; two Indian movies from the local rental shop for a quid. They were always cheap copies and Harry had to get up every half-hour to adjust the tracking on the VCR. He and Ronnie would lie on the carpet, arguing over whose turn it was next.

Simpler, happier times.

Now nothing more than nostalgia.

Harry directed Billy into Bierley, the estate in front of Euroway.

At the bottom, he told him to head towards the warehouses. Harry removed the knife from his sleeve, then his phone.

The Euroway estate housed several cash-and-carries, none of them Ronnie's but Harry knew the area well. He had spent his youth traipsing around here with his father and had been given his first unofficial driving lesson by him in the car park.

Now the estate had been left to rot, the buildings abandoned and disintegrating. Seemed to be the same story right across the city.

Harry directed Billy to the far end, where the streetlights were out and he knew the warehouses were empty. Putting the phone to his ear, he pretended to talk to his brother, organizing a pick-up location. As instructed, Billy pulled over outside the metal gates of an abandoned warehouse.

The second Billy engaged the handbrake, Harry leaned forward and put his arm around his neck, the blade of the knife across Billy's throat. 'One fucking wrong move.'

Billy tried to struggle and Harry put his weight into the sleeper hold.

'Hey, hey!' Harry pushed the blade up Billy's nose until he hit bone. 'You want to try me?'

Billy stilled. Harry told him to remove the GPS tracker and radio from its power source and turn it off. He twisted the knife so Billy got a shock and frantically obeyed.

'Turn the car off. Throw the keys into the passenger footwell.'

Billy did as he asked.

Harry told him to put his hands on the steering wheel. He tightened his grip around Billy's neck, removed the knife from his nose and grabbed his handcuffs, perfectly placed at his side. With the fluidity of a seasoned pro, Harry slapped one half across Billy's left hand then told him to thread the other side under the steering and secure his right, trapping Billy where he sat.

Billy didn't flinch. He was either resigned to his predicament or, more worryingly, he wasn't afraid.

'Very clever,' said Billy. 'What now?'

'Where's your phone?'

Billy hesitated until Harry leaned back into his seat, his full weight on Billy's windpipe.

'Inside pocket,' said Billy, wheezing.

Harry relaxed his grip and slipped his hand inside Billy's pocket, removing his phone.

Billy gritted his teeth. 'What now, *benchaud*?' It was the most vulgar Asian profanity.

Harry got out of the car, walked around to get in the front next to Billy. He put the knife on the dashboard, picked up the keys from the floor and looked towards the driver's seat. Billy was smiling.

'Something funny?'

'You're making a big mistake.'

'I hope so.'

Billy shook his head and swore again.

Harry pulled up a recent picture of Tara on his phone, one Ronnie had sent him that morning. He thrust the phone in Billy's face, watching him intensely.

No reaction.

He was either very good or he'd never seen her.

'You know this girl?'

Billy kept looking at the screen. 'I pick up hundreds of girls every week.'

'I mean personally. Do you know this girl personally?'

'No.' Billy looked away.

'Not what I heard.'

'You heard wrong. That all this is? Some *randi*?'

The word meant slut in Punjabi.

Harry grabbed the back of Billy's head and smashed his face into the steering wheel; his nose gave a sickening crunch.

'*Benchaud!*' shouted Billy, his eyes blinded by tears, blood streaking down his face.

'This is my niece,' said Harry. 'You repeat that word and I'll break the rest of your face.'

'What do you want?'

He waited for Billy to stop thrashing.

'She was found murdered yesterday morning.' Again, no reaction.

Billy used his shoulder to wipe the blood from his nose. 'So? In this city, that's not news.'

'I heard you'd taken a liking to her.'

'I told you.' He was struggling to steady his breathing through a bloodied nose.

'You're not lying to me, are you, Billy?'

The use of his name momentarily threw him. His eyes flickered towards the badge on his dashboard.

Bilal Musa.

'I told you,' Harry read what was going through his mind, 'someone said you know this girl.'

'Why are you here?'

'Last time, Billy. You sure you've never seen her?'

He shook his head.

Harry reached for the phone on the central console. He pressed Billy's thumb into the iPhone's home button, unlocking the screen.

'Sure you've never seen her?'

'Fuck off.' Billy was glancing nervously at his phone.

Harry removed Tara's phone from his pocket, the one Sarah had given him in the New Beehive, and accessed Tara's number. He punched it into Billy's phone and pressed the call button. A selfie of Tara and Billy flashed on the screen.

Billy glanced worriedly at Harry, who nodded slowly. He threw Tara's phone on the dash, grabbing the knife instead and jammed the tip under Billy's chin.

'Your night just got a whole lot worse, *benchaud.*'

TWENTY-SIX

'YOU'RE GOING TO TELL me you don't know how you got her number. Right?' Harry trawled Billy's call logs and saw two dozen calls over the past week. He focused on Saturday night when Tara had been murdered.

She'd called him six times. All around midnight. He hadn't answered once.

Billy remained quiet, staring out of the windscreen.

Harry accessed the photographs on Billy's phone. Hundreds of pictures of young girls – opportunistic shots taken while they weren't looking. In his taxi, at a playground and several in some-one's living room, but no pictures of Tara.

'You like them young?' he said, turning the phone towards Billy, who just smiled back.

Harry scratched the stubble on his face. Billy's arrogance was causing his anger to rise. 'We really going to play this game?'

'Fuck you.'

Harry scrolled to 'Recently Deleted' photos on Billy's phone. He knew what he'd find before he opened the folder: Tara.

Harry's temper fractured, his face tense, eyes burning.

'How much do you think this car weighs? Got to be, what, ton and a half?'

Billy looked perplexed. Harry threw the phone on the dash, an image of Tara blowing a kiss filling the screen, and got out of the car.

Harry's blood was on fire as he opened Billy's boot and removed the car jack, all sense of reason lost.

He rolled up his sleeves, ignoring the rain, ignoring the warning at the back of his mind. 'You want to play, let's fucking play,' he whispered.

Ten minutes later, Harry had raised the front of the car a foot off the ground.

He opened the back door and got in carefully, mindful not to jump the vehicle off the jack. Harry wrapped his arm around Billy's neck and pulled back, choking him until he faded into unconsciousness. The taweez hanging from the mirror caught Harry's eye again. He ripped it from its perch and shoved it in his pocket.

Outside, Harry opened the driver's door and unlocked the hand-cuffs. He pulled Billy's unconscious body from the vehicle, allowing him to crash to the ground. The car shuddered on the jack.

The impact roused Billy. Harry was caught flat-footed as he scrambled to his feet.

'Now you're done,' said Billy, taking huge gulps of night air and massaging his neck.

Harry calmly lifted the handcuffs from the steering wheel, put them in his back pocket and closed the door. The interior light went off, plunging them into darkness.

They stood a few feet apart, waiting. Harry kept his arms arrogantly folded across his chest. Under the jacket Billy was wearing, his shalwar kameez was flapping against his body, revealing a meaty frame.

Billy inched forward until he was close enough to throw a punch. Instead he grabbed at Harry, who stepped aside, leading Billy away from the car. The punch that followed hit only air, inches from Harry's face.

Billy lunged again, leaving himself wide open. Harry slapped him; a full palm-strike, a sudden explosive crack.

The ultimate insult to an Asian man: to be slapped like his father would have done.

Billy, enraged, launched himself at Harry, who again moved out of the way.

Another slap.

They repeated the charade, Billy grew angrier and lost all sense of battle-readiness. Harry kept it up until he heard the one thing he had been waiting for.

A wheeze.

Billy was slowing.

A minute later, Billy was stationary, huffing and puffing like he'd sprinted the hundred. His face showed angry red marks where Harry had struck him, the blood was still leaking from his nose.

This time Harry didn't slap him. Instead he coiled his body, then threw an elbow into Billy's face.

Another crack, Billy's cheekbone imploded before the big man hit the ground.

When Billy came round, the side of his head was trapped under the car tyre. Harry had used the jack to lower the car just enough to hold Billy's skull firmly to the concrete.

The panic was immediate.

Billy tried to push the wheel but it was futile, the weight of the seven-seater was inescapable. If Harry kicked the jack from underneath the car, it would shatter Billy's skull.

Harry was sitting beside him, his hand on top of the wheel. He applied sudden downward pressure.

Billy screamed as the impact hit him.

'Let's start with an easy question,' said Harry, and waved Billy's phone in the air. 'What's the unlock code?'

Reluctantly, Billy gave Harry the pin.

'That's the kind of cooperation I'm looking for, Billy-boy. Now, let's try something else. Did you kill my niece?'

He screamed he hadn't, swore every kasam he could think of.

'You lied to me. Your kasam, your promise, means nothing,' said Harry, giving the tyre another shake.

Billy grew angry. 'You don't know who you're fucking with. You're dead – even if you kill me, you're dead.'

The confirmation Harry needed. There were others.

He stood up and wound the carjack down a quarter-turn.

Billy's head compressed into the tarmac, the pressure causing blood to run down the side of his face.

'No!' he screamed.

'I'm not going to kill you,' said Harry. 'Not my style,' he added truthfully. He repositioned himself next to Billy. 'Everything so far tells me you killed my niece. So start talking or I'm going to keep turning that jack until your skull cracks – which by my reckoning is two more quarter-turns. Bone will pierce your brain, causing it to bleed. Once you're brain-damaged I'll drop you at the hospital – you'll suffer the rest of your miserable life.' Harry shook the tyre again. 'We're not far off, are we?'

'Please!'

'Did you kill my niece?'

Billy screamed that Tara had been hanging around the taxi rank, wanting free rides. Billy had looked after her.

'Bet you did,' spat Harry. 'Why did you lie to me?'

'You know why.'

'No, I don't.'

'You'd think I was taking advantage.'

'Were you?'

'No.'

Harry thought about the other pictures on Billy's phone. He was a nonce. Through and through.

'Look at me,' said Billy, desperate now. 'If I knew something, I would tell you.'

Harry got up suddenly and started to turn the jack.

Billy felt the force: immediate and life-threatening.

'No!' he screamed. 'I know who did it!'

Billy writhed on the floor. No longer angry, flat-out petrified.

'I'm listening.'

'Take this off.'

'Tell me what you know.'

'Not like this.'

'Think I'm stupid?' Harry completed the quarter-turn. Several teeth in Billy's mouth suddenly cracked. 'Quit trying to buy yourself time.'

'Ali! Ali!' groaned Billy, and spat a bloodied tooth on to the floor, coughing wretchedly as more blood oozed from his mouth.

Harry reversed the turn.

'Ali?'

Billy spluttered his words. 'Taxi driver. Not on the books! Let me out, I'll tell you everything!'

Although it tallied with what Sarah had said, Harry needed to be sure.

'Bullshit. You did it, Billy. I know you did.'

'When was she killed? Tell me!'

'Saturday night.'

'Call my dispatch! I took a group of girls to Birmingham, stayed at a friend's house – I was there until Sunday afternoon. It's all on the tracker!'

'If you're lying, Billy—'

Harry was distracted by a car heading towards the derelict estate. Instinctively he crouched and tore off a piece of Billy's shalwar, stuffing it into his mouth.

The vehicle skidded to a halt next to the Peugeot.

Ronnie and Enzo climbed out of the Range Rover.

'Harry.'

'What the fuck, Ron?'

'Just passing.'

'Don't do this,' said Harry.

Ronnie looked down at Billy. 'Nice touch.'

Harry glared at Enzo. 'You're tracking me.'

'Prefer to think of it as protecting an asset,' said Enzo.

Harry stepped closer to his brother so they were toe to toe. 'Spying? Really?'

Ronnie put his foot on Billy. 'This our guy?'

'This isn't how it works.'

'Is this our guy?' Ronnie screamed, shoving Harry square in the chest.

The smell of whisky hit Harry like a slap. He looked hard into his brother's eyes.

Never met an alkie who could fight the thirst . . .

Nash had been right.

Ronnie removed a gun from inside his jacket.

'I'll take it from here,' he said.

TWENTY-SEVEN

SARAH'S PHONE WAS OUT of reach on the other side of the room.

She waited.

Fifteen minutes after Harry had left, there was a knock on her door.

'Let yourself in,' she cried.

For a moment Percy, the barman of the New Beehive, simply stared at Sarah, who made the handcuffs rattle against the bed frame.

'Could be worse, I suppose,' he said, before turning to leave.

He returned with a battered old bag, unzipping it on the dressing table. He removed several metal picks before stepping across to Sarah and sitting on the bed.

'How was he?' Percy asked.

'Angry,' she replied. 'You sure you can open these?'

He shrugged and smiled at her. 'Let's find out.'

'I need to leave, Granddad. Now.'

'I know,' he said, sighing. 'Did he buy it?'

Sarah rolled her eyes.

Percy slipped a pick into the lock of the handcuffs and nodded. 'Didn't strike me as a stupid man.'

'He's not. But when Billy doesn't talk, Harry will have to come back.'

'*If* Billy doesn't talk?' said Percy, gently manoeuvring the pick inside the lock. 'Is this whole thing dependent on Billy not talking?'

'Would you?' she asked.

'Given who the boss is?' Percy shook his head. 'Billy's dead either way.'

'Exactly. He'll take his chances with Harry.'

Percy cursed under his breath. 'Almost had it,' he said, moving back to his bag and selecting another tool.

'You could unscrew the bottom of the frame so the cuffs will slide off,' she said.

'Twenty years in this trade, never found a lock I couldn't open yet. What time's your meet?'

'Soon,' she said, trying not to sound impatient.

'Easy,' whispered Percy almost lovingly at the lock. 'Easy . . .'

The handcuffs slipped open.

'Thanks, Granddad. Did you sort his car?' she asked.

'As briefed,' he said. 'It should be showing on your phone.'

While Harry had been in the basement with Sarah, Percy had left the bar, walked across the street and stuck a magnetic GPS tracker to the underside of Harry's car.

'Technology's amazing, huh?' he said.

Sarah reached for her phone, checked the tracker app.

'Got him,' she said. 'He took my key. Said he was coming back. You can't let him in while I'm gone.'

'I'll have the night-staff bolt the back door from the inside so he has to buzz. He comes back before you do? They'll ignore him and you can come through the front. OK?'

'Perfect,' she said.

Percy got off the bed and rearranged his tools in his bag. Before he zipped it closed, he removed a knife with sharp serrated edges. He paused then handed it to Sarah.

'There's no going back after this,' he said solemnly.

Sarah typed a hurried text message then took the knife from him and concealed it under her burka.

'Are you having second—'

'Never,' said Percy coldly.

'Has Victor called?'

'Aye. The farmhouse is quiet. They're still there. I'll close up and head out to see him now.'

Sarah concealed herself inside her burka with practised efficiency.

'Kid?' said Percy quietly.

She paused and looked at him. 'Yes?'

'I'm proud of you and of what you're doing,' he whispered, nodding and wiping his eyes.

Sarah pulled the top of the burka over her head, tucking her blonde curls inside, then walked over to him, her steely eyes momentarily softening as she slipped her arms around her grand-dad. 'What *we're* doing,' she said, burrowing her face into his chest.

Sarah walked down the hill opposite the New Beehive Inn. A bitter wind chilled her skin, combating the burning in her cheeks, and a light drizzle continued to fall. Eighteen months' work, and it all came down to the next twenty-four hours.

She passed the Jamiyat Tabligh-ul-Islam mosque and kept her head down, her feet quickening, her heart racing as she saw her destination in the distance, one of the largest derelict mills in the city: Conditioning House. Each year ambitious plans to redevelop the colossal structure faded into familiar broken promises.

Outside, towering iron gates kept out the drug addicts and whores who used the many dilapidated mills in the city as shelter. Sarah paused to check she was alone.

The chain securing the gates had been cut open; *he* was already here.

She hurried across the open courtyard, the metal gates casting a shadow across the yellow stone walls of the crumbling building.

This place had a haunting quietness to it.

She reached the central courtyard, where four floors rose dramatically on all sides, casting ground level into an unearthly darkness. Three metal bridges crossed the space, each one above the other on the way up to a web of interlinked steel meshes that once formed a ceiling. Sarah was always struck by the vast emptiness. *This is what the end of the world would look like.*

At the far end of the mill, she saw a torch flashing in her direction.

'Salaam alaikum,' she said.

He had waited for her, his Asian garment thin against the cold, black wavy hair flopping down the side of his handsome face.

Yasser simply nodded, turned off his torch and pushed a black bag towards her with his foot. Sarah glanced at it, then at him. 'I feel ready,' she said. 'You?'

'I do,' he nodded, putting his hands in his pockets and leaning back against the wall. A gentle breeze revealed the muscular physique beneath his clothes. 'Next time we meet?' He looked up, through the crisscross of metal girders supporting the ceiling to where, high above, dark clouds moved across the sky.

Sarah joined him, looking at the heavens. 'Anywhere is better than here,' she said, unwavering in her resolve to see their plan through.

Sarah crouched and unzipped the bag. 'May I?' she asked.

He handed her the torch.

'This is amazing,' she whispered.

Yasser crouched beside her. 'It is my best work,' he said, 'for the greatest thing we shall ever do.'

His hand found Sarah's, tentatively enclosing it with his own. She allowed him to feel her skin, turning her hand over and grasping his.

'I can't begin to express how much you've helped me,' she said.

'No,' he said, again glancing to the heavens. 'Not me.'

Sarah pulled her hand back and zipped up the bag. As they stood, she looked towards the top of the mill. 'The roof,' she said, staring intensely at him and stepping closer until their bodies touched. She ran her hand through his hair. 'Will you come with me?'

'What for?'

Sarah took his hand. 'It's our last night,' she said, and looked at him in a way she knew would get his attention. 'We can't let this depressing courtyard be our last memory together. Let's . . . remember how we used to be.'

'We are not allowed,' he said, his voice unconvincing even to his own ears.

'We are no longer just soldiers, Yasser,' she whispered, putting her hand on his chest. 'We have given so much for the greater good, but tonight? On our last night before we complete, I want to remember what it feels like to have you close to me.'

For the first time since he had owned the New Beehive Inn, Percy had closed up early.

He had driven to the Cow and Calf Rocks in silence, using the forty-minute journey to go over the plan.

The Cow and Calf comprised one large and one smaller sandstone rock sitting close together. In his youth, Percy had scaled the four hundred metres to the top of the Cow for the breathtaking views across Ilkley Moor.

With the dark shadows of the rocks concealing his presence, Percy walked purposefully from his car into an adjacent field, his boots familiar with the route.

The field was barren, overgrown marshland which the rain had churned into a bog. A quarter of a mile later, Percy saw a familiar Jeep tucked behind a large row of trees, not exactly hidden but not easy to see from the road.

'It's bitter out there,' said Percy, getting into the passenger seat and handing Victor a flask. 'Any movement?'

'Just the boy, Billy. He came by earlier this evening with their dinner. Other than that, nowt.'

Victor looked cramped in the driver-side of the Jeep, his

six-foot-five, solidly built frame filling the space, knees touching the bottom of the steering column.

Percy pointed to a puzzle book on the dashboard. 'That yer war book, is it?'

Victor grunted, unscrewed the lid of the thermos and poured himself a cup of steaming tea. 'Keeps my brain sharp.' He frowned. 'This got sugar in it?'

Percy slipped a hand into his bag and removed several sachets he had lifted from the pub. 'Couldn't remember.'

'Eleven years in the force, forty-two years of camaraderie and you can't bloody remember the sugar?'

'Christ, I've got to take more pills than I've got fingers these days. Be grateful I remember your name.'

They grunted stifled laughter. 'You don't have to tell me. I didn't take my water tablet today so I wouldn't have to piss out there every hour.'

'Smart thinking.'

'Doc says I've got to exercise my bladder,' continued Victor. 'Pelvic strengthening, he calls it. I told him: last thing that strengthened my pelvis cost me three hundred grand in a divorce.'

This time they let themselves howl, Victor only stopping when he spilled tea on his pants.

'Christ!' he yelled, and spilled even more.

'It's good to laugh, particularly on a night like this.'

Victor calmed down. 'She gone to see the boy?'

'Aye,' replied Percy. 'And the detective fella was round earlier.'

'And . . . ?'

Percy shrugged. 'As per the brief,' he said, looking at Victor and forcing a smile. 'As per the brief.'

'Should hope so. Eighteen months in the planning, I'd expect it to go like clockwork.'

Victor opened two sachets of sugar, poured them into his tea and used his finger to stir it. 'If this city – shit, if this *country* functioned as it should, we could have stayed retired.'

'Different times. Different war,' said Percy, removing a lunch box from his rucksack and placing it on the dashboard. 'Cheese and pickle,' he said.

'You say that like it's something for me to look forward to.' Victor smiled.

'I'm going to miss these times, old boy.'

'Don't talk like that. We're not going anywhere. Plenty of life in these veins yet,' said Victor, raising a wrinkled fist.

'For you, maybe.' Percy removed a crumpled packet of Capstan Full Strength cigarettes from his pocket.

'How many left now?' asked Victor.

'Three.'

Victor took the packet from him. 'Greatest pack of cigarettes in existence.'

'Absolutely; opened on a war-torn field in eighty-two. Lasted thirty-four years. Let's have a couple.'

'You sure?'

'The night before we experience the night to end them all? It's time.'

Victor nodded solemnly, removing one and handing the pack to Percy.

They wound their windows down a little, smoking in silence, staring into the darkness where half a mile away Olivia Goodwin and her mother were spending what might be their last night in Bradford.

'Tastes like eighty-two,' said Percy.

'Nothing tastes like eighty-two,' whispered Victor.

'Not that part.'

'It's only ever that part for me. Eighteen good 'uns, we lost. If Thatcher had've of waited instead of throwing her weight behind a war to save her political career, well . . . ?' Victor stirred his tea with his finger again, then repeated, 'Eighteen good 'uns.'

'We were taking fire from all corners. You ever wondered why we didn't fall?'

'Suppose not. Never seen a man face death in quite the way you did. Held 'em off for what? Thirty minutes?'

'I had the ammunition hoard.'

'And I had you.'

'Nothing's changed there, friend.' Percy took a deep drag on his cigarette and coughed.

Victor smiled. 'Been a while?'

'Maybe ten, eleven years?'

'Still taste as good as they always did?'

'Tastes like a barman's backside to me.' Percy wheezed a laugh.

'Tomorrow night,' Victor said. 'Are we certain?'

The weight of everything they'd left unsaid bore down on them both.

Percy nodded stiffly. 'We didn't come this far to stop now.'

'And Sarah?' said Victor.

'Without this, she'd have tried to slit her wrists again.'

Percy struggled to remove a piece of paper from his pocket and handed it to Victor.

'I didn't just come to see if you could still see through those binoculars,' said Percy, nodding at the pair hanging around Victor's neck and keeping hold of the document. 'We . . . need to talk.'

'I don't like that look,' Victor replied. 'What you got there?'

'A change. For tomorrow.'

'Late in the day.'

'I know. Listen . . .' Percy faltered now it came to the next part. 'What I'm going to say? It stays here. Sarah doesn't need to know.'

'I don't like that look on your face.'

'Then you definitely won't like what I'm about to show you,' said Percy, and he handed over the paper.

Standing hundreds of feet above the ground on the roof of Conditioning House, Sarah and Yasser could see for miles in every direction. The wind had calmed and the black plastic sheeting across sections of the roof was rattling softly. Bradford almost looked beautiful. Yasser pointed to St George's Hall in the distance. The oldest concert hall in the UK with a capacity of fifteen hundred people, tomorrow night it would be packed for a Bonfire Night theatre extravaganza.

'They won't know what hit them,' he said. 'Can you picture it?'

'Forget about that for now. This is our moment,' replied Sarah, putting her hands on his face and turning it towards her.

'If I closed my eyes, wiped this city from my mind and opened them again, I could almost believe I was back in Islamabad,' said Yasser, facing her and holding her hands.

'Big city. Bright lights. We could be anywhere,' she replied. 'Close your eyes,' she said.

'Why?'

'Trust me.' She smiled.

Sarah removed a white rag from her pocket and wrapped it around his eyes, tying a loose knot at the back of his head.

'Are you going to throw me off the roof?' he asked teasingly.

'Remember the game we used to play when we were training?'

He smiled as she took his hand and slipped it underneath her clothes, placing it on her skin. 'Tell me,' she whispered, stepping closer to him.

The lights of the city sparkled.

'Your stomach,' he said.

'Yes,' she said, whispering gently in his ear and moving his hand higher.

'Now?'

'Your chest.'

'What can you feel?'

'Your heart beating.'

'Tell me how.'

He paused, finding the rhythm. 'Ba-bum. Ba-bum. Ba-bum,' he chanted quietly.

'Keep it there,' she said, letting go of his hand.

'Ba-bum, ba-bum, ba-bum,' he whispered, smiling broadly.

Sarah pulled Percy's knife from under her burka.

'Is it getting quicker?' she whispered, stepping back an inch and catching sight of the tattoo on her raised hand.

GZ.

'Yes,' he said.

'Do you love me, Yasser?'

'From the first moment I saw you,' he replied.

'And I love you?' she asked him.

'Yes,' his brow creased momentarily, confusion washing over his face.

'Then,' Sarah replied, plunging the knife into his throat, warm arterial blood spraying across her, 'perhaps you trained me too well.'

TWENTY-EIGHT

'PUT IT DOWN,' SAID Harry, 'that's not how this works.'

Ronnie kicked Billy, who was staring in disbelief at the gun. 'Did he do it?'

'I don't know yet,' replied Harry.

'Who are you people?' asked Billy.

Harry stepped into the firing line. 'A word,' he said, and pulled Ronnie away from the car.

'Oi,' Harry shouted at Enzo, 'watch him.'

He hauled Ronnie away.

'What's got into you?' asked Harry, when they were out of earshot. 'You're drinking again.'

'No—'

'Don't. I can smell it.'

'When one of your kids ends up dead, you see if you want a fucking drink.'

Harry couldn't say much to that.

'And I don't share my location with you so you can babysit me,' said Harry, removing his iPhone, accessing the Find My Friends app and disabling the function.

'I told you: I want the guy. My way. You haven't exactly shown willing, ignoring my calls and messages.'

'Micro-managing me isn't going to help us.'

'Did he do it?' asked Ronnie, nodding towards Billy.

'Says he didn't. Says there's another player.'

'Who?'

'I'd got as far as the name "Ali", and then you interrupted me.'

Ronnie made to push past Harry. 'You're not thinking straight.'

Harry wouldn't budge.

'I'm always thinking straight. That's why I run this city.'

'This morning, with Nash? Now, arriving here like this?' Harry snatched the gun from Ronnie and waved it in his face. 'Carrying a loaded weapon when you didn't know what you were coming into?'

'Tara's dead,' whispered Ronnie, stepping closer to Harry. 'My kid is dead.'

Harry pushed his fist into Ronnie's chest. 'I'm on it.'

'I want his fucking head on a stick.'

'I'm on it.'

'I'm not a patient man,' replied Ronnie. 'My wife wants to slit her wrists. Old man's wandered off, and Mum . . .'

Harry tensed at the mention of their mother.

'Sitting by the window, like she used to after you left,' said Ronnie. 'Hasn't spoken. Hasn't eaten. Hasn't slept.'

He tried to snatch the gun back from Harry, who moved it out of reach.

'Keep it,' said Ronnie, and barged past Harry towards Enzo and Billy.

'Shit,' Harry hissed and followed. All the ground he'd covered was about to be lost.

'Weapon,' snapped Ronnie. Enzo produced another revolver.

'Now,' said Ronnie, crouching on the floor by Billy. 'You want to deal with him? Or me?'

Harry tried to get close, but Enzo blocked his route.

'We spoke about this earlier,' said Harry, starting to lose his temper. He had one eye on Ronnie.

'Don't take orders from you.'

'Last guy who came between me and my brother?' Harry reminded Enzo of Ronnie's previous business partner. 'No longer with us.'

'Times have changed.'

Harry saw Ronnie press the gun to Billy's temple.

Forced into the move, and with the revolver to hand, Harry fired a shot into the ground. Enzo jumped and Harry jammed his fingers into his bared throat. As Enzo staggered backwards, gasping for breath, Harry kicked his feet from underneath him, sending the big man thundering to the ground.

Harry stepped past him and snatched the other revolver from Ronnie's hands, raising both weapons, one at Enzo, the other at Ronnie.

Billy remained pinned to the ground, helpless, watching the unfolding drama.

'I asked you this morning if you were with me or against me? Looks like I got my answer,' said Ronnie, standing up.

Enzo was coughing on the ground, trying to get his breath back.

'One: I don't like your poodle crossing me. He's *your* bitch, so keep him on a damn leash. Two: don't spy on me. And three . . .'

Harry stepped closer to Ronnie, leaving only Billy's body between them.

'. . . She was mine too,' snapped Harry, losing his composure. 'Mine! *I* held her for the first twenty minutes of her life. *I* was the one she came to when she was scared of the dark and *I'm* the one who failed her when I left that godforsaken house! So don't tell me I'm against you, Ronnie, or I will knock you the fuck down and make sure *you* don't get back up.'

Harry lowered the weapons, eyes blazing furiously at Ronnie.

'Are we fucking clear?' he shouted.

'I'm sorry,' said Ronnie.

The brothers were sitting in Ronnie's Range Rover.

Enzo was watching Billy, who still had his head trapped under the tyre of the Peugeot.

'You should be bloody sorry,' replied Harry. 'Christ, we're supposed to be a team.'

'Guilt,' said Ronnie, and wiped his eyes. 'It's my fault. All of it. I let Bradford take her.'

'You're not the only one. Tara tried to call me – I never answered.'

'When?'

'A few months ago. I told you I wouldn't be in contact with her and I kept my word.'

'She called you? Why the hell didn't you answer?' snapped Ronnie, ignoring what Harry had just said.

Both men stared uncomfortably at each other until Ronnie started pounding the dashboard.

'Shit!' he hissed. 'This fucking family!'

'I know,' said Harry, and waited till Ronnie calmed down. 'I feel like part of me died yesterday. She looked so helpless. I wanted to hug her, bring her back to life. I just . . . can't stop picturing it.'

'Jesus, we're both losing it,' said Ronnie.

'I'm not,' said Harry.

'Don't bullshit me.' Ronnie rubbed his hand across his face and sighed.

'When did you fall off the wagon?' asked Harry.

'Does it matter?'

'It does to me,' said Harry, remembering the detox programme Ronnie had been through. 'I can't let you go back there.'

'I'm not like I was.'

'Says every alcoholic. I can't have you hitting the bottle with this over our heads. I need you ready, not obsessing about where the nearest off licence is.'

'I won't touch it, OK?'

Harry stared outside. He could see Enzo pacing, still rubbing his throat.

'Fucking Elmo, when will he learn?' said Harry.

'You going to hurt everyone who helps me run things?'

Harry looked at his brother.

'Easier if you just joined us. Look at you: you stick a guy's head under a car and you think you're not like me?'

'We're not having this conversation again.'

Ronnie shook his head. 'Tell me about him.'

Clearly Ronnie didn't know who Billy was. Harry struggled to hide his relief that his brother hadn't expanded into child trafficking. He told him everything he knew about Billy.

'So he's complicit in something and he's a nonce?' said Ronnie.

'Exactly. Says he was in Brum on Saturday night and the guy we need is called Ali.'

'Ali?'

'That's as far as I got when you arrived.'

'Let's get back to it,' said Ronnie.

Harry put his hand on his brother's arm.

'One thing?'

'I know – it's your show.'

'Not that.'

Ronnie raised his eyebrows.

'Put Elmo in your car. I don't need an audience.'

'On one condition.'

'What?'

'Stop fucking calling him that.'

Outside, Harry took the lead with Ronnie a few steps behind.

'Who's Ali?' asked Harry.

'Who are you people?' Billy asked again. Blood had pooled on the concrete below his chin, in the shadow of the tyre.

'People you shouldn't have crossed,' said Harry. 'Ali?'

Billy was struggling between his fear of what might happen if he didn't talk and what would happen if he did.

'OK, I'll help you out. Here's what I've got so far,' said Harry. 'Olivia Goodwin is the target. Tomorrow night you complete a deal which sees her disappear. Tara got in the way, put the transaction at risk and you guys killed her. Sound about right?'

Billy tried to move his head to look up at Harry.

Harry put his hand on the jack and started to turn it.

'Do it!' screamed Billy. 'If I talk? I'm fucking dead anyway.'

'Poor choice,' said Harry and gave it a quarter-turn.

Another sickening scream from Billy.

'Harry,' said Ronnie, stepping forward, his breath warm on Harry's ear. He put his hand over his brother's. 'Step away. One more and he'll be no good to us.'

Harry couldn't believe Billy still wouldn't talk.

'Let me take him,' Ronnie continued. 'Few hours in the black hole will do the trick.'

Ronnie was right, but the clock inside Harry's mind was racing.

Tomorrow night Bradford loses another girl.

Tara had died trying to protect Olivia Goodwin. Harry couldn't let her efforts go to waste.

He couldn't let Tara's murderer walk free.

Harry stepped away, breathing heavily, trying to regroup. 'I need him to talk, Ron, however you do it. He's the key. There's another player, called Riz. See if you can get his details.'

'You got other things to chase down?'

Harry nodded.

'You focus there. I've got this.'

Ronnie used the jack to raise the tyre from Billy's head and crouched by his side.

'They worth dying for, these people you work with?'

Billy didn't reply.

'You think this is as bad as it gets?'

He smiled warmly then grabbed Billy's face, squeezing his cheeks. Billy spat out a bloodied tooth.

'You've got about thirty minutes before we hit the black hole.' Ronnie let go of Billy's face and stood up, towering over him. 'Thirty minutes before you're begging me to kill you.'

TWENTY-NINE

AT MIDNIGHT ALI KAMRAN was parked outside Detective Inspector Harry Virdee's home, a simple three-storey end-of-terrace Victorian house on Oak Lane in Manningham.

The house was dark. The orange glow of the streetlight fell on the pavement just in front.

Ali walked to the back of Virdee's house, through a narrow snicket. No CCTV cameras out the back either.

Come on, Detective.

He opened the gate and hurried down the path. The back door was locked but he had expected that. Ali tested the letter box. It opened easily; a decent-sized gap to pour petrol through.

He was out to make sure the next twenty-four hours passed without incident.

He was not prepared to risk his plans.

Ali glanced through the kitchen window. He could see a picture frame but in the darkness he couldn't make out its contents. The window came away from the frame as he pulled; it wasn't locked.

He held his breath, half expecting an alarm but there was nothing. Slipping his hand inside, he picked up the picture, brought it close.

Detective Inspector Virdee, his wife and their baby.

A perfect family photograph.

Ali slid his hand across Saima's face, the outline of her body.

A wife. A child. A family.

Tomorrow night, in a farmhouse by the moors, Ali would seize his opportunity and take Olivia Goodwin. He replaced the photo, pushed the window shut and walked away. If Detective Inspector Virdee threatened what Ali had been planning for over a year, he wouldn't hesitate.

Back in his cellar, as Gori slept, her naked, cold body tucked under a loose white bedsheet, Ali stood with his hands in his pockets, staring at a shelf at the opposite side of the room.

Hidden at the back of the shelf was a glass jar, covered in a thin layer of dust.

A jar Ali Kamran so desperately wanted to bring out.

No.

He wanted to smash it against the wall. His breathing quickened, sweat trickling down his face.

Ali rubbed angrily at his face, disturbing the make-up, leaving his skin naked and exposed.

He stepped closer to the shelf, eyes fixed on the hidden jar.

'Just you wait until tomorrow night,' he hissed. *'Just you wait!'*

THIRTY

HARRY PARKED BILLY MUSA'S Peugeot in a dark side street off Thornton Road, a couple of hundred metres from Triple B's dispatch office. He went inside and asked Pamela, the driver coordinator, to confirm Billy's location over the weekend. Despite Harry's ID, she refused to cooperate until he removed the wad of cash Ronnie had given him and put a fifty-pound note on the table. Then another.

Billy hadn't been lying. He'd driven to Birmingham on Saturday afternoon and hadn't come back until Sunday afternoon. Harry made her double-check the log, then left the office. Billy was out of town while Tara was murdered. He wasn't the guy Harry was looking for.

Back in his car, Harry contemplated his next move.

He took out his phone and found the photo he'd taken of the logbook at Manningham Lane Autos. He could just about make out Omar's phone number.

He'd kept Billy's phone – he'd have no need for it at the black hole.

Harry found Omar saved under OMG. There was a goofy-looking photo of Omar grinning with a cigar in his mouth.

'There it is,' Harry whispered.

In the last hour and a half, it looked like Omar had been trying to get hold of Billy. There were several missed calls listed.

Back on his own phone, Harry went to check the GPS tracker for Omar's location. But it failed to connect.

The damn thing wasn't working.

Harry accessed Billy's text messages, scrolling down to find the last thing they had sent each other. Harry went back through their conversation log to get a feel for how the two of them communicated. Then he started to type.

U sleepin? Don't buz. Still drivn.

Harry's heart was racing.

Billy's phone beeped with an instant reply.

Yo. Bowt time.

Letz meet. Now.

Wher?

Harry quickly checked the location services on Billy's phone, choosing 'frequent locations'. He scrolled the history and replied.

Water Lane.

Harry pulled up in front of the derelict Crabtree & Sons mill on the corner of Water Lane and Wigan Street.

A crumbling six-storey monument to Bradford's past.

On the passenger seat were two things Ronnie had refused to let Harry leave without. A taser and a rare eight-chamber .357 Smith & Wesson revolver wrapped in black cloth. Ronnie loved anything out of the ordinary. Why have a six-chamber gun when he could have eight?

Rain battered the road, the surface shimmering, the sound a calming prelude to Omar's arrival.

Harry wasn't thinking about Omar. He was thinking about Tara, about the Candy Club. If Nash was right, he could understand why Tara had been so desperate to move out from home. Why she was so determined to follow her own path, free from the Asian traditions that her grandparents and her parents would be forcing on her. It was an all-too-familiar scenario for Harry.

A car coming the opposite way interrupted his thoughts. It slowed and flashed its lights twice. Harry started the car and pulled forward, taking an immediate left turn. Victorian cobbles gleamed golden in the streetlight.

Harry pulled into the courtyard at the back of the mill, reaching for Ronnie's weapons. Omar killed his lights as he pulled in alongside. He got out of his car and darted towards the passenger side of the Peugeot, opening the door, hurrying in out of the rain.

Harry locked the doors and pointed the gun at him. 'One wrong move.'

Omar jumped towards the door, fumbling for the handle.

Harry jammed the gun into Omar's crotch. 'What did I just say?'

'You? What the fuck is with you, man? You crazy? What's going on?'

'You tell me.' Omar was bigger in the passenger seat than he had seemed at the garage.

'Where's Billy?' asked Omar.

'Busy.'

'What do you mean?'

'You need me to draw you a picture?'

'Listen, man—'

Harry raised the gun, striking Omar in the nose. It shattered instantly.

'Fuck! What's wrong with you?'

Harry had expected rage. Instead, Omar cowered.

This kid was no hero; the bulk was to compensate.

Harry sat more comfortably in his seat.

Omar was cradling his nose, pinching the top, trying to stem the blood flow.

Harry glanced over at Omar's car; there was somebody inside.

'Who'd you bring with you?' asked Harry.

'Nobody.'

'She looks young.'

'I was giving her a lift home.'

'At midnight? From where?'

Omar fell silent.

Harry's temper started to fracture. 'How old is she?'

Nothing.

'How fucking old, Omar?'

'Eighteen,' he mumbled.

'Bullshit.'

Harry fired the Taser into Omar's neck. He slumped unconscious against the door. 'I'm not done with you, pretty boy. Not by a long way.'

He handcuffed the big man's wrist to the passenger door and went to Omar's car. As he got into the driver's seat, he startled the little blonde girl in the passenger seat.

'Who's you?' she asked, slurring her words, alcohol ripe on her breath.

'Omar's friend,' he replied, thankful the Peugeot had tinted windows, obscuring what Harry had done.

'We just seen his friends. I'm aching. Get laid someplace else, bro. He said we was done.'

'I'm mates with Billy too. You know Billy?'

'Everyone knows Big Bee.'

'You seen him lately?'

'Why's you askin'?' She was squinting at Harry, her head bobbing drunkenly on petite shoulders.

'He owes me. Said you owe him. Said we could work it out.'

'Told yous, I'm aching. I done enough tonight.'

Harry gritted his teeth, afraid of the answer to his next question.

'How old are you?'

'However old yous want me to be.'

'The truth.'

She shrugged. 'Like, nearly fourteen.' She lifted a bottle of vodka from the floor and clumsily unscrewed the top.

'Where are you heading tonight?' said Harry, taking the bottle from her. She didn't protest.

'Not wiv yous.'

'Omar's?'

'Mmn.'

Harry nodded. 'I got some business with him. Let me drop you home?'

'Forget dat. My ma gonna bust my ass.'

'So where?'

'Shit, I don't know.' She leaned against the passenger door, closing her eyes. 'I just chill here.'

Harry reached into the back seat and grabbed a coat, Omar's presumably, and placed it protectively across the girl. 'When you wake up, it'll be better.'

Outside, Harry took a moment, hands in his pockets, head down, staring at the cobblestones, venting, his breath white in the bitter night air. Few crimes got to Harry as much as the kind Omar and Billy were involved in. These vulnerable girls would be damaged for ever.

Harry marched to the passenger door of Billy's Peugeot and opened it. He uncuffed Omar, who was starting to come round, and dragged his body out of the car, letting it collapse on to the water-logged ground. Omar rolled over and stood up on unsteady legs. He swung a clumsy fist at Harry, who easily avoided it before ramming his elbow into Omar's solar plexus.

Harry drew his weapon.

'On your feet, dickhead.'

Omar was back on the ground, struggling to breathe. It took him a minute to get up. Blood was streaming from his nose.

'I can get you girls!' shouted Omar, raising his hands, afraid another blow was coming his way. 'More white pussy than you ever dreamed!'

Omar knew it was a mistake as soon as he looked into Harry's eyes.

It was all Harry could do to resist the urge to pull the trigger. He slapped Omar hard across the ear.

'You think 'cos we share the same skin colour I share your sick tastes?'

Harry spat on him and threw another slap, which missed its mark as Omar jerked away.

'Pieces of shit like you keep this city down. Touching young girls, ruining lives. You deserve what's coming to you.'

'Please, I . . . didn't mean it like that. What do you want?'

Harry towered over the cowering fool. 'It's not what I want, Omar, it's what I'm going to get.'

The top floor of the Crabtree building was an unearthly space last used as a chicken farm. Harry grimaced as the rancid odour hit him.

He marched Omar to the far end of the floor, where most of the windows were nothing but jagged edges linked by huge cobwebs. This high up, streetlights attached to the building opposite were on a level with them, forcing an amber glow into the room. The wind channelled past, screaming a tortured melody.

Omar was naked. Recalling how he disliked the cold, Harry had forced him to strip outside. When they got to the end of the room, he ordered the big man to turn round. Omar's teeth were chattering, his body shaking as he used his hands to preserve his modesty.

'What's wrong with you?' Harry raised his voice above the wind. 'You need a thirteen-year-old girl to get you off? What happened?' He waved the gun in Omar's face as his anger rose. 'You get some shitty arranged marriage and your wife won't blow you? Think that justifies it?'

Omar shook his head, looking pleadingly at Harry, but if he was hoping for sympathy he was wasting his time.

'Stop fucking crying. Take what's about to happen like a man.'

Omar sobbed louder, his muscles shaking violently.

'There's some shit going down in Bradford tomorrow night and you know something about it.' Harry took a chance: 'Billy tells me you're the guy to ask. Says you know where Ali lives.'

For the briefest of moments Omar stopped shivering, adrenaline exploding through his body, which told Harry everything he needed.

'Thought that would get your attention. What is it? Surprised your mate Billy likes to talk?' Harry smiled and opened the barrel of the gun, emptying the bullets into his hand.

'Russian roulette. Know how to play?'

Harry didn't wait for a response; he put a single bullet in the firing chamber. 'Never did understand it – one-in-eight chance. I'll give you a one-in-one chance.'

He raised the gun and Omar instinctively raised his hands, exposing his flesh to the cold air.

'No! No!'

'Good start. You want to live, Omar?'

'Yes!'

Harry looked around the abandoned floor. The wind dropped suddenly, leaving them in an eerie silence. 'Kids would have died young here, Omar. Factory work. Long hours. Sometimes, they dropped dead—' Harry snapped his fingers. 'Just like that.'

He stepped closer to Omar. Harry's eyes were raging.

Unlike Omar, he wasn't shivering.

He was on fire.

'Now, you know something about my niece.'

Omar nodded eagerly.

Harry moved the gun away from Omar's temple. 'Open your mouth.'

Omar shook his head. More sobbing.

'Open. Your. Mouth.'

Harry forced the tip of the gun into his mouth. 'You taste that?'

Omar's body was practically convulsing.

'I like this place.' Harry knew exactly what he needed to say to ensure Omar's cooperation. 'Every time I've killed someone here, it's felt right,' he lied. 'Like this is the place to end lives that don't matter. Now? With my finger on the trigger, I so desperately want to pull it, Omar.' Harry leaned closer, his next comment perfectly weighted. 'You see, this is *my* sickness. Like yours is the girl downstairs.'

He pulled the gun from Omar's mouth. 'I don't do second chances. I don't tolerate people lying to me. This is it.'

Harry thought about the list of names in Tara's diary and the one he was yet to receive any information on.

'Riz. Who is he?'

'He's a businessman. Runs forty taxis in Bradford. Manages the money.'

'And the girls?'

Omar shook his head. 'He just controls the money. Doesn't get his hands dirty on the streets.'

'Where can I find him?'

'I don't know! Honest! He's careful! You think I've got his address?'

Harry stepped a little closer.

'Did Billy kill my niece?'

Omar clamped his eyes shut.

'Ali,' he mumbled. 'It was Ali. He wasn't meant to. He . . . I . . . I don't know what happened. I swear!'

'Ali what?'

Another shake of the head. 'I don't know.'

'You don't know your mate's name?'

'It's how it works, man! We only know what we need to!'

Sweat was pouring down Omar's temple. He'd stopped shivering.

'How what works?'

Omar started crying again. 'Please,' he said pathetically, 'I'm not involved like they are! I just get them flash cars to impress the girls. Honest.'

'You're lying. You collected Lexi and Olivia Goodwin from their home on Friday night. Where did you drop them?'

'Bradford Interchange, exactly like I told you. Billy took them from there.'

'How do you know Ali killed my niece?'

'I don't.'

'What?'

'I just know you don't fuck with Ali. Girls give Billy shit, Ali takes care of them – that's all I know. I'm not really involved.'

'No,' said Harry. 'You just fuck them?'

'I look after my girls!'

Harry cocked the gun. Omar let out a sob and pissed himself.

'Jesus,' whispered Harry, backing off. 'What do you know about Olivia Goodwin?'

'She's . . . she's . . . the one!' said Omar. 'Never been touched. They . . . got plans for her.'

'Plans?'

Omar started crying hysterically. Urine pooled around his bare feet.

'Do I look a patient man?' shouted Harry, raising the gun again.

'They selling her, man,' he said, crumbling to the ground as if he *had* been shot. 'But I don't know how it goes down.'

'Fuck's sake,' said Harry, stepping away from the urine snaking its way across the wooden floorboards.

'I'm sorry,' sobbed Omar.

Harry gritted his teeth and shook his head.

Sarah had been right. *The fuckers.*

'I'm sorry,' repeated Omar, his voice nothing more than a whimper.

Harry stepped to the side of his sobbing body and crouched to his knees.

'Not yet, Omar.'

He put the safety on the gun and slid it into his jacket pocket, glancing around at the destitute space.

'But you will be,' he whispered. 'You will be.'

THIRTY-ONE

SARAH ARRIVED AT THE Cow and Calf Rocks and parked beside Percy's car. She'd changed out of her bloodstained burka and left it with Yasser's body in a corner where he wouldn't be found until they redeveloped Conditioning House – likely not for years.

She took the bag he had given her and began the quarter-mile walk to Percy and Victor, grateful for a bright moon to guide her path.

'Hey,' she said, climbing into the back seat behind her granddad.

'You OK?' asked Percy, his eyes still on the farmhouse in the distance.

'Fine,' she replied, closing the door. 'Is he out?'

Victor was snoring heavily in the driver's seat.

'Old fool needed a kip.'

'What time are you leaving?' she asked, pushing the bag further along the back seat.

'You checked it?' Percy asked, ignoring her question, turning to inspect the bag.

'Obviously.'

'I'll give him a couple more hours' kip. You sure he can go when the sun rises?'

'Yes,' she replied. 'Too risky to stay here on the day they complete.'

'He hasn't been spotted so far.'

'They'll be on high alert before the boss arrives, and they've got all day to prepare for his arrival.' Sarah patted the bag then looked at Percy, concerned. 'You sure he will take care of it?'

'I've fought wars with the man. And look how much time and money he's put into this operation,' replied Percy. 'Are you're sure they won't move on the farmhouse until evening?'

Sarah shook her head and reached for the handle of the back door. 'Trust me,' she said, opening it. 'Bad things only happen after the sun sets.'

Sarah didn't get into her car; instead she hurried past it. She knew this place well. The rocks were the perfect vantage point to look out over the place where her torment had begun eleven years ago. The farmhouse. She could clearly remember her mother, lying in the upstairs bedroom with needles dotted around the floor.

Sarah scaled the larger rock, confidently navigating the natural toe-holds until she reached the summit. Panting heavily, she walked to the edge and lay down.

Being able to stop them selling Olivia, to keep that young girl from going through everything that Sarah had been forced to endure, everything she had fought so hard to escape was . . . a bonus. It wasn't her motivation.

Sarah was here for revenge.

Tomorrow night, she would take out every player in the chain.

And there was nothing they could do to stop her.

They couldn't fight what they didn't know existed.

She checked her phone; the GPS signal from Harry's car hadn't moved. He was still at Bradford Royal Infirmary. What was he doing there with Billy?

Tomorrow night, Sarah would end all this.

Not just the boss and his chain of lowlifes. She was going to take Harry Virdee with her too.

She knew everything about him. His dark secrets, the secrets that had killed Tara.

Tara would still be here, if it wasn't for Harry.

Tara.

Sarah got to her feet and stood tall, raising her arms, feeling the wind rush past her body. She was angry and she was free.

She stared out towards the farmhouse.

A reckoning, eleven years in the making.

Tara had been innocent; just like she had once been.

'I'm coming for you,' she whispered, the wind whipping her words away. 'Every last one of you.'

THIRTY-TWO

HARRY HADN'T EVER SPENT so much time at Queensbury Tunnel.

He shoved Omar on to the uneven ground, firing a brutal kick into his back.

'Where's the rest of his clothes?' asked Ronnie, staring at Omar's semi-naked, cowering body.

Harry threw a bag on the floor and heard the scuttle of rats.

'What's he know?' asked Ronnie.

Harry was looking at Billy, bound to a rickety chair, bleeding heavily.

'Said the same as him,' he replied, kicking the chair. 'This Ali is our guy.'

'How do we find him?'

'Dunno. It's how they protect themselves. Apparently,' Harry said.

Ronnie threw down the baseball bat he had been using on Nash that morning.

Who knew about it and was it worth killing for?

Nash's words flashed into Harry's mind.

Harry shrugged and rubbed his eyes. 'I haven't slept in . . .' he checked his watch, '. . . twenty-four hours. Not sure how much more I've got in me.'

Did Ronnie know about Tara visiting the Candy Club?
Did it make a difference?

'He been crying like that all night?' said Ronnie, pointing at Omar.

'Pretty much. If he knew anything, he'd have spilled. Already pissed himself.' Harry nodded at Billy: 'What about him?'

'Night's young.'

'Nothing?'

Ronnie shook his head. 'More afraid of whoever he works for than me.'

'That's not good,' said Harry, looking at Billy's battered, bleeding face. 'Doesn't this place break everybody?'

'Until tonight.'

'Guy he's protecting has to be a big fish,' said Harry, rubbing his eyes again, the thick air of the tunnel stinging his eyes.

'Not big enough to stop me,' said Ronnie.

'Where's Elmo? You taken your hand out his arse?'

Ronnie frowned. 'Gone for supplies.' He turned his back to Harry. 'You hear that, Billy? My night's just getting started.'

'I'm done,' said Harry. He wanted to press Ronnie and see what he knew about Tara, but this wasn't the time or place. 'I need a lift back to BRI. Got a plus-one too,' he said, and put his hand in his pocket, checking he still had the key to Sarah's room at the New Beehive. 'And my night's not over – let's move.'

'Plus-one?'

'Young girl in Omar's car.'

Ronnie raised his eyebrows.

'Thirteen.'

'What was she—'

The look on Harry's face answered Ronnie's question.

'She's comatose on vodka. Hopefully, she won't remember a thing. I'll hand her in to A & E.'

'Bind him,' said Ronnie, nodding at Omar. He handed Harry a roll of duct tape.

'You think he raped the girl outside?' he asked.

'Him and others.'

'You a rapist, Omar?' asked Ronnie.

There was no response, just a soft resigned sobbing.

'Built like a shithouse and cries like a baby,' said Ronnie.

'Not sure you'll get anything out of him. He's as scared as I've ever seen anyone.'

Ronnie grunted. 'He's a vain lad. He'll want to protect that face of his. Trust me, he'll talk,' he said, smiling devilishly, 'don't you worry about that.'

Harry didn't push for details. Truthfully, he didn't want to know. He removed the .357 revolver Ronnie had given him, wiped his fingerprints from it and handed it back to his brother.

'Go,' said Ronnie, pulling up outside Bradford Royal Infirmary and turning his car off. Harry hesitated in the back with the little girl lying unconscious by his side. 'She all right?' asked Ronnie, genuinely concerned.

'Paralytic, damaged, vulnerable. Aside from that?'

'Fucking cockroaches.'

Harry still didn't move. 'There's something big at play here,' he said eventually.

'Yeah.'

'You think they know who they're protecting?' asked Harry.

'Billy does. Omar? I'm not sure.'

He looked at the little girl. 'She going to be OK?'

Harry pointed towards the hospital. 'Best possible hands.' He dropped his voice, now unmistakably laced with venom. 'These bastards . . . You get something, you ring me.'

'Oh, I'll get something, don't you worry,' Ronnie said.

'Billy's Peugeot's outside the tunnel. You'll sort it?'

Ronnie nodded.

Harry had lifted the child into his arms and was about to close the door when Ronnie called to him.

'Your boy,' said Ronnie. 'Aaron. You . . . you . . . look after him, Harry.'

'With my life,' said Harry, closing the door behind him.

*

Harry told the staff he'd found the young girl comatose on the street. Then he went looking for Balraj. His friend was three hours from finishing his night-shift and looked as jaded as Harry did.

'If it's a competition to see whose night's been shittier, I'd say it's a close-run thing,' said Balraj.

Harry rubbed his tired eyes, his vision blurring slightly. 'This city is killing us both.'

'We should leave. Before Bradford drags us down with it.'

'Institutionalized,' replied Harry. His eyes stung. Queensbury Tunnel had a way of leaching into every part of his body. He breathed a deep sigh before he locked eyes with his friend. 'So?'

'She's got an A & E file,' Balraj said, handing him some papers.

'Stabbing?'

Balraj shook his head as his pager started to bleep.

'Shit,' he said, clicking it off. 'I've only got a few minutes, Harry.'

'Tell me,' said Harry.

'Self-harm. Two attempts.'

'When?'

'Back in 2014. She was nineteen.'

'How?'

'Wrists.'

'Bad?'

'Cry for help. Superficial.'

'That's all? Nothing more?'

Balraj shook his head.

'Anything written about why?'

'Psychiatry notes aren't here. She was referred on.'

'Can you pull those notes?'

Balraj shook his head. 'Not quickly, and not without questions.'

Harry nodded. 'Got it. That helps, mate. Just to be clear, there's nothing in 2013 to do with lacerations across her neck?'

'Nothing like it.'

'Thanks,' said Harry, and shook Balraj's hand. 'I owe you.'

'I'll add it to the list, Harry,' he replied.

Back in her room, Sarah saw Harry pull up outside the New Beehive just before four a.m.

Handcuffed to the bed once again, Sarah had quickly spilled vodka on to her clothes and the bed, hoping Harry would believe she had fallen asleep drinking. As she heard a key collide with the lock, she closed her eyes.

Harry paused outside Sarah's room. He felt light-headed, weak, his vision blurring.

Streetlights outside made the dark room appear amber. Sarah was asleep, her hand still cuffed to the bed frame, her bottom lip vibrating as she breathed deeply. The bottle of vodka by her side was empty.

Harry unlocked the cuffs and gently examined her wrists, seeing faded scars.

He picked up the empty bottle from beside her and set it on the floor, then grabbed a pen and scrawled on a notepad by the bedside cabinet:

Call me in the morning . . . Harry.

At half past four in the morning, Harry stood in his kitchen scrubbing Omar's blood from his hands. He noticed the window was slightly ajar and a photo frame had fallen over. Saima must have left it open. She was sometimes so tired from being up with Aaron all night that she would have left the front door wide open if Harry hadn't learned to go round and check these things. He closed the window and righted the photo frame.

Upstairs, Harry sat beside Aaron's cot, watching the rise and fall of his little chest.

He had taken the stairs two at a time, desperate to see his son. The sound of Aaron's snores restored his balance and was the perfect antidote to a city determined to drag Harry to its darkest corners.

Harry wanted change for Bradford, so his son might grow up in a better place than he'd known as a kid.

The thought kickstarted the familiar battle in his mind:

I haven't turned. I'm not like Ronnie.

But if I turned, would Aaron have a better life?

Harry inhaled deeply. He got off the bed and lifted Aaron from his cot, cradling him and putting his lips to his son's forehead.

'My boy,' he whispered, and thought of the times he had done this with Tara – on nights when Mandy hadn't realized Uncle Harry had snuck into Tara's bedroom for half an hour to revel in the warmth of his niece's tiny form.

'My boy,' he repeated, sitting back on the bed and trying to wipe the last thirty hours from his mind. The tiredness felt like bricks in his pocket, pulling him to the ground.

'Harry?' Saima stood half-silhouetted in the doorway. She crept into the room and sat cross-legged on the floor by his feet.

'Just . . . needed a cuddle,' he whispered.

'You need to sleep.'

'I know.'

'Why don't you sleep in here?'

Harry shook his head. 'My dreams might infect his mind.'

'Don't be silly. It might help you relax.'

'A shower will fix that.'

'Any . . . you know . . . progress?'

'Not in here, Saima. How was he? I'm sorry I missed bathtime.'

'He missed you. Kept looking at me, like, "You're not my daddy."' She smiled and put her hand on Aaron, next to Harry's.

'I used to do this with Tara,' he said, his voice unsteady. 'We were all crazy about her, but I always felt like, I don't know, she and I had a special bond? You know?'

Saima nodded. 'She was precious, Harry.'

'I wasn't there for her, Saima.'

'It's not your fault.'

Harry didn't tell her that Tara had tried to call him. That he hadn't answered.

'How can I help?' said Saima.

He shook his head. 'Nothing.'

'Tea?' she offered.

Harry smiled. 'You and your "Indian tea fixes everything".'

'Always did in my mum's house. Something bad happened, you put the tea on the stove.'

'Mine too. My mum would be proud of you.'

'Do I make it better than her?'

'Not this again,' he said, and smiled.

'One day I'll get to make her a cup,' she repeated the line she had said for years now. 'It's a daughter-in-law's rite of passage. And when that day arrives, it's got to be the greatest cup of tea she has ever tasted. I want to be prepared, Harry.'

'It will be.' He leaned forward and kissed Saima on the forehead. 'Get back to bed, it's late.'

'And you? You look ready to collapse.'

'A shower, then bed,' he promised. 'When I wake up, that cup of Indian tea will be just the thing.'

Harry kissed his fingers and put them on Aaron's face.

My boy.

In a bathroom full of steam, Harry's mind was racing. Something was amiss, a whisper in his mind too soft to hear. It had been there all evening, but only now in the calm of his home could Harry try to focus on it.

Sarah was hiding something.

Why?

Harry got out of the shower, the rancour of Queensbury Tunnel washed away.

He climbed into bed and felt Saima roll over and slip her arms protectively around his body. All the doubts and whispers vanished from Harry's mind as he fell into an exhausted sleep.

THIRTY-THREE

THE STEADY DRIP OF water from Queensbury Tunnel was the only thing disturbing the silence as Ronnie Virdee stood in the darkness watching the cowering bodies of Billy and Omar.

Rule number one; no one dies.

Not his rule . . .

He held a Stanley knife, flicking the blade in and out, thinking.

Billy wasn't going to talk. Ronnie had done this enough times to know. But Omar? He was frightened, out of his depth and vulnerable. Omar would talk.

What does he know?

Ronnie was glad for the distraction of the tunnel. He couldn't go home. His wife hadn't yet said anything, but it was only a matter of time before he would have to face her accusation that he was to blame for Tara's death; a father who allowed his daughter to face the streets of Bradford alone.

He felt it too.

The only thing left for Ronnie was revenge.

The rhythmic dripping was disturbed by the arrival of Enzo, accompanied by a brutishly built man they simply referred to as 'Hobo'.

'Got anything yet?' he said, pointing at Omar and Billy.

'Nope,' replied Ronnie, still absent-mindedly toying with the Stanley knife.

'You want me to?' said Enzo.

Ronnie shook his head. 'I'll take this.'

'You sure, boss?'

'Yeah. In fact, you head home.'

Ronnie stepped into the path of Enzo's torch and put his hand out.

Enzo handed his boss a clear bag filled with tablets of two different colours.

'Blue and yellow. Up to you,' said Enzo. He looked over at his friend. 'Or, maybe up to him?'

Hobo stared back at them, dishevelled as always. He knew this tunnel, one of the few people Ronnie invited here and allowed to leave afterwards. Not quite one of the team. But a man who could be relied upon and had a certain sickness, one Ronnie only ever utilized in extreme circumstances.

'And?' asked Ronnie expectantly.

Enzo hesitated.

'Boss, you know—'

'If I wanted a lecture, I'd have asked Harry to stay. Hand it over.'

Enzo fished a brown paper bag from his other pocket and gave it to Ronnie. 'Sure I can't stay?'

'It's almost five in the morning, Enzo,' replied Ronnie, taking the bag from him. 'I need you fresh for whatever the next twenty-four hours brings.'

'What about you?'

Ronnie waved the bag of tablets at Enzo. 'This won't take long,' he said. 'Never does.'

'You cold?' Ronnie asked Omar, kneeling in front of his trembling body.

Omar nodded, his face undeniably blue now, eyes drowsy but

wet with tears running down his face on to the gag across his mouth.

'Here,' said Ronnie, wrapping Omar's coat around him. Beside them, Billy was watching closely, his mouth gagged, old blood crusting across his face.

'Nonces? That's what you both are? Right?' Ronnie pointed behind him. 'Same as my friend over there.' Then he shook his head. 'Well, similar.'

He opened the bag Enzo had given him and spilled a pool of yellow and blue pills into his palm. 'Know what these are?'

Omar and Billy looked at them but didn't respond.

'I call 'em C5s and V50s, but you might know them as Cialis and Viagra.' Ronnie smiled. 'I make nearly a quarter of my money selling these. Amazing, huh?'

Omar looked at the bag, then at Ronnie. His eyes settled on Hobo.

'I reckon there's things that you're not telling me about this Ali. And your boss. What I can't work out is why you think they need protecting more than you do.'

Omar shook his head. Ronnie took the gag from his mouth.

'Told you everything. Honest! I just get the cars!'

'Come on, you do more than that.'

'I never did nothing bad. I treat 'em all good!'

'Screwing a thirteen-year-old "ain't bad"?'

'They wanted it, I swear – they're not like kids any more, you know?'

Ronnie scowled. 'You got kids?'

Another shake of the head.

'When my . . .' Ronnie struggled momentarily, 'when Tara was thirteen, she was still a kid.'

'I wasn't involved in that shit! I swear! I told you, I just get the cars—' He broke off with a sob.

Ronnie looked over at Billy but continued talking to Omar. 'The girl you helped take – Olivia Goodwin. What's so special about her?'

'There's a buyer, that's all I know!'

'A buyer. That's all? And you still think you're not involved?' said Ronnie, smirking. 'You fuck little girls. You supply the vehicles to help with whatever this deal is? Selling some kid. And you think you're not a player? You think you've got a clear conscience, you dumb fuck?'

Omar groaned. 'Look, just hand me in to the police, yeah? I'll do my time.'

Ronnie stood up and chose two pills from his hand, one blue, one yellow. 'You know the difference between these?'

Omar shook his head.

'Blue ones last maybe a few hours. Yellow? Shit lasts for days.' Ronnie turned to Hobo. 'Which one are you thinking?'

He stared greedily at Omar, then lifted the yellow one.

'He likes you,' said Ronnie, turning to face Omar and smiling.

'No,' said Omar, shaking his head, realization suddenly hitting him, panic clear across his face. 'No! I swear, I told you everything! Billy's in charge, not me!'

'Don't you worry about Billy – he'll get his go,' said Ronnie. He checked his watch. 'Five o'clock,' he said, yawning. 'How long you want with them? Ten? Twenty?'

The man took his grimy coat off and threw it on the floor, grinning stupidly.

'Tell them!' screamed Omar to Billy. 'Tell them I don't know shit!'

Billy remained stony-faced, staring at each of them in turn. He tried to talk, but the gag was tight across his face. Ronnie removed it.

Billy shocked them all when he started laughing.

'You're dead,' he said finally. 'You want to know who you're taking on?'

'Amuse me,' replied Ronnie.

'They'll be coming for you. No police, no military, not even God can save you. You hear, *benchaud*?'

Ronnie smiled. 'Got it. You tell me if any of that shit matters when your kid's been murdered.' He turned to Omar. 'Looks like your mate Billy wants to watch.'

The sound of a belt unbuckling, a zip lowering filled the tunnel.

Omar started to scream.

Ronnie snatched the coat from Omar's body and threw it across the tunnel.

'What the— Please! Look, you can't do this – the girls, they wanted it, I looked after them, I never did anything to your daughter. Look, I—'

Ronnie slapped him, sending Omar's head thudding into the wall.

'Not my usual thing this, Omar,' said Ronnie, softening his voice a little. 'It's important you know that. Certainly not the sort of stuff my brother would condone. But the punishment needs to fit the crime. That's my world. Now, last chance before my friend here gives you nightmares you'll never wake up from,' said Ronnie coldly. 'He's dirty. The things he's got crawling all over his skin? Shit, even this tunnel's got more chance of salvation.'

'Ali! Ali! I . . . I . . . dropped him off one time,' shouted Omar.

'Where?' said Ronnie.

'I . . . don't know exactly, he's . . . he's . . . really secretive. Really weird, never shows his face. Doesn't want anyone knowing anything about him.'

'So where'd you drop him?' asked Ronnie, noticing the way Billy's body had suddenly tensed.

'Off Leeds Road.'

'Fucking hell,' said Ronnie. 'Leeds Road? That's not an address, that's an area.'

'It was outside Mughal's. There's some houses at the back of the restaurant . . . I'm sure he headed towards one of them. I tried to look, but it was dark so I didn't see properly . . . I swear,' he said, gasping for breath between his sobs. 'I swear, that's all I know!'

Ronnie believed him. Omar was about as afraid as anyone he'd ever seen.

'Tell him to stop,' shouted Omar, flinching. 'Tell him to stop!'

'That what the girls say?' asked Ronnie, his voice thick with contempt.

'Please,' sobbed Omar. 'I . . . I . . . don't deserve this.'

Ronnie grabbed his coat and a spare torch and stepped away from the trio. 'I don't like this, you know,' he said to Omar. 'Not one bit. But you brought it on yourselves.'

Ronnie switched on his torch, the beam lighting up the dark route which would lead him out of the tunnel. 'Before I go, I'll give you one last chance, Omar. Who killed my daughter?'

'Ali, it was Ali,' he sobbed.

'Olivia Goodwin, where is she?'

'I don't know.'

'Who's the boss of your gang?'

More of the same.

'What time does this shit go down tonight?'

'Eight! Eight o'clock – I know that much! I heard them talking about it. I swear, that's all I know.'

'You know what I'm looking for,' Ronnie said. Hobo nodded. 'See if you can jog his memory.'

Ronnie took the brown paper bag he had got from Enzo out of his pocket, removed the bottle of bourbon and walked into the darkness, listening as Omar started to scream.

THIRTY-FOUR

FOUR HOURS AFTER HARRY fell asleep, he opened his eyes to find Aaron standing unaided by his bed, grinning broadly and mumbling.

'Bah?'

Harry froze, savouring the sight of his son standing alone.

Aaron then took his first step.

And another.

'Bah!' he said, waving his hands excitedly and arriving by Harry's bed, throwing his arms triumphantly on to it.

'My boy,' whispered Harry, shuffling out of bed and scooping Aaron into his arms, kissing him repeatedly. 'Show me again.'

He placed him back on the carpet, a foot from the bed, leaving him standing. Aaron teetered unsteadily, then sat down, then crawled rapidly away towards the bedroom door.

'Hey,' said Harry, going after him, 'where's your mum?'

Aaron's chubby arms and legs ate up the ground as he entered the spare bedroom, where Saima was on her knees praying and whispering in Arabic. He raced towards her, head down, bum swaying until he head-butted his mother, who continued undistracted.

'Leave your mum alone,' said Harry, taking him back into his bedroom and getting into bed.

Harry was surprised to see Saima praying, she usually only performed Friday *namaz* worship.

'Nine a.m. prayers,' said Harry to his son, resting him on his chest, 'what have you done to make that happen?'

'Bah,' said Aaron.

'Bah,' replied Harry, and stared into his son's eyes. They were identical to Saima's. 'Have you eaten?'

'Bah.'

'Got it. Slap-up meal for two. Say, porridge with banana? Or shall we head out to that café where the cute brunette was giving you the eye last week? Think you're in there, my son. Mum'll freak if you bring a white girl home, but Dad's got your back.'

Aaron tried to pluck hair from Harry's chest, mesmerized.

'Sorry,' said Saima, coming into the bedroom. 'You got in so late last night; go back to sleep.'

'Nine o'clock prayers?' said Harry, raising an eyebrow.

'Ramadan starts tomorrow. Getting in the routine. Should have done it at sunrise, but Aaron woke up and wanted feeding.'

'He took a step,' said Harry, lifting Aaron high in the air.

'What?'

'Just now. Stood up over there and walked to the bed.'

'And I missed it!'

'Didn't the all-powerful interrupt your prayers to tell you?'

'Don't be a shit! I can't believe it, I tried for hours yesterday, he was so close!'

'Training paid off.'

'You're sure you weren't dreaming?'

Harry frowned and Saima took Aaron from him, standing him a few feet from the bed. 'Come on,' she said, patting his bottom. 'Let's see it.'

Aaron stared inquisitively at them, smiling stupidly. Then, hesitantly, he took three steps to the bed, where Saima threw her arms around him and kissed him like it was the first time.

'Told you,' said Harry.

Tears had formed at the corners of her eyes and she peppered Aaron with kisses, ignoring his struggles to break free. *'Bismillah,'* she said, thanking God in Arabic and continuing her religious start to the day.

'Why don't you go back to bed?' said Saima, putting Aaron into a playpen in their living room.

'Got work to do,' said Harry distractedly. Last night's events had finally broken through and were flooding his mind. He was scribbling in a notepad, looking for patterns in the information he'd gathered so far.

'You only slept for four hours,' she said.

'I'm fine, Saima,' he said, with just enough bite that she stopped.

Harry underlined the word 'taweez' several times. He found it in his pocket.

Aaron started to whimper, so Harry reached for the TV remote. 'The Wheels on the Bus' got Aaron excitedly making circles with his hands.

'That bloody bus,' whispered Harry, before walking over to the bay window where he could see the paperboy delivering newspapers, his fluorescent yellow bag in stark contrast to the morning's gloom.

'Twenty-six minutes,' whispered Harry to himself. 'Beat that boy's ass by three minutes. Never could catch me.'

As teenagers, he and Ronnie had competed to see who could finish their paper-round first, their father starting his stopwatch as soon as they stepped outside the corner shop.

'Tea?' shouted Saima from the kitchen.

Harry made his way through to her, taking Aaron with him. He handed his son a spoon to keep him occupied in his arms . . .

'Indian or English?' he asked.

'Either.'

'Indian. Might be the last decent cup I get for a month, once Ramadan starts.'

'I'll still make it if I'm fasting.'

'No taste test, though,' said Harry. 'It's never quite the same.'

'You get up with me at three in the morning, it's perfect then.'

'I'll pass.'

'Toast?'

'Just tea.'

'You've got to eat something. You're going out again today, I can see it in your face.'

Harry thought about Queensbury Tunnel and what might have happened there overnight.

'You heard from Ronnie? How's Mum and Dad?' asked Saima gently.

Despite everything, she still referred to them as Mum and Dad.

Harry didn't answer. He evaded a looping spoon to his face, taking it from Aaron and replacing it with a plastic one.

Saima put a pan of water on the stove, added cardamom seeds and threw in two tea bags. She placed a tava, an Indian frying pan, next to it and turned the gas on.

'Before you start,' said Harry, placing the taweez he had taken from Billy's Peugeot on the counter. Saima didn't look at him; she carried on spooning a lump of butter on to the tava, making it sizzle. She buttered both sides of a piece of a bread, added ajwain seeds to it and placed it in the centre of the pan.

She looked at Harry, then at the taweez.

Saima stared at it, puzzled.

'You know what this is?' he asked.

'A taweez?'

'I got it from someone I'm investigating.'

'Give me Aaron,' Saima said sharply, almost snatching their son from him.

'Hey!' said Harry, momentarily stunned.

'What the *hell* are you doing, bringing something like that into this house?' Her face flushed worriedly and she glared at the piece of string suspiciously.

'Come on, you know I don't believe in that crap.'

'But I do, and it's not right to take these things from people. You don't know what it might do.'

Saima was cradling Aaron protectively, kissing his head.

Harry sighed. He hadn't predicted this reaction. 'I need to know what it says. What it . . . does.'

'I'm not touching it.'

'Saima, would you stop. It's a piece of paper, not some sort of devil.'

'You wouldn't understand, you never do. These things can be dangerous.'

'You know I don't believe in black magic.'

Saima shook her head and carried Aaron into the living room. She put him in a high chair, strapped him in, and poured some Rice Krispies on to the tray to keep him occupied.

'I don't mock what you believe in,' she said, coming back into the kitchen, slamming the door behind her.

'But I've seen you with these things before.'

'I know what mine are for. They guard us, our family, give us strength.'

'That might be what this is.'

'Did you get it from somebody nice?'

Harry didn't reply.

'Did you get it from somebody dangerous?'

The look on his face said it all.

'Get rid of it. Now.'

Harry shook his head. 'I can't. I need to know what it's for.'

'No way.'

The bread on the tava was starting to burn. Saima lowered the gas and flipped it over, sighing at the sight of burned toast.

'Shit,' she said, grabbing another piece of bread.

'Christ, Saima, I need your help,' said Harry, taking the bread from her and setting it down.

'What for?' she said, turning to face him, her face flushed, muscles in her jaw flexing. 'You don't believe in them – you just said so.'

'I don't. But it might tell me something about the guy I took it from.'

Harry scrunched the taweez in his hand and grabbed a plastic bag, placing it inside and wrapping it firmly. 'I need you to take this to the old man around the corner.'

'The peersaab?'

'Ask him what it's for.'

'He might not know. Only the person who wrote it can really know its intentions.'

'There can't be many people in Bradford who are proficient in this . . . art,' said Harry, finding the right word. 'Even if he can't read it, he might know who wrote it—'

'You shouldn't mock what you don't understand,' she said quietly. Turning away from Harry, she once again picked up the piece of bread and started to butter both sides furiously.

'OK,' he said, trying to get her back onside. 'I shouldn't have brought it here.'

'No. You shouldn't,' she said, slapping the buttered piece of bread into the tava. 'You've only seen the ones I've had written. What if it's an ulta-taweez?'

'Ulta?'

'Opposite. Ones intended to harm.'

'Look, Saima,' Harry put the bag on the counter and stepped closer to his wife. 'I'm sorry. I didn't realize. I don't understand this shit.'

Saima was eyeing the bag suspiciously.

'I need you to go see him. I won't understand the language or the meaning.' Harry put his hand on her shoulder. 'It might help me nail the guy who killed Tara.'

Saima stiffened. 'Did you get it from him? A suspect?'

'Yes.'

'Then it's definitely evil.' She looked into his eyes. 'I'll go on one condition.'

'Anything.'

'I'm getting the peersaab to make me a taweez to undo whatever it is you brought here.'

'Fine.'

'I'm not finished.' Saima turned the gas hob off and turned to him. 'I'm going to get one written for you. I want you to wear it around your neck while you're out there. To protect you.'

Harry sighed. 'I'm not putting anything I don't believe in around my neck.' He saw Saima's lip curl. 'I'll carry it, OK? In my pocket. Compromise?'

Saima nodded. She snatched the bag from the counter, pushed past Harry and waved towards the cooker. 'Make your own breakfast,' she said.

In the living room, Harry sat at the table, next to his son. There were cardamom seeds floating in his tea and ajwain seeds all over his toast. Harry tried his tea and frowned. 'Crap,' he said to Aaron. 'Mum left in a huff and Dad's no good in the kitchen.'

Aaron left the Rice Krispies and waved his hands excitedly at Harry.

'OK, OK.' Harry broke a small piece of toast, picked the seeds from it and tried to feed it to Aaron, who snatched at the food, wanting to feed himself.

'Don't like any help, do you?' Harry whispered. 'Stubborn, like your old man. Try and park that?'

Aaron looked suspiciously at the bread, then put it in his mouth.

Harry sipped the tea and turned his chair towards his son. 'Two things: one – keep away from religious nuts. Your mother isn't quite a nut, but she has her moments.'

Aaron was staring at Harry, sucking on the bread, his face serious.

'Yeah, tell me about it.' Harry broke another piece and put it in Aaron's outstretched hand.

'Two?' Harry paused and leaned closer. 'When you're bigger? When you're ready to leave?'

Tara's empty house flashed into Harry's mind.

'Go far,' he said.

The whisper in his mind from the night before was surfacing.

I'm missing something.

'Bah?' said Aaron.

'Nope,' said Harry, shaking his head at the Rice Krispie clutched in Aaron's hand. He watched as his son put it down, chose another and held it out to him.

'Bah?'

Harry stood up and looked at the notes he had written.

'Something's not right,' he said, picking up the phone and calling the HMET office. Harry had an awkward conversation with a detective sergeant working Tara's case. He dodged his questions, claimed he couldn't talk.

What did they know that Harry didn't?

Harry stared at the phone in disbelief; he'd been cut off.

Nobody fobbed Harry off like that, especially not a junior.

He tried calling back, but nobody picked up the phone. He dialled DI Palmer and was about to press call when he glanced down at the table of notes he had made earlier.

Harry put the phone down.

'Shit,' he whispered. 'Shit, how did I not see that?'

His palms hit the table.

Tara found 03:00 Mon.

Sarah called 03:30 Tues.

No press release had gone out.

How had Sarah known about Tara's death?

With everything going on, Harry had missed it: there was no way Sarah could have known about the murder.

Unless she'd been there when it happened.

Saima arrived back ninety minutes later, walking into the living room and removing her headscarf. She didn't wear one routinely, but it was mandatory when visiting the peersaab.

Harry was desperate to get to the New Beehive, to Sarah, but on seeing Saima's face he knew he wouldn't be leaving for a while.

'Kitchen,' she said quietly.

Harry lifted Aaron from the floor and put him in his play area. When he got to the kitchen, Saima was pacing.

She shook her head. 'Nasty thing. Nasty, nasty thing.'

Harry massaged his temple. 'Go on.'

'It's about the dead.'

'What?'

'It's a black-magic pendant, not a real taweez. This protects against the dead. Against ghosts and jinns. Whoever you took that from is haunted by the dead.'

'Eh?'

Saima nodded. 'It's a . . . reverse taweez. It pushes the spirits of the dead on to others. It protects the one it was given to from their rage.'

'The rage of the dead?'

'Yes.'

'Can taweezes even do that?'

'It's not a real one. The peersaab wasn't impressed. He said it's not what they are meant for. He hadn't ever seen one like that. He was very upset, he's spiritually cleansing his house now.'

'Where is it? The taweez?'

'Outside in the bin, where it belongs.'

Harry approached his wife, but she backed away.

She put her hand in her pocket and removed a piece of string, attached to a wrapped-up scroll, encased in a plastic green sleeve. 'For you.' Saima pulled her top down, exposing her neck. 'This is mine and Aaron's.'

Harry put it in his pocket. 'I didn't know what it was, Saima.'

'I know.'

She allowed Harry to embrace her.

He hugged her tightly. 'I love you, you know that?'

'I don't like this,' she whispered.

Harry's phone was ringing in the living room. 'Come on,' he said breaking away. 'Everything's fine.'

In the living room, Harry took his phone to the bay window, where reception was clearest. He couldn't shake the burning question in his mind: had Sarah been there when Tara was murdered? Harry needed to get down to the New Beehive urgently; something was amiss.

'Morning, Sarge,' he said, answering the call.

Harry listened. Eyes widening, skin paling.

He lowered the phone, the voice on the other end still speaking, all thoughts about Sarah now banished.

Saima looked at him, unnerved by the expression on his face. 'Harry, what's wrong?'

He didn't reply. Saima could see that his hand, still clutching the phone, was shaking.

'Harry?' repeated Saima more forcefully.

'My father,' he said, unable to look at her.

'What? Is he OK?'

Harry shook his head, Nash's words from the night before suddenly booming inside his mind.

Who knew about Tara and was it worth killing for?

His voice was no more than a whisper.

'He's just been arrested for murder.'

THIRTY-FIVE

WEDNESDAY MIDDAY, EIGHT HOURS before everything would be made right, Sarah entered the city centre in her burka, hidden from the world.

The day she had been waiting for had arrived.

She'd found Harry's note that morning.

Call me.

She suspected he'd found inconsistencies in her story, but she couldn't go to him. She needed him to return; he was the final piece to this puzzle.

She entered the towering Bradford Cathedral, the oldest building in the city.

Once inside, she walked down the nave, imposing stained-glass windows on all sides. As a child, she had been afraid of them; a small part of her still was – those harrowing images of life and death, bright and petrifying.

But the windows also reminded her that, amongst the darkness of civilization, human beings could be exceptional. Centuries ago, when these windows had been installed, simple men with simple tools had created something extraordinary.

Sarah looked to one window in particular, where two angels cloaked in white stood side by side.

Today the words across the top held new meaning.

I am he that liveth and was dead, and behold I am alive for evermore.

She continued into the darkness of the cathedral, past the peace chapel, which had been set up for prayer against the war on terror; an attempt to show cross-faith solidarity with the largest Muslim population in England.

In the front pew she found Percy, head down.

'Hey,' said Sarah, sitting beside him.

'I was waiting for a pretty young girl to come and distract me. I suppose you'll do.'

Sarah smiled and put her hand over her grandfather's, squeezing it tightly. 'Have I ever told you that I love you?'

'Aye. You might have mentioned.'

'You seem . . . calm?'

He nodded, looking up at the altar. 'I am.'

She squeezed his hand a little tighter. 'You don't have to, you know? If you're having doubts.'

'No doubts.'

'Why do you look so sad?'

He thought about the letter he had shown to Victor, the guilt over lying to his granddaughter causing a pain in his chest. 'You know, I just wish things had turned out differently.'

'Thought you said only hard work makes things happen.'

'Good advice.'

'It was. *It is.*'

Sarah removed her hand from his.

'Don't,' he said, taking hold of it and putting it back. 'Warms an old man's heart.'

'How's Victor?' Sarah checked her watch. 'He will do his end, won't he?'

'It's a certainty. I think, in a strange sort of way, he's enjoying this.'

'Enjoying it?' she asked, raising an eyebrow.

'Not like that,' he said, shaking his head. 'I told you about eighty-two, right?'

'Falklands? Sure.'

'Well, Old Man Victor always wondered why we survived that day when everyone else died. Haunts him sometimes. Then you came back.'

'He thinks he survived for this?'

'He does.'

'Do you think that?'

Percy sighed. 'I think,' he said, blinking away tears, 'if I'd been a better granddad this might never have happened.'

'Don't do that,' said Sarah, shifting in the pew so she could look him straight in the face. 'You're not responsible for what they did to me. Or to Mum.' She paused, trying to find the right words. 'You always told me that we can only look in the mirror and judge what *we've* done.'

'That's right.'

'So, tonight? After all this is finished? We'll look in the mirror together and realize we changed the fate of many girls in this city for ever.'

Together.

Percy thought about what he'd told Victor the night before.

He looked away from Sarah. 'How'd you get so smart?'

'From you.'

He faced her and smiled. 'If tonight doesn't go—'

'It will,' she said fiercely, squeezing his hand. 'Are you sure you're up to your end? Because—'

'I think I should be with you,' he said, returning to a discussion they'd had many times before.

'No,' she said firmly, shaking her head.

'You've got so much to worry about, Sarah.'

'You're wrong,' she said, squeezing his hand again. 'Harry is going to come and see me – it's inevitable. I tried to book Billy's seven-seater earlier, but it's unavailable. Harry obviously got to Billy.'

Percy nodded.

'Billy won't have talked,' she went on. 'He's too involved, and there's no way he'd cross the boss.'

He nodded again, slowly.

'What is it?' Sarah asked.

'I did all this for you, Sarah. For the little girl I used to know and for the woman I hoped you'd become.'

Sarah looked away, blinking rapidly.

'You told me once that you'd died so many times, there was nothing left to do but actually die,' said Percy, thinking back to the trauma of her suicide attempts.

'I remember,' she said quietly.

'And now?'

'What do you mean?'

'I need to believe you are going into tonight in order to come out to better things.'

'I am.'

His body relaxed at her words.

'Give your granddad a hug,' he said, putting his arms out.

When he released her from the embrace, he got up. 'Be careful,' he said.

Sarah watched him leave, the sound of his footsteps gradually fading.

She rubbed the *GZ* tattoo with her finger, then closed her eyes.

The tattoo focused her mind away from memories of blood staining a machete. More than once.

She had escaped being the boss's child-whore in a foreign country straight into an alternative nightmare, where Yasser had obsessively trained her for an unprecedented mission and Sarah had drawn him close, making him believe their relationship was for real.

Sarah focused on the Epiphany window and saw similarities.

The detailed paintings told the story of the birth, the crucifixion and the resurrection of Jesus.

Christ was born. He died. He was re-born.

The parallels to her life were clear.

She left her pew and walked down the nave, to set off for Undercliff Cemetery.

Death wasn't coming to Bradford: *it had already arrived.*

THIRTY-SIX

HARRY PULLED UP OUTSIDE Trafalgar House, police divisional headquarters in the centre of Bradford, parking carelessly across a restricted bay before rushing into the building.

This cannot be happening.

But he couldn't be sure.

If his father had thought Harry marrying a Muslim was bad, where would he stand on Tara's sexuality? What might he have been capable of?

Right under my nose.

What about Olivia Goodwin? Some sort of bizarre coincidence?

The awkward phone call with the DS earlier now made perfect sense. Harry had been purposefully kept out of the loop.

Inside, DI Simon Palmer was waiting. He put his hands out, instinctively placating.

'Harry, you need to—'

'Inside!' Harry collided with his shoulder on the way past.

Palmer stayed with him as Harry stormed through reception to the back of the building.

The office was bustling; Harry could feel eyes awkwardly

glancing his way before they hurriedly looked elsewhere.

When he reached an empty interview room, he stepped inside, and waited for Palmer. No sooner had the door closed than Harry pinned Palmer against it, dropping his voice. 'What the fuck, Simon?'

'Listen, you best get a grip, Harry. This isn't about to get any easier.' Palmer's voice was strained; he was trying not to panic. 'Sit down, Harry.'

'I'm fine standing.' Harry let him go and backed off a step.

Palmer moved to the other side of the room, putting the table and chairs between them. Harry locked the door. Palmer glanced at it nervously. 'Are we going to have a problem?'

'Why would we? I trained you, so I assume you've got something concrete on my father. I want to know what, and I want to know why I wasn't kept in the loop.' Harry slammed his fist on the table, unable to shake the fear that his father might have murdered Tara, a possible honour killing – far from fucking honourable in Harry's eyes.

He thought of the night he had left home. He knew what his father was capable of.

'You know why. The DS told you, this isn't your case.' Palmer kept his voice even.

'I thought you of all people would have kept me up to date. You know how many times I've bent rules for you, Simon? You want reminders?'

Palmer shook his head. 'No.'

'So start talking.'

Ranjit had been placed at Tara's house on the night of her murder. Text messages proved they had arranged to meet, and CCTV cameras showed his vehicle parked outside her home for forty-five minutes while he was inside.

'Tara was found at Wapping School,' said Harry.

Palmer nodded. 'He might have moved the body.'

'You'd have seen it on the cameras.'

'Not if he used the back entrance. No cameras there.'

'Fuck's sake, Simon, you've got nothing.'

'There's more. He denied meeting with her that night.' Palmer suddenly looked nervous. 'He got angry. Said we were hassling him because he doesn't get on with you. That you put us up to it.' Palmer didn't know about Harry's issues with his family. Nobody at work did. 'So, we brought him in for questioning.'

'When?'

'Yesterday.'

'You arrest him?'

'No. He was happy to cooperate. At first. Voluntarily gave his clothes and jewellery for Forensics to examine. The usual.'

Harry nodded. 'You kept him overnight?'

'Yes. We . . . arrested him. Held him incommunicado.'

Incommunicado, which is why Harry hadn't heard about it. Palmer had been worried Harry's loyalty to his father might have swayed his better judgement, causing him to tamper with possible evidence. The arrest wasn't known to anyone outside of the investigation team.

'We got the forensic results, Harry.'

Palmer's face said it all. Harry didn't want to hear it.

'We found Tara's blood under your dad's ring.'

Harry had a vivid flashback. His father's ring on his right hand, accelerating towards his face. A back-hander: his father's preferred choice of discipline.

Harry slumped into a chair.

He'd received that particular blow many times in his life. The last time, the night he left home.

'Harry?'

'Huh?'

'You OK?'

'Fine,' he croaked, unable to look at Palmer. 'Keep going.'

'We asked him about it – told him we had proof he'd been there – but still he denied it. He got angry, Harry. That's some temper.'

The room was spinning. Harry knew that temper.

'Fuck,' he whispered.

'Listen, Harry, we had no choice. Look at the facts. We've got him at the scene, there's DNA, and he won't cooperate. Plus, he's shown us he's capable of violence.'

Harry felt sick. He wanted to stand up but didn't trust his legs. 'Does my mother know?' he whispered.

'No. You're the first person we've told.'

'My brother?'

'Nobody. Like I said, just you.' Palmer hesitated, then said, 'We're raiding the house, Harry. You know the drill. It's why I told you. Knew you'd come storming down here. I'm doing you a courtesy because of who you are. Because . . . I wanted you to know before it happens.'

Harry nodded. 'When are you doing it?'

'The team's assembling at the moment.'

'What have you charged him with?'

'Nothing yet – he's looking at a murder charge today.'

Harry's breath caught in his throat.

'I want to see him.'

'Not a chance.'

Harry stood slowly, keeping his palms on the table for support. 'I'm not asking.'

'You know I can't.'

'Let me help you out here.'

'How so?'

'His temper?'

Palmer nodded.

'I sit across from him and you're really going to see fireworks. There's bad blood there.'

'So he said. He reckons you're fitting him up.'

Harry laughed, a dry sound.

'I can't, Harry.'

'You don't trust me? Come in with me.'

Palmer leaned against the wall, stuffed his hands in his pockets and sighed.

'Listen.' Harry stepped closer. 'I don't want to do this, but you're forcing my hand. We both know there are things you've done that you'll want to keep secret.'

Palmer's face flushed and he looked to the floor. 'Don't know what—'

'Fuck off, Simon,' said Harry, jabbing his finger into Palmer's chest, all patience abandoned. 'You've screwed half the station. Now put me in that room with him.'

Palmer met his gaze but said nothing.

'You want a confession? There's only one person who is going to get it.'

'I'll bring him to interview room three,' whispered Palmer. 'You step out of line—'

Harry walked out.

In the kitchen, Harry waited for the kettle to boil. He had tried to call Ronnie but his phone was switched off. Harry didn't want to send a text.

He couldn't have done it.

The voice in Harry's mind wasn't convincing.

Shit, Ronnie wouldn't have evidence of who he really was at his house, would he?

He pulled a mug from the cupboard, one eye on the corridor outside the kitchen.

There was a moment's lull. With the corridor deserted, Harry grabbed for the little wooden door stop wedging the kitchen door open, putting it in his pocket and closing the door. He made a coffee, more out of habit than thirst, and held it to warm his hands.

Of all the shit he'd shovelled dealing with murderers in this city, none of it compared with the raw fear now rooting inside of him.

Palmer opened the door. 'We're ready, Harry.'

'Does the DS know?'

'Are you serious?'

Harry put his coffee down. 'Keep it that way.'

He followed Palmer down the corridor.

'We're clear. It's lunchtime, quietest this place is going to get.'

'Appreciate it.' Harry paused outside the room. He could see his father's orange turban through the glass panel.

Harry's legs were unsteady.

'Ready?' said Palmer.

Harry barged him out of the way, sending the DI sprawling to the ground.

Harry stormed into the room, closed the door and wedged the door stop he'd pocketed into the gap between the bottom of the door and the floor.

Palmer was back on his feet and desperately rattling the door handle. His attempts to open it only secured the door stop in place.

'You give me ten minutes, Simon. Or I burn you,' Harry said through the glass.

Palmer couldn't cause a scene; he was too afraid Harry would make good on his word. He mouthed objections at Harry who turned to face his father.

A man he loved.

A man he resented.

A man he needed to break.

THIRTY-SEVEN

ALI WAS SICK OF waiting.

Parked at the rear of the farmhouse where Olivia Goodwin and her mother were staying, he checked the time on his dash again. Only a minute had passed.

His agitation growing, he played with the toggles on his hood.

Five more minutes.

Why this had to be done at exactly one p.m., he didn't know. But he wasn't about to rock the boat now.

Seven hours.

The back door of the farmhouse was drawing him in.

She's in there.

He looked over at the kit on the passenger seat.

One large syringe for Lexi; it would keep her unconscious long enough for them to complete their deal.

The smaller syringe was for Olivia.

Olivia.

His thoughts were disturbed by the hurried arrival of a car he recognized. Mud sprayed from its wheels as it ate up the ground and parked hastily beside him, back wheels skidding in the dirt. Even through the blacked-out windows, Ali could feel Riz's eyes on him.

Riz got out of the Mercedes, tapped the bonnet of Ali's Ford and pointed to the empty stables behind.

'Billy and Omar are missing.' Riz got straight to the point.

'Missing?' said Ali, sitting down on an old packing case. He turned his face away, conscious of weak streaks of sunshine coming in through the stable windows.

'Billy disappeared off the grid about eleven last night and Omar never showed up for work this morning.'

From under his hood, Ali's eyes were burning intensely.

He couldn't lose the girl.

'Sure?' he said quietly, his heart hammering in his chest. He didn't like dealing with Riz. He acted like the one in charge, but he was nothing more than a dog on a lead.

'Virdee visited the garage last night. Spoke to Omar, then left.'

Ali nodded slowly.

'So it's over?' he asked, waiting anxiously for an answer.

If Riz pulled the deal, he'd be forced to act.

End this now.

'Don't be stupid,' said Riz.

Ali's shoulders relaxed.

Riz carried on. 'Billy's the only other person who knows this location. He won't talk.'

'Omar?'

'He's got nothing.'

'How d'you know Billy won't talk?'

'You don't know the boss.'

Ali shook his head.

'Anyway, this is all on you, you little fucker,' hissed Riz, stepping forward.

'On me?' Ali said, springing to his feet.

'The Virdee girl. What the fuck were you thinking?'

'Billy told me to make sure she disappeared.'

'*Disappeared* didn't mean sticking a knife in her chest and leaving her to be found in the middle of the city. What's wrong with you?'

What's wrong with you?

Ali took a step closer, pushing his mother's favourite phrase from his mind. 'She's quiet now, isn't she?' he said.

Riz backed off, shaking his head. The pressure of the next seven hours was suddenly bearing down on him.

'Girl's not secure in there with Omar and Billy gone,' said Ali, pointing to the house, an idea forming in his mind.

'No choice now,' said Riz. 'Knock them out, and if anyone arrives before eight o'clock, you bail.'

Ali shook his head.

'I'll put Mum to sleep,' he said. 'Leave her in there, and I'll take the girl someplace safe.'

Riz shook his head. 'Don't be stupi—'

'You're being stupid,' Ali snapped. 'There's a serious chance this has all gone to shit and you want to leave them here while we wait for Virdee to arrive with all his mates?' Ali paused, unsure if he could pull this off. 'I'll take the girl. You get here early. If we're clear, you call me and I'll bring her.'

'Where are you going to take her?' asked Riz.

'My place.'

'Where's that?'

'Bradford.'

'Don't get smart.'

'Makes no difference. I could give you any address. You trust me with the dirty work, but not this?'

'This—' Riz started.

'I'm your only option,' said Ali.

He was right. Riz hated being backed into a corner but he didn't have a choice.

Too much money at stake for Ali to screw this up.

'She's . . . pure,' he said, staring intensely at Ali. 'Understand?'

'I know,' replied Ali, stifling a smile under his hood.

'You fuck this up . . .' Riz closed the gap between them.

He got his phone out and typed in a search before turning it around so Ali could see the screen.

'You see this guy?' he said.

Ali glanced at the screen and although Riz couldn't see much of his face, he saw Ali's mouth drop open.

'What?'

'Yeah,' said Riz, relieved. Ali's reaction had been exactly what he needed. 'That's our fucking boss. So now you're in the loop – make sure you behave.'

THIRTY-EIGHT

ALI PAUSED BY THE back door of the farmhouse.

The boss.

Jesus.

Could he do this?

He needed time to think it through, but time was the one thing he didn't have.

He opened the door into the kitchen, slamming it behind him to ensure he was heard.

Ali saw the note Billy had left on the counter:

Don't 4get, heating man coming in morning Billy x

He called out.

'In here!' came a young voice.

Olivia.

'Where's your mum?' He wandered through to the hallway.

'Upstairs,' the voice said. Ali stole a glance into the living room where Olivia was watching television. Having caught a fleeting glimpse of a prize he had coveted for years, Ali felt suddenly overwhelmed.

Focus, Ali, focus.

'I . . . need to go upstairs first,' he said. 'Billy said I was coming? Right?'

'Yeah.'

'Is your mum asleep?'

'She won't be bothered,' the girl replied. 'She's on medicine.'

'Thanks,' said Ali, and hurried away, the syringes burning a hole in his pocket, his heartbeat deafening inside his head.

Upstairs, he found Lexi Goodwin asleep in the end bedroom.

The boss. His identity had sent shock waves tearing through Ali.

He hurried over to the bed, afraid he might lose his nerve. He shook her shoulder.

Lexi didn't respond, her breathing shallow, dried saliva around her lips.

Ali pulled out the syringe, rolled Lexi on to her front and, seeing she had no underwear on, jabbed the needle into her backside.

In the living room, Ali was relieved Olivia still had her back towards him, focused on the television. He was holding a syringe in his hand; he was loath to use it to pierce Olivia's flawless skin, but it was a necessary evil.

This was about to happen.

Ali marched purposefully towards Olivia, adrenaline searing through his veins.

Her reaction was instinctive as Ali grabbed her and dragged her to the floor. He used his knees to pin her shoulders and used a rough hand to turn her face away from his. Olivia thrashed wildly, almost sending Ali toppling over. His knee slipped from her right shoulder and she raised her hand and clawed her fingers into his face, covering her hands in his thick make-up. Ali plunged the needle into her thigh, waiting the few minutes it would take the drugs to work.

Panting heavily, hood dislodged and with blood running down

his face where Olivia's nails had caught his fragile skin, Ali moved away to wait until she had faded.

Then at last he came face to face with his prize.

The revelation of the boss's identity had taken the ground from underneath him, but now with shaky hands stroking Olivia's face, Ali Kamran could think of only one thing:

He was going to keep this girl, for ever.

THIRTY-NINE

HARRY REMAINED BY THE doorway as his father sat stony-faced, ignoring the objections of DI Palmer outside.

Harry walked to the empty chair and sat down. Both men stared at each other. Harry took in new details about his father: wrinkles across his forehead, grey hair escaping his turban and painfully hollow eyes.

He didn't do it.

The first thing Harry thought.

He can't have done.

This was why he had not been allowed to work the case: the risk of loyalty undermining his objectivity. He was searching for an opening sentence when his father shattered the silence.

'You killed her,' he said in Punjabi.

Of all the things he could have said, Harry hadn't expected that.

'What?'

Ranjit was calm.

'What you did. It paved the way for Tara. Leaving home, breaking your parents' hearts, disgracing your community.'

'Did you kill her?'

There was no emotion on Ranjit's face. No reaction at all.

It hit Harry, like a brick.

Jesus Christ, you ruined him when you left. He's broken too.

'Do you think,' Ranjit asked softly, 'that I did?'

Harry didn't reply. He'd been expecting fireworks.

'I hate you,' said Ranjit calmly, quietly. 'With everything inside of me. Every bone, every cell, every memory you ever created – all of it.'

Harry felt light-headed.

Christ, not this.

He needed anger – fury, not guilt. He had enough of that on his own.

'I brought you home, from the hospital. January first, 1979. New Year. New life. I raised you. I fed you. I clothed you. I worked in that damn shop, fourteen hours a day, to give you the best of everything—'

'You've said all this before,' said Harry, not wanting to repeat the conversation they'd had four years ago.

Ranjit pointed to the door Harry had sealed. 'You think you're going to get some confession from me? No.' Ranjit shook his head. 'You're going to *suffer*, same as me.'

Harry blinked profusely. *Don't crack. Not here. Not in front of him.*

'I see it,' said Ranjit. 'In your eyes. I gave them to you. You think I cannot see your pain? I'm your father.'

Harry clenched his teeth, grinding his jaw, thinking of Tara's secret.

'What were you doing at Tara's?' he asked.

'Having a conversation I should have had with you a long time ago. Before it got out of hand.'

Don't. Don't say it.

'I asked her to come home.'

Harry felt pain in his chest, heat spreading.

'I asked her to think again about what she was doing,' Ranjit continued.

'What she was doing?' Harry could only manage a simple question.

'I told her not to do what you did. She had moved out, she had shamed her family. I did not want her going against our community like you had. Our girls do not leave home until they are married. It is *not* how our culture works.'

'Why didn't you tell that to the guys who interviewed you?'

'I wanted to tell you. I wanted you to know that you killed her.'

'I didn't,' whispered Harry, feeling drained. He put his hand in his pocket, feeling for the keyring of the candle and crescent-moon Saima had given him for Diwali. He found Saima's taweez instead.

'If you hadn't done what you did, if you'd married someone respectable, Tara would still be at home and this . . . tragedy wouldn't have happened. You started it all – you gave Tara all the ammunition she needed.'

'You disowned me,' said Harry, searching his other pocket and finding the keyring, squeezing it tightly. 'Tara knew nobody would tolerate her independence. Not after what happened with me.'

'Her father tolerated it. Ronnie never had the strength to do what I did.'

'Strength?' Harry dug the edges of the keyring into his fingers, trying to keep calm. 'Strength? Is that what you think it was?'

'What would you call disowning a son? You think it's easy?'

'Weakness. That's what I call it.'

'When the boy in your house grows to be a man, you decide whether it is strength or weakness.'

'There's nothing my son could do to make me disown him.'

'You allowed the *devil* into your house and you think—'

Harry got to his feet and leaned over the table, towering above his father.

'Don't you call my wife that. Ever,' snapped Harry, letting go of the keyring and pointing angrily at his father.

'Not your wife. What she believes. It is incompatible with everything *we* believe,' said Ranjit, unmoved in the chair.

'It's not incompatible with what I believe.'

'You have converted?' Ranjit spat on the floor.

'No.' Harry tried not to lose it. 'I believe what I always have. There's no place in *my* world for religion, but I'm not going to stop anyone else believing.'

'And the boy in your house?' Harry was sure his father knew Aaron's name, but he refused to use it.

'When he's a man? When he's old enough to decide, he'll make up his own mind.'

'That's not how *those* people work.'

'Those people? You can't even bring yourself to say the word "Muslim"?'

Ranjit looked away.

'And the woman in your house, she agrees with you?'

'She puts family before religion.'

Ranjit shook his head, smiling patronizingly. 'You are so misguided and foolish. This decision will be the end of your life.'

'Guess we'll see.'

'Did I really raise you so badly?'

'How have you not figured this out yet?'

'What—'

'You forced me to go.'

'I did not.'

'You came at me with your kirpan.'

'I wish your mother hadn't stopped me.'

'What kind of father wishes his son's death?'

'I gave you life. It is for me to take it away.'

Momentarily lost for words, Harry stared at him in disbelief. His legs felt unsteady but he remained standing. 'Do you want to know the truth?' he said.

'My conscience is clear.'

Harry put his hands on the table, steadying himself for what he was about to say.

'Let me tell you why me marrying a Muslim is all your fault.'

Ranjit met Harry's gaze. 'Show me how the woman in your house has *twisted* your view of your own family.'

Harry took a breath, his temper crumbling when his father spoke about Saima.

'You moved to this country. You left your parents in India, so that you might have a better life. You never had to worry about them – your brothers were left to look after them. All you ever worried about was making money and raising your family.'

'I'm proud of what I achieved.'

Harry continued, determined. 'Good education, mixing with English people from all backgrounds. We became English citizens in a country where this religious melodrama of yours is laughed at. You bought us that education, you were proud of this open upbringing you'd got for us. But you had one rule: be tolerant, mix with everybody, but never associate with Muslims. It was totally flawed. It was never going to work. We don't live in India, we're not "Indians" like you think we are. You can park your bullshit, Dad.'

Anger started to show on Ranjit's face, but Harry continued. He couldn't have stopped if he wanted to; it felt as if his blood were on fire.

'If you wanted that life, you should have stayed in your own damn country,' said Harry.

Ranjit cursed loudly and smashed his fists on the table, making Harry jump. 'Ungrateful bastard! I gave you the best of everything!'

'My wife, Saima—'

'Don't say her name in my presence! That dog took my son from me!'

'Don't. Call. Her. That.'

From outside, DI Palmer must have seen the mood shift. He started urgently knocking on the door.

Harry pointed at his father. 'Get up.'

Ranjit didn't move.

'On your fucking feet!' shouted Harry, losing control. 'Before I drag you.'

His father stood.

Ranjit wiped his eyes, unwilling to shed tears in Harry's presence. 'She took you from me! Look at you, choosing her over me. Again!'

Harry smashed his own fist down on to the table.

'I'm standing right in front of you, Dad. There is no choice. There never was. I'm still your son.'

Both men glared at each other, the ice they were standing on fracturing. Harry's fists were still clenched, digging nails into his palms, sweat bleeding into his clothes.

'Tara's blood,' hissed Harry, suddenly remembering why they were in the room. 'How did it get under your ring?'

Ranjit looked past Harry to the far wall, then fell back into his chair, his anger and energy suddenly drained.

'If you don't tell me, they're going to do you for her murder,' said Harry.

Ranjit rubbed both hands over his face and wiped his eyes. He looked as broken as Harry felt.

'She cut her hand on a glass,' he said dejectedly. 'I grabbed it to look at it, because she was crying. That is how. Very, very simple.'

'I don't believe you.'

'I don't care. It's the truth.'

He hadn't killed Tara.

Relief flooded Harry's system. He hadn't realized how fearful he'd been of the possibility it was true.

'Why didn't you tell them earlier?'

'Four years ago I lost a son. Now, a granddaughter.' There was a tremor in his voice as he continued: 'I'm broken. That day . . .'

Harry nodded.

'I wouldn't have done it. I wouldn't have hurt you. I'm weak. I should have been able to. But I know I couldn't have.'

Harry had never seen his father cry.

'Not having the ability to take your son's life doesn't make you weak,' he said, his voice softer now.

'I didn't kill Tara. You think I could take my granddaughter's life when I couldn't even take yours?'

Harry didn't. 'You need an alibi for Saturday night, after you left her place.'

'That's easy.' Ranjit dropped his head on to his chest, tired. 'I was at the temple all night until Sunday morning. There was a do. Hundreds of witnesses. I got a lift home at nine o'clock and I didn't go out all day. We have CCTV cameras at the house – you can check.'

'You could have saved a lot of trouble by saying all this earlier.'

Ranjit lifted his head. 'I wanted you to come here to see what you have done. We are all dead inside and now we have lost another part of the family – because of you. Your mother is no longer the woman I married.' Harry looked away, unable to maintain eye contact with his father. 'Damn you, Hardeep. Damn everything about you. Your kismet is black like your blood. The woman in your house will ruin you, just like she did us.'

There was no anger any more. These were the facts as he saw them.

'You're a foolish old man,' whispered Harry, shaking his head. Then he walked towards the door.

Palmer stepped aside, glaring at Harry, waiting for the door to open.

'And you're wrong about Saima,' said Harry, remembering his wife's words. He kicked the wooden block from the base of the door, but kept his foot pressed against it. 'You don't hate her because she's a threat. You hate her because she isn't. Because if you met her, she would shatter your preconceptions and then . . . And then what the hell would you do with all your hate?'

Harry opened the door, and stepped outside.

'All yours,' he said to DI Palmer. 'All fucking yours.'

FORTY

ALI GENTLY LAID OLIVIA'S body on the single bed in his cellar, having moved Gori's lifeless body on to the floor.

He stroked Olivia's hair, gently sliding a pillow under her head and spreading a blanket over her little body.

Then he sat beside her, a calmness stilling his thoughts.

He couldn't wait for her to open her eyes.

Over the course of the last year, Ali had worked tirelessly in his cellar. Much like his face, he had transformed it from a ruin. The walls were painted warm pink and he'd stuck glow-in-the-dark stars across the ceiling. He'd loved them as a kid, counting them every night to relax his mind from the torment of surviving another bruising day at school.

Ali lifted Gori's body from the floor; her skin, as usual, was icily cold. He dragged her upstairs, her feet bouncing clumsily on the stairs. Unsure what to do with her, for now, Ali laid her on the kitchen floor and hurried upstairs.

He needed to get ready.

He took far more care than he usually did. He needed to look just right for when Olivia woke up and saw him for the first time.

There was no time for the bath. But Ali painted, smudged and repainted his face until it was perfect. He lifted a piece of broken glass from the floor, hesitating in his excitement. One deep breath.

He looked good.

Olivia would be pleased.

He even allowed himself to smile.

Back in the cellar, he paced the floor while Olivia slept.

'I have the most beautiful girl anybody in our community will ever have seen, Mother.'

He scratched at his hands.

Why did you curse this family?

'I didn't curse this family.' Ali fell silent, dejected. 'I knew you wouldn't believe me. Look, let me show you.'

Ali's hands were shaky as he stood in front of the shelf he usually shied away from at the far end of the room and pulled back the black cloth. The jar sat alone. Two eyes floated in yellow liquid. They didn't shine like they once had, but they had at least lost some of their judgement over the years.

'Look at me,' he whispered, his voice unsteady. Look!' he hissed, stepping aside and pointing at Olivia's body, which was starting to move on the bed.

'I knew you'd have nothing to say.'

Ali returned to his pacing.

'She's mine, Mother. I proved everyone wrong. She'll love me and I'll no longer be an outcast.'

Olivia was starting to come round, mumbling incoherently. Ali hurriedly covered the jar with the black cloth.

'You don't get to see her any more, Mother,' he hissed, then stepped aside, looking into a mirror hanging on the wall to check his appearance. He pulled his hood down. *Good.*

Nervously, excitedly, he crept towards Olivia and knelt by her side as she started to awaken.

He smiled and reached out his hand, lovingly tucking her hair behind her ear.

'Hi,' he said as she opened her eyes.

Their eyes locked and for a moment, nothing happened.

Then, as if Ali was viewing it in slow-motion, her eyes narrowed, her body coiled and she did the one thing that was guaranteed to break Ali's heart: Olivia screamed.

She pushed her body back, away from Ali, until she felt the wall behind her.

Stunned, he got to his feet. He marched around the room, showing her how he had provided for her. Urging her to stop screaming.

She wouldn't. She couldn't. Between screams, she gasped for air, struggling to breathe. Terror was etched into every inch of her face.

'It's OK,' said Ali, turning his face away. 'I . . . saved you,' he said pathetically.

'Mum,' she sobbed. 'Where's . . . my mum?'

Ali backed off a step and put his hands out. 'No,' he said. 'You're going to stay here with me. We're going to be happy.'

He gestured around the cellar, at all the toys he had bought, and pointed at the new outfits, hanging pristine in the wardrobe.

'Look . . . *all this work.*'

But Olivia would not stop screaming. Ali balled his hands into fists.

Why couldn't she see?

All this for her!

He began panting. He looked at Olivia and instead of the little girl he had coveted for so long, he saw the girls in the playground, screaming and running away from him. That fear had seemed so exciting then, but it was devastating now.

'Just like them!' he hissed at Olivia, who cowered in a corner of the bed.

Ali snatched a bottle of chloroform from the shelf, seething as Olivia's face merged with others who had ruined him. He searched for a cloth – he couldn't use the one covering the jar containing his mother's eyes; she didn't need to see this.

He grabbed one of the new pink towels and unscrewed the bottle.

Ali descended on Olivia, all sense of reason lost.

'You are mine!' he hissed. 'And you *will* love me.'

FORTY-ONE

HARRY STEPPED OUT OF Trafalgar House to see Ronnie's Range Rover in the car park. The family had been notified within the past hour.

He checked his phone; twelve missed calls from Ronnie and four from Sarah. She'd also sent him a text.

Meet me at Undercliffe Cemetery. We need to talk.

Harry replied before he hesitantly climbed inside the Range Rover.

Ronnie's eyes were red, his hair a mess. Harry wondered if he'd even been home.

'What the fuck, Harry?' he said, even before the door had shut.

'I know,' replied Harry, bracing himself.

'Did you do this?'

'Don't be stupid. We'll get to that. First, they are raiding your home.'

'What?'

'Standard practice. Are you clean there?'

'They're raiding—'

'Are you clean there?' snapped Harry.

Seeing the panic in Harry's face, Ronnie nodded. 'Home is home. Nothing to do with work there.'

Harry relaxed a little. Now that was out of the way, he was finding it difficult to know where to start.

'Dad didn't do it,' he said.

'No shit, Sherlock! Mum's going crazy.'

'She'll be worse when the police arrive for the raid. You need to get back there.'

'You've seen him?' asked Ronnie.

Harry explained what had happened.

'When will he be out?'

'Once the alibi checks out, they'll bail him. Probably later today.'

'Bail?'

'It's only a formality.'

'Get him out,' snapped Ronnie. 'And stop the raid. I can't deal with this right now.'

'I can't. It's not my call.'

Ronnie looked to the ceiling in despair.

'You enjoyed seeing him in there, didn't you?'

'Hey,' snapped Harry. 'I might not like the guy, but he's still my father.'

'Is he safe?'

'Nobody's letting him suffer. His alibi – temple all Saturday night into Sunday morning – were you there too?'

Ronnie nodded. 'I'm going in there to tell . . .' he checked his phone, 'DI Palmer.'

'Good,' said Harry.

'That gets him out?'

'It helps.'

'What is it? Do you want him to stew?'

'Enough, OK! I told you – I'm on it. He should have at least told *you* he visited Tara on Saturday night. What's that about?' asked Harry incredulously.

Ronnie hesitated.

'What are you not telling me?' Harry pushed.

'Nothing,' Ronnie whispered, closing his eyes.

'Send it elsewhere, Ron.'

'The old man and I aren't the greatest of friends right now.'

'Because of Tara?'

'Yup.'

'Looks like you finally understand what it's like to be me.'

'He blamed me for her leaving. Said I was weak, that I should have shut it down. We had . . . an altercation.'

There was a flashback in Harry's mind.

Ronnie read his thoughts: 'Nothing as dramatic as what happened with you.'

'How bad?'

Ronnie shrugged. 'We haven't spoken since I let Tara leave.'

There was silence. The brothers looked each other over.

'You know, don't you?' Ronnie whispered.

Harry sighed. 'Fuck me,' he said, shaking his head. 'Fuck me.'

'How?' asked Ronnie.

'I bumped into Nash.'

Harry turned to face Ronnie and dropped his voice. 'Gay Asian girl moves out of home, family disapprove, girl ends up dead,' he said bluntly. 'You see how it looks? They're going to come for you, Ron.'

Ronnie pulled a joint from his pocket, put it between his lips and wound the window down.

Harry snatched it from him. 'We're outside the damn station! You're about to go in there as Dad's alibi. Think!'

'Then stop looking at me like that. This shit's hard enough to say without you glaring at me.'

Harry shoved the joint in Ronnie's pocket then turned to stare out of the passenger window.

'Tara was at my warehouse,' said Ronnie. 'I had this prick working for me, in charge of Bradford West distribution. Never liked him. Bastard picked a fight. There was just me, him and Tara. The argument got heated and he told Tara what we really did.

I denied it, but he opened a container, showed her the drugs.'

'What did you do?' said Harry, still looking out of the window.

Ronnie shuffled in his seat.

Harry turned to face him. 'In front of Tara?'

'She wouldn't leave.'

'Ronnie, you *fucking*—'

'Hey! I messed up. I know. I tried to explain it to her. Tried to . . .'

'Turn her?'

'I guess. There was nothing else I could do, Harry. I wasn't about to lose my daughter.'

The brothers looked at each other.

'I made her an offer.'

'Life-long riches?'

Ronnie shrugged. 'Instead, she saw her opportunity. She told me she was gay and that she wanted out. I was cornered. But I couldn't tell the family. Couldn't do shit except give in.'

'Christ, Ronnie, does Mandy know that Tara was gay?'

'No.'

Harry looked at his watch, he needed to get back to Sarah.

'I envied you then,' whispered Ronnie. 'After she'd gone.'

'Envied me?'

'Inside the four walls of that little house you live in, it's happy, right?'

Harry nodded.

'You picked the woman you loved. And even though the world collapsed around you, you never wavered. I envied that selfishness to protect you and yours at all costs.'

'What are you talking about? You and Mandy are—'

'Arranged. I was out of jail, drinking heavily. She was a traditional girl. We fell into it, but we don't love each other like we should. Throw in living with your parents and then you'll understand why I work like I do. I need something to focus on – something *I* own, Harry. Something *I* control.'

Harry had never realized his brother felt this way. 'When I lived with you guys, you were the happiest couple I knew. Shit, before I met Saima, you guys gave me faith in arranged marriages.'

'We put on a good show.'

Harry's head was starting to pound.

'Finding the bastard who did this to Tara is the only way I might get some respect back.' Ronnie looked at the floor. 'I know what you feel like now.'

'No. You don't. But you soon might, if this life drags you under, Ronnie. You might actually lose them. You need to stop.'

'I know,' he replied.

Harry stared at him in disbelief.

'Yeah, you heard me,' said Ronnie. 'I know. But first? I need the son of a bitch who did this to Tara. After that? We'll see.'

The brothers let another silence linger. Harry wasn't sure what to believe.

'What happened with Billy and Omar?' asked Harry finally.

'Not much,' said Ronnie. 'Shit goes down at eight o'clock tonight. No idea where. And this Ali guy? Freak show, apparently. Omar reckons he knows where he lives.'

'Where?'

'Not exact. Houses behind Mughal's restaurant? One of them, he thinks.'

'Thinks?'

'These guys are ghosts to each other.'

'You look ready to collapse, Ronnie.'

'Don't. Just check out the location, OK?'

Harry glanced at his watch. 'Sure. But I need to see Sarah first.' *How did she know about Tara's death?*

Harry wasn't sure he could accept everything she'd been telling him. Perhaps she hadn't been one of Billy's girls either.

'Anything I can help with?'

'No, no. Sort Dad's alibi, then get home and tell Mum everything's under control. She'll be a mess once the raid starts.'

'She already is.'

Harry couldn't go there.

'I've an idea how we can break Billy,' he said.

'How?'

Harry produced Billy's taweez. He'd taken it from the bin outside his home where Saima had dumped it. Now, he handed it to Ronnie, telling him his plan.

'It's . . . ambitious,' said Ronnie, handing it back.

'Got any better ideas?'

Ronnie shrugged. 'I can't go home and be there for them when the raid starts if you want me at the tunnel in an hour?'

Harry sighed and drummed his fingers on the dash. 'Leave them to deal with it,' he whispered, almost ashamed of himself. 'There's no time for you to get bogged down. Are you up for this, Ron? You look like hell.'

'I'm on it.'

'Good,' said Harry, opening the door to leave. 'It's about time the dead came back to life.'

FORTY-TWO

HARRY ENTERED THE CEMETERY, once an exclusive burial ground for wealthy wool merchants, but now anyone could be laid to rest inside the grounds. Scattered amongst grand, awe-inspiring tombs decorated with serpents and eagles were more modest granite headstones.

He went in through the open gates; the place was deserted. He headed towards the newest tombs at the far end and saw an outline of a lone figure, clad in black, familiar blonde curls resting on her shoulders.

Sarah didn't move as Harry arrived by her side. She was looking at a small grey tombstone with a fresh white lily laid across it.

Amy Brewster, 1980–2010, aged 30.

No embellishments or kind words. Just the facts.

Sarah was crying. Harry stood beside her and waited. Finally she broke the silence.

'You know, don't you?' she said quietly.

Harry pointed to a bench away from the graves. 'Can we?' he said.

She nodded, kissed her fingertips and touched the headstone before following Harry.

'You weren't just one of the girls they hung around with,' said Harry, sitting on the bench beside Sarah.

'No.' Sarah's body deflated as she admitted the truth. 'They groomed us. When Mum was at her weakest, Billy promised her a new life. So stupid not to have seen it,' she hissed angrily.

'How old were you?'

'Eleven.'

'Don't think any eleven-year-old would have seen that coming.'

'I worshipped him,' she said, turning to Harry, her face flushed in the cold air. 'He treated me like I was his daughter. Spoiled me. Made me laugh. I loved him like he was my father.'

They both fell silent as a teenage boy walked past, hands deep in his pockets.

'What happened?' Harry turned towards her.

Sarah shrugged. 'We packed up. We'd moved a couple of times. Lost all our friends. Nobody really gave a shit. Mum had me when she was fifteen. She was . . . difficult. She had a few boyfriends after Dad left, and then Billy came on the scene. He isolated her, ruined her. He . . .' Sarah pointed towards the tombstone in the distance.

'Why did you lie to me?' he asked bluntly, an edge to his voice that he didn't try to hide.

'I needed you to see it yourself.'

Harry shifted uncomfortably in his seat. He needed to go through all of this before he could get her to talk about Tara.

'So you were taken?'

Sarah met his gaze and nodded.

'We went to some farmhouse on the outskirts of Bradford – I can't remember why. Billy said we had to stay there a few days before heading to London. It was a nice place, big TV, I thought it was great. One evening I went to sleep and the next time I woke up, I was somewhere else . . . captive, with the others.'

'Others? You weren't the first?'

'No. I was the first white girl though. The others were Asian.'

'Asian?'

'From Pakistan,' she said. 'Kashmir.'

'Who kept you, Sarah?'

She looked away, back towards the gravestones where an elderly man crouched to lay flowers at a headstone.

'A big Asian man. Fat, hairy, a bit of a beard, and he had a finger missing on his left hand. I never saw more than that. He kept his face covered when he came to . . . use us.'

'How many other girls were there?' asked Harry.

'When I arrived, there were six Asian girls, but they soon disappeared. Once he had me, he lost interest in them. They were all fair-skinned and made to look white, their hair was coloured and they wore western clothing, but they weren't the real thing. Melissa arrived a year later, then Anna. Then Lena, Zara . . . and by that point, I was sixteen. I'd outgrown my appeal.'

'So he just let you go?' Harry asked incredulously.

Sarah shook her head. She turned her body to face him, raising her knees, folding them on the bench.

'Let me go?' she said sarcastically. 'Would you?'

'No.'

'Some low-life was supposed to take me down to the river and drown me. But he didn't.'

'Why not?'

'A sixteen-year-old white girl in that part of the world? I was worth something and he knew it. He sold me.'

'To whom?'

'Some other low-life,' she said, thinking of Yasser. He'd spent four years teaching her how the debauched ways of the western world had led to her being trafficked. He taught her that she needed to return as a messenger of God to take her own revenge. She'd listened and learned, knowing that, if she proved her worth, she'd be sent back to the UK eventually. But Sarah didn't tell Harry any of this.

'Just another low-life,' she repeated. 'But he wasn't as careful. I ran.'

Harry sighed again, overwhelmed by the scale of it. If Sarah was right, they only had a few hours before another girl vanished.

'How did you get back here?'

'I crossed over to India and managed to get to the British consulate in Delhi. By then I was nineteen. I told them I'd been doing charity work and lost my passport. They didn't believe me. I had no evidence, but I made a big show, cried a lot and caused them a headache. After a few weeks, once they'd contacted my grandfather and verified who I was, they brought me back.'

Sarah had rehearsed that part many times, it came out as easily as truth.

'Your grandfather?'

'Percy,' she replied. 'You met him at the New Beehive.'

Harry sighed and got up. He began pacing the path in front of the bench.

He thought about Tara charging down the street outside Gerard House, frantically trying to save Olivia.

'So Tara knew all this?' asked Harry.

Sarah nodded.

'Where did you two actually meet?' he asked. He knew what she'd say before she opened her mouth.

'The Candy Club,' she replied.

He nodded. 'Were you two together?'

'Yes.'

He looked at her. Really looked at her. Determined not to let his pity for her get in the way.

'You were there when Tara was killed, weren't you?'

Sarah placed her feet back on the ground and leaned forward. 'Yes,' she said.

A current went through Harry's body, forcing him to clench his fists.

'And you didn't st—'

'Don't. I need you to understand. Tara knew she could never tell her family the truth about being gay unless . . . she became hugely successful or did something to make everybody proud. It's the way your community works, isn't it? Shame is only countered by success, right?'

Harry nodded.

'She was out for revenge, not just for me but for herself too.'

'So how the fuck did she end up dead?' Harry began pacing again, his shoes crunching slowly on the path.

Once Tara had seen Olivia being driven away, she'd panicked. She knew they didn't have long because it was all happening on Wednesday, so she arranged to see Billy on Saturday and he suggested Wapping School.

'And no alarm bells went off then? Fuck's sake, why would she agree to that?' said Harry bitterly. If only he'd returned Tara's calls.

'She didn't have much choice, which is why I insisted on going with her.'

'So what went wrong?' asked Harry.

'It wasn't Billy that turned up,' said Sarah.

Harry thought back to the night before, how he'd confirmed Billy had been in Birmingham.

'Who was it?'

'A small guy, big hood. I thought he was a junkie passing through, but . . . ' she struggled to finish the sentence. 'He just walked up to Tara and . . . you know.'

'What?' said Harry.

There was a pause. 'He stuck a knife in her chest.'

'And you—'

'I . . . froze.' Sarah started to cry, guilt spreading across her face. 'I . . . ran . . .'

Harry stopped pacing, looming large over Sarah.

'I panicked, OK!' she snapped. 'You think I haven't relived that moment a thousand times? I . . . I was terrified.'

'You left her?' Harry yelled.

For a moment, the cemetery fell silent as they stood glaring at one another.

'Why didn't you call the police? An ambulance?' Harry continued, still towering above her.

Sarah rose to meet him. 'We've both made errors where Tara was concerned,' she said, and pushed him angrily in the chest. 'I ran because I knew nobody would believe me. I didn't know who I could trust. You're not exactly proving me wrong, are you?'

Harry turned away from her, his mind overwhelmed with conflicting emotions. Guilt, anger, suspicion.

'I spent the whole of Sunday obsessing over what to do. Then I decided that even though Tara hadn't managed to contact you, I had to try. I went back, and when I saw nobody had found her, I called the police.'

Harry breathed in icy air, trying to calm his mind.

'Put yourself in my shoes,' he said, finally turning to face her. 'Just for a moment. Can you hear yourself? How crazy this whole thing sounds?'

'That's exactly the point!' She couldn't help but raise her voice again.

'What's that supposed to mean?'

'Celebrities have been screwing young girls for years. Politicians, policemen? Go as high and as far as you can and it's there.' She stepped towards him. 'We live in a world where my voice is ignored because you don't want to believe it. Because you prefer to tell me how crazy it sounds, and that's the end of it.'

Her face had changed. Her eyes were cold. 'The greater the scandal, the more nobody wants to hear it.'

She took another step closer, so they were almost toe-to-toe. 'Posh, educated white men have been doing this for decades. What makes you think an Asian gang couldn't repeat it?' she asked. 'Don't you dare fucking doubt it's possible. I saw Tara murdered in front of my eyes and I'm telling you, we need to end this now or she died for *nothing*.'

Harry recognized the anger raging behind her eyes, but he couldn't hold her gaze. Turning away, he walked until he reached the nearest headstone. Then he stopped, dropped his head on to his chest.

'See, what I now have to ask myself,' said Harry, 'is what does *your* definition of justice look like?'

'I don't want Billy in handcuffs,' she replied.

Harry grimaced. Now he had two people who wanted blood.

'I've been through hell,' she said, 'which is where I want to send Billy – and more importantly, whoever the bastard is at the top of this chain.'

'It doesn't help,' he said.

'Easy for you to say. I am so sick of losing to these fuckers, Harry. I want them dead.'

He repeated himself, something in his voice making Sarah look at him differently. 'It doesn't help.' Harry was thinking of the door of 19 Belle Avenue.

'No?'

'No.'

'You've . . . crossed that line?'

Harry told her about what he had done when he was fifteen, the weight of the last forty-eight hours weighing heavy on his shoulders.

'Why are you telling me this?' she asked when he had finished.

'Honestly? I don't know. Maybe because I want you to know everything in life isn't black and white.' Tara had trusted her and Harry wanted to.

'You're saying that after what I've been through?'

'No,' said Harry. 'You don't know what killing someone will do to you. What it might trigger. There are consequences, even if you can escape the law.'

'You mean like your brother becoming a criminal?'

'Yes. And . . . what I did to that boy's parents.'

'I don't think I'm up against the same issues here,' she said petulantly.

'Just think about it,' was all Harry could say.

He put his hand in his pocket and found Billy's taweez. Tara had died trying to unravel this mess and Harry intended to see it through.

'I need your help if we're going to get to Olivia before it's too late.'

Sarah's eyes locked on to Harry's. 'In exchange, you need to let me decide what happens to him.'

Harry started to shake his head.

'Listen, I'm not sure I could even do it . . .' She looked down at her shoes, then up into his eyes. 'But I want the choice.'

Harry checked his watch again, five hours.

Trapped between two impossible choices, he was forced to concede – for the time being.

'Fine,' he said.

Sarah smiled.

'What do you need me to do?'

Harry pointed to the nearest row of tombstones and dropped his voice. 'You have to die.'

FORTY-THREE

RONNIE VIRDEE WAS ALONE in the wine and spirits section of his cash-and-carry, having sent the staff home and closed up early. He walked back and forth along the rows of whiskies.

He'd ignored the dozen or so calls from his wife, along with several text messages that their house was being raided. Ronnie could not do anything to stop it anyway. His thoughts were too crowded.

Every day, he worked in the shadow of this seemingly limitless supply of booze. He had to ignore the whispers from the bottles day in, day out. Tara's death had turned the whispers into deafening wails.

Ronnie selected a bottle. Chivas Regal, a twenty-one-year-old Salute edition which retailed at £110. If he was going to drink, may as well drink the best.

Ronnie pulled a wooden step over to a powerful heating unit that blew warm air down from the ceiling. He put the bottle on the floor in front of him and stared at it.

For fifteen years he had been sober. Until yesterday.

Ronnie could remember little of his eldest daughter before she turned five; he'd been enslaved to the golden poison now just inches away. He looked at his hand resting on his knee and saw something he hadn't experienced for years; his forefinger and thumb were involuntarily rolling an imaginary pea, something only alcoholics experienced.

Ronnie could picture Tara standing there, right there by his office door, screaming at him after she found out about what he did. She had been disgusted by him, the hatred clear in her eyes.

Ronnie felt empty.

Tara was gone.

His marriage was a lie.

And his brother didn't understand.

Ronnie had put everything he had into his business.

And what had he got?

Nothing.

He took a slow glance around the warehouse, packed from floor to ceiling but empty – no one in there but him.

He closed his eyes and screamed until his voice gave way.

He jumped to his feet, snatched the bottle from the floor and launched it at a steel girder where it smashed. Glass and whisky covered the floor.

Ronnie screamed again and picked up the stool.

He lashed out savagely, smashing everything within reach, only stopping when the lactic acid boiling in his arms forced him to. He found himself on his knees, his head drooping, in a pool of pungent liquor.

This was where he had done it. Ronnie looked up, past the metal sheeting that screened off the rest of the cash-and-carry from where he sat. Tara had stood at the end of this aisle.

How could he have done such a thing?

So carelessly shown his daughter just how far power had corrupted him?

Harry's words were suddenly loud in his mind.

Karma; that shit has a way of hunting you down.

'Fuck you, Karma,' he whispered, getting to his feet. 'I write my own.'

FORTY-FOUR

AT EXACTLY SIX P.M. Victor parked in the car park of the Cow and Calf Rocks.

He'd be glad never to return to this place again. The beauty of the moors had been forever ruined for him by the knowledge of what took place in the farmhouse.

Not after tonight.

On the passenger seat, Victor had the black bag Sarah had given him.

He knew what he had to do.

By the base of the rocks, Victor gathered a dozen or so stones and placed them carefully in a second bag before starting his ascent.

It took him almost thirty strenuous minutes but he never wavered. Failure now would jeopardize everything. At the top, Victor looked to the heavens, casting a disparaging glance at darkening clouds.

In a corner close to the lip of the rock, Victor pushed the bag Sarah had given him deep into the shadows and carefully concealed it behind the smaller rocks from his other bag. Satisfied that it was well hidden, he stepped back, ensuring a cursory sweep of the area would not reveal it.

Pulling his binoculars from his bag, he moved to the far side of the rock for a final look at the farmhouse. From here it almost looked inviting.

He spat on the floor.

'She's going to burn you to the ground,' he said, the wind slicing at his words. 'Send you bastards straight to hell.'

FORTY-FIVE

SAIMA VIRDEE WASHED HER hands, rinsed her mouth out and inhaled water into her nose, performing her ritual cleansing before she prayed. She scrubbed her face, then her lower arms from wrist to elbow, before cleaning her head and wiping her ears inside and out. Finally, she washed her feet. Each stage was repeated three times.

Ramadan began the following day and she was starting the month of five times daily prayer early: it helped to still her worries about Harry. Aaron had hauled himself up in the bathroom, teetering precariously by a laundry basket, trying to repeat his earlier steps.

'Learning to walk when your mum's about to starve herself for a month,' she said, grabbing a towel to dry herself. 'Nice work, little man.'

Aaron grinned before falling on to his backside.

'Come on,' she said, scooping him up from the floor.

In the living room, Saima lowered Aaron into his playpen, put cartoons on the TV and rolled out her prayer mat.

'Praying with the wheels on the bloody bus in the background,' she muttered. 'As if I'm not halfway to hell already.' She turned the volume down low. Aaron stopped watching the wheels on the bus and stared at his mother.

'Maa,' he called out. 'Maa?'

Saima read her prayers quickly, ignoring the singing from the television and Aaron's babbled commentary.

She stepped off the mat and turned to her son, crouching beside him and blowing gently across his face. Aaron started laughing. 'Everything's a game to you,' Saima said warmly.

She had learned this from her mother. Saima walked to all four corners of the room, blowing her now purified breath at each point. From his playpen, Aaron puffed out his cheeks and copied.

'Better get used to it,' she said when she'd finished. 'Five times a day for thirty days.'

Aaron picked up a lone Rice Krispie from the floor and held it out for her.

'Der,' he said proudly.

'Yes, der,' she said, picking him up.

In the kitchen, Saima strapped Aaron into his high-chair. He grabbed at the taweez around her neck, pulling it sharply.

'Ow!' she said, raising her voice suddenly. Aaron immediately started to cry.

'No, no, no,' she said, getting on her knees and kissing his cheeks. 'Mummy didn't mean it like that.'

His cheeks were streaked with tears.

'Here,' she said, taking it off and putting it in his hands. 'See, nothing to be scared of.'

Aaron stopped crying once he held the taweez. He put it in his mouth.

'It's to protect our family from Daddy's nasty work,' she whispered, wiping tears from his face.

Saima pinned a Ramadan calendar to the fridge and secured a red pen underneath. As a child, she had been in charge of crossing out each fasting-day as it passed, counting down to the festival of Eid. It had been her favourite time of year: presents, new clothes and celebrations with family and friends.

Now, it was a more sombre affair. Like Harry, Saima had made her choice. She'd struggled to leave her family who, like Harry's, had refused to accept their inter-faith marriage. But while Harry carried his anger on the surface, Saima swallowed her pain. She put on a good show, but Ramadan was difficult, lonely. Harry tried to help by ensuring they ate together in the evenings, but it didn't fill the emptiness in her heart when faced with a lonely month-long fast.

Saima opened the freezer and looked at its overloaded contents. At home she had done the family Ramadan shop for years and still hadn't adjusted to her new family's size, once again buying far more than she needed. She'd hoped that with Aaron's arrival, things might have changed. The sight of the bulging freezer made Saima suddenly sad.

She took the red pen and put a big round dot next to the first date, blinking away tears as she heard her mother's voice.

You're the only person I know who looks forward to fasting . . .

Saima had found it exciting as a child; waking up early, her brothers and sisters all meeting in the kitchen while the rest of the street was asleep. It felt secretive and special.

'Thirty days to go,' she whispered to Aaron. 'I might envy you those jars of baby food by tomorrow afternoon,' she said, waving one at him. Aaron put his hands out for it and Saima swapped it for the taweez.

'Too easy,' she said.

She warmed a small portion of daal and when it was ready, carried Aaron's high-chair into the living room, parking him in front of the television.

Two spoonfuls down, the doorbell sounded.

'Crap,' she said, putting the food aside. 'Amazon need to work on their timing.'

The doorbell went again.

'Coming!' shouted Saima, and hurried to the door.

Aaron started to cry as soon as she left the room.

'Keys, keys, keys,' she said, searching the hallway for them, knocking Harry's mother's slippers to the floor as she looked.

'Come on,' she said, hurriedly picking them up.

The doorbell went again and Aaron's crying became more frantic.

Saima finally found the keys.

She flung open the door and stared in confusion at the short hooded figure on the step.

Time seemed to stop. With Aaron screaming from the living room, Saima was confronted by a face that made her heart stop.

FORTY-SIX

HARRY AND SARAH WERE standing outside Queensbury Tunnel just as the evening sun started to set and swollen grey clouds threatened rain.

'What is this place?' she asked Harry.

'Hell,' he replied, looking towards the metal fencing around the mouth of the entrance where Ronnie was making his way towards them.

'When you said your brother was a criminal, I wasn't imagining this,' whispered Sarah.

Ronnie stopped just short of them. He nodded awkwardly at Sarah, not sure what to make of her. Harry had updated him on the phone on the way over.

'We set?' asked Harry.

Ronnie's eyes darted between Sarah and Harry, then to the skies. 'Going to rain,' he said. 'It gets noisy in there when that happens. Makes talking difficult. We haven't got a lot of time.' He paused, scrutinizing Sarah. 'Some story you've got.' His voice was neither accusatory nor sincere.

'Stories start with once upon a time and end with happily ever after,' she said quietly.

Ronnie nodded.

'Your show,' he said, holding out a kitchen knife, waiting till she took it from him. He pointed to the tunnel entrance over his shoulder. 'You sure you can do this? That place is hell without the fires.'

Sarah felt the weight of the knife in her hand, her eyes darting between Harry and Ronnie. 'I'm not unfamiliar with this type of place,' she said bitterly.

Droplets of rain started to fall, slow and heavy, thudding as they hit the already saturated ground.

'Not much time,' said Ronnie, turning to lead Sarah into the tunnel. 'He's about two hundred metres down on the right.' He pulled a pair of night-vision goggles from his jacket pocket and handed them to her. 'I'll be waiting here, just inside. Shit gets too much, you come straight back.'

Sarah nodded, spinning the handle of the knife in her hand.

Harry handed Sarah the taweez and a torch. 'Remember, he needs to believe the dead have risen, that you've returned to drag him to hell.'

Sarah turned to face the entrance. Her voice was steady.

'Don't worry,' she said. 'I have.'

The brothers watched Sarah disappear into the tunnel just as the clouds unleashed a torrential downpour. They followed her inside, watching the light from her torch bounce off the walls until she vanished into the darkness.

'She's not right,' whispered Ronnie. 'Never hesitated once.'

Harry was thinking the same thing. He was beginning to worry about the deal he'd made with her.

He checked the time on his watch. 'Five o'clock,' he whispered. 'Three hours before this goes down.'

'Whatever *this* is,' said Ronnie.

'You good here?' Harry asked. 'I'm going to check what Omar said about the houses behind Mughal's restaurant, in case what we're trying here doesn't work.'

'You be careful,' Ronnie said. 'I'm not sure we know everything we need to know here.'

Outside in his car, Harry picked up his phone to access Google Maps; he wanted to get a better feel for the area behind Mughal's restaurant. With only three hours before Olivia's supposed sale, he had to pursue every lead.

He didn't get to open the app. There were eight missed calls from Saima, all within the last six minutes, and a single text message which made him drop the phone, start his car and tear away from Queensbury Tunnel.

Billy was freezing. The tunnel was unlike any place he'd ever been. The noise of water flowing above the roof and the heavy crescendo of rain were sending him mad. How long had he been here? A day? More? Had the deal gone ahead uninterrupted?

Billy was going to die, of that he was certain. He'd seen what had happened to Omar.

Taking on the boss would have only one outcome, no matter how powerful the Virdee brothers thought they were. The thought warmed Billy.

Sitting silently in a dry section of the tunnel, watching him through night-vision goggles, Sarah revelled in every shiver of Billy's body. His hands and legs were bound, and he seemed to be muttering something. The tunnel was noisier than she'd expected, but that had worked in her favour: she'd been able to get close without him realizing.

Dangling the taweez from her fingertips, she made her approach.

When she was a foot or two away she took off the goggles. Then she gripped the knife hard, knelt in front of Billy and put the torch under her veiled face.

Eleven years.

She turned it on.

The sudden glare made Billy scream. He turned away, raising his bound hands to his face, eyes closed, gasping.

Sarah remained deathly still; her burka made her look like the grim reaper.

Billy turned his face, looking through splayed fingers at the hooded figure, too afraid to speak. Sarah set the torch down on the ground, positioning it so she could see him, then held out his taweez, swinging it in front of his eyes like a noose.

Billy's thoughts immediately went to the children who plagued his dreams; they rose from freshly dug graves, fingers sharp as razors, baying for his blood. A bony hand reached up into the darkness.

The dead had risen.

With her face uncovered, Billy stared at her speechless.

Sarah.

'You've been dreaming about me,' she said. She was close enough that her voice reached him despite the rain. She pushed the tip of the knife into Billy's chest. He closed his eyes, shaking his head and whispering what sounded like a prayer.

'Look at me,' she said. And when he refused, Sarah leaned forward, her lips almost touching his face, and let out a blood-curdling scream that echoed around the tunnel, so loud that even the rain could not compete. She didn't stop until her breath gave way.

Billy started crying, shaking his head, terrified.

'You . . . you . . . you . . . are . . . a . . .'

'A spirit?' said Sarah.

'I . . . I . . .'

She slapped him with the blade, slicing his cheek. Billy yelled, blood running down his face.

Sarah hesitated, waiting to see if Ronnie would intervene.

'I'm here to take you, Billy,' she said. 'They've sent me.'

'Who?'

'You know who. It's time for you to pay.'

He shook his head, cowering away. 'I . . . I'm . . . sorr—'

Sarah sliced the other side of his face, the sight of his blood encouraging her.

'Don't say that,' she hissed.

Billy couldn't even scream this time.

'You'll like it down there,' she said, pointing to the ground. 'Where you're going? It's hot – you like it hot, right?'

Billy sobbed, loud wails of regret.

Sarah revelled in every shudder of his body. 'You want to save yourself?'

He nodded, desperate. 'Anything. I'll do anything.'

Sarah checked over her shoulder.

'I know,' she replied. 'When does Faisal come to collect Olivia?'

'The boss? What . . . what day is it?'

'Wednesday. Five p.m.'

'In three hours, eight o'clock.'

He wasn't lying to her.

'Who else will be there?'

'Ali and Riz.'

Sarah looked at the blade of the knife, dull in the torchlight.

'I'm not dead,' she said. 'You know that, right?'

Billy didn't answer her, his head drooped heavy on his neck.

'Look at me,' she said. 'I escaped.'

Billy's eyes widened in the dark.

'I worked hard to get back. I've come to rid Bradford of scum like you.'

Billy opened his mouth to say something but Sarah lunged at him, expertly slicing his carotid artery. Watching as his life eked away, her hand went instinctively to her wrist, to her tattoo. GZ.

She whispered one final message, the rain still loud in the tunnel, Billy fighting for one last breath.

'Don't worry about your pal Ronnie either,' she said. 'Just like the rest of you, he can't see Girl Zero coming right for him.'

FORTY-SEVEN

HARRY CHARGED THROUGH HIS front door.

In the living room, he found Saima with Mandy and his mother, Joyti.

Aaron was on his grandmother's lap.

It was an occasion he had longed for, that he had pictured a thousand times. But the timing could not have been worse.

Three cups of untouched tea stood on the coffee table by a plate of chocolate digestives. Harry could tell Saima had been crying. It looked like the past thirty minutes of their married life might have been the hardest for her.

'Bah,' Aaron said, waving his hands at Harry and trying to wriggle free from Joyti's hands.

'*Beta.*' His mother held Aaron close and stood to greet her son. Harry was so overwhelmed, he forgot to stoop and touch his mother's feet. Queensbury Tunnel was far from his mind, though the tension did not leave his shoulders.

'Let's talk in the kitchen, Hardeep.' Joyti put her hands to her son's chest.

Harry looked at Saima, then Mandy, clearly uncomfortable about leaving them alone.

'We'll be fine,' said Saima unconvincingly, forcing a fake smile.

'I know you will,' said Harry firmly, his eyes on Mundeep. She didn't meet his gaze.

'Do you want me to take Aaron?' asked Saima.

Joyti shook her head, smiling. 'Allow me the seconds God has given me.'

Harry left the kitchen door ajar behind him. Four years ago, when he got married, Mundeep had made her feelings towards Saima clear.

I can't allow you to be close to Tara and the twins because it will look as though I accept your marriage. I don't and I never will.

He would never forget her words.

'It is my own cursed kismet,' his mother said in Punjabi.

'Mum,' he said, suddenly acutely aware of everything else he had going on. 'I really—'

'I see my son twice in two days after four years of nothing and both times, my heart is broken,' she carried on, ignoring his protests. 'The night you left was my darkest – until today when the police told me they have arrested your father! They came to our home, Hardeep – they are going through everything!'

Harry took Aaron from her and hugged his mother, kissing her forehead. 'I know,' he whispered, unable to find any comforting words.

'Help your father,' Joyti sobbed, her voice muffled by Harry's body. 'Get him out of that jail, Hardeep. Please, I beg you.'

In the living room the silence was unbearable. Mundeep had moved to the window where Harry usually stood and was looking out across the street.

'Your tea?' Saima spoke softly from the sofa. Each second felt like minutes.

'I'm fine,' replied Mundeep, without turning around.

Saima wondered whether Mundeep wouldn't drink it because

she had made it. Harry had told her about the poisonous sermons they had all heard repeatedly from his father. Accepting food or drink from an Islamic household was considered unclean.

'I . . . I'm so sorry for your loss,' said Saima.

Mundeep didn't reply.

From the kitchen, Saima could hear voices, but she couldn't make out the words.

'Harry told me a lot about Tara. She sounded—'

'Please don't,' said Mundeep, her voice flat.

Saima looked down at her hands and took a breath. 'A mother cannot console another mother?' she said, getting to her feet, determined not to feel like an imposter in her own home. She cut the gap between them, mustering enough courage to whisper her next sentence: 'What did I ever do to deserve your silence?'

She heard Mundeep's breathing quicken, saw her body stiffen.

'I . . . know I cannot ever change your perception of me,' said Saima, stepping closer still, 'but here? Now? I'm just a mother offering sympathy.'

'I don't want your sympathy.'

'Why?'

'What is it like?' said Mundeep sharply, suddenly turning to face Saima.

'What is what like?' she replied, taking a step back.

Mundeep swallowed the lump in her throat.

'Living with the man I once loved.'

Saima's eyes narrowed.

Was she . . . ?

'Despite all this, he is still your brother-in-law,' she said, her voice composed. 'You can still love him.'

Mundeep looked back across the street, shaking her head.

Saima moved closer, staring intently at the side of Mundeep's face until she turned to looked at her.

And when she did, in that single moment, Saima Virdee understood everything.

*

Joyti was holding Harry's hands as if every moment she could touch him was precious, pleading with him to get his father out of jail. Aaron was by her feet, pulling himself up using the bottom of her coat.

'Ma, he's fine.'

But Joyti's understanding of detention in police custody had been formed by television dramas; she was convinced her husband was holed up in some maximum-security prison with inmates who'd jump at the chance to get the guy wearing the turban.

'Ma, stop. They may still release him today.'

'No, Hardeep. No more "maybe". You must get him out right away,' she said in broken English. 'Terrible people are in jail!'

'He's not in danger. Trust me.'

Harry wanted to tell her that he had seen his father, reassure her that all was well. But too many questions would follow. He couldn't risk it tonight, not with Tara's killer still out there and time running short.

'Trust me,' he said again.

'You have friends down there?' she said, switching back to Punjabi. 'You must do, you're well respected. I've seen your name in the paper many times.'

He smiled in spite of himself.

'I know, Ma, but it's not that simple.'

'Why not? He has done nothing! Why did they take him?'

'Ma, stop,' he snapped, embracing her tightly again while Aaron held up his arms to be hugged too. 'I told my friends to look after him. I'm the boss, Mum, everybody is scared of me.'

'You told your friends this?'

'Yes. I'm sorry, but I really have to go now.'

She relaxed in his arms and finally let herself cry.

'I am so sorry for what has happened with us.'

'I chose this life.'

'It is my duty to honour your father. I cannot disobey him.'

'I know.'

'But I miss you,' she said, crying harder. 'I miss my Hardeep.'

Harry hugged her tighter.

'I miss you too, Ma.'

His watch beeped. Six p.m.

'I loved him because he was everything Ronnie is not,' said Mundeep, once again staring absently out of the bay window at the gloomy street outside.

'I married a weak man,' she continued, her voice shaky. 'I didn't know he'd been in prison until after we were married, and I was pregnant within a month. There was no way I could leave after that.'

Mundeep turned to face Saima, arms folded across her chest, trying not to cry.

'The only thing that made me happy was spending time with Harry,' said Mundeep, seeing the look of horror creep into Saima's face. 'He made me laugh. He looked after me. And then he met you and just like that,' she said, clicking her fingers, 'I lost the only bit of comfort that I had in that godforsaken house.'

Saima opened her mouth to speak but Mundeep raised her hand, cutting her off. 'I don't hate you because you're Muslim,' she said, shaking her head, letting a tear fall. 'I hate you because you took him from me.'

The kitchen door opened and Joyti carried Aaron back into the room. Harry was close behind.

'What's wrong?' he asked accusingly as Mundeep dropped her gaze to the floor and hurriedly wiped tears from her face.

'Nothing,' Saima said with a forced smile. 'Nothing,' she repeated.

Harry didn't buy it.

'We need to go,' said Joyti, giving Aaron a last cuddle.

'Yes,' said Mundeep, stepping awkwardly past Saima. She paused in front of Harry, just for a moment, before taking her mother-in-law's arm and leading her towards the door.

'You didn't drink your tea,' Saima called after them.

'Try it,' Harry said to his mother. 'Give your daughter-in-law a memory she can cherish.'

Joyti walked towards Saima, reached out and cradled her face in her hands.

'Not only today are you my daughter,' said Joyti, pulling her close and kissing her, 'you have always been so. Forgive an old woman her sins. I will answer for them when I die, but my hands are bound.' Joyti raised them in front of Saima. 'They still are. We choose our husbands and stand by them, whether we like it or not.'

'I know,' whispered Saima. 'I know.'

'It is your eyes that got my boy. Green like emeralds. He always liked girls with pretty eyes.'

'Don't be a stranger,' whispered Saima pleadingly.

'I am a stranger only by my presence. In your heart, I can never be so.'

'Thank you,' said Saima, embracing her.

'Your tea?' said Joyti, breaking away and picking up her mug. She sipped it, smiled and looked at Saima.

'With both my daughters-in-law in the same room for maybe the only time, let me say no finer tea has ever passed my lips.'

FORTY-EIGHT

THE SUN HAD SET over Bradford; light had given way to dark.

For the second consecutive night, Percy had closed the New Beehive early. He sat in silence with an untouched pint. He might never stand behind his bar again. The letter in his hands was from his doctor, confirming lung cancer. Terminal. The doctor gave him six months.

Victor was now the only other person who knew.

Percy raised the pint to his lips but put it down again without taking a sip. He didn't feel like drinking it any more. Instead, he plucked his favourite old beer mat from the wall – a faded red Tetley's – and put it in his inside pocket, patting his chest.

He ran wrinkled hands across the smooth surface of the bar. Images of the past rushed out of the darkness: the pub alive with people, laughter, women. He hadn't recognized the broken little girl inside a woman's body when Sarah had come home. He hadn't recognized her dead eyes.

One final look at the old place.

Percy turned off the lights.

He picked up a heavy rucksack from the floor and made his way to the front door, leaving his solitary, untouched pint on the bar.

'Cheers, my darling,' he said into the darkness. 'That one's for you.'

Twenty minutes later, Percy got out of a taxi somewhere on the outskirts of Bradford.

He walked towards Victor's haulage office, the night breeze fresh across his face. The weight of his bag was heavy on his back: lock-cutters, a bottle of rum and an old packet of Capstan Full Strength, one cigarette remaining.

At the entrance, Percy cut the padlock and slipped inside the depot.

He knew it well; he'd worked here before he'd taken over at the New Beehive Inn. Six acres crammed with machinery, ghostly in the night-time quiet. Percy hurried through to the office where he could see the lights were on.

He found Victor sitting at his desk with a bottle of Navy rum and two glasses.

Percy smiled as he closed the door, pulling his own bottle from his bag. 'Great minds.'

'Always were. We've got a few minutes, haven't we?'

'Aye. You ready?'

Victor laughed. 'Ha – I've been waiting decades to repay you for eighty-two. Must say, I never thought it would be something like this.'

'You always said you owed me. Not any more.'

'If I'd known then that this is what repayment would look like, I might have thought it better to fall like the rest of 'em.'

'You don't mean that,' said Percy.

'The Lord works in mysterious ways,' replied Victor, almost throwing his Bible on to the table from where he had been resting it in his lap.

Percy pointed to it. 'Does that help?'

'Old Testament maybe,' said Victor, smiling. 'An eye for an eye and all that?'

'We're giving this city its honour back,' said Percy.

Victor opened the bottle of rum and poured two measures. 'Let's drink to that.'

'Aye,' said Percy, lifting a glass.

The two men clinked glasses.

'To the repaying of a debt,' said Victor, his glass still hovering above the table.

Percy shook his head. 'Can't toast our final drink to that, old boy. It wasn't a debt, saving your life, it was my bloody duty and an honour.'

Victor's eyes glossed over. 'Pah! You always were good with words.'

'To Bradford?' offered Percy.

'Aye. We can drink to that.'

Percy savoured the rum, while Victor simply swallowed it back.

'What to do with this?' said Victor, pulling an enormous file from the shelf next to his desk.

'I'll take it,' said Percy, putting his hand on it. 'Hell of a lot of work you put into this, Victor. I don't know how to thank you.'

'There's no need, fella. Hell of a trauma your girl's been through. Can't say I believed it at first, but' – Victor raised his palms – 'it's all there.'

Victor's help had been vital in identifying Ronnie Virdee. Initial research had suggested that Bradford's drug trade was now being routed through the city's hundreds of convenience stores, a shift away from restaurants. Victor had established haulage contracts with all the city's cash-and-carrys, including Ronnie Virdee's, and a painstaking process of elimination had finally resulted in finding proof that Ronnie was Bradford's biggest drug lord. All the details of his investigations were contained in the file.

With his identity confirmed, Sarah had then set about trying to get close to Ronnie via his daughter. Having followed Tara Virdee to the Candy Club, Sarah befriended her. She hadn't needed to turn the girl against her father; Tara was already angry.

'Right,' Percy said, placing his glass on the desk and checking his watch. 'I've been in here long enough for it to look like a robbery on the CCTV.'

Victor got reluctantly to his feet and came around the desk.

'It's the first tanker on the left,' he said, putting his hand in his pocket and handing Percy the keys. 'Don't know what to say, old friend. Be safe?'

'Always. You ready?'

Victor nodded and took a couple of breaths.

'Close your eyes,' said Percy.

'No need.'

'For me.'

Victor did as asked.

Percy punched him square in the face, holding him steady so he didn't fall.

Victor didn't make a sound. The blow split his lip and bloodied his nose. He blinked away reflex tears. 'Good?'

Percy nodded and embraced him tightly. 'Give me an hour before you call the police.'

Victor nodded.

'Thank you, old boy,' Percy said. 'For everything.'

Outside, Percy made his way towards the trucks. The first on the left, a forty-four-tonne refuelling truck, carried fifty thousand litres of petrol. He climbed inside, threw his bag on the passenger seat and revved the engine. Adrenaline burned through his veins.

Fifty thousand litres.

One key location.

One epic bonfire.

FORTY-NINE

RONNIE VIRDEE LET HIS breath out slowly as Sarah walked towards him, blood splattered across her face. She threw the soiled knife at Ronnie's feet where it clanged noisily against the rusted train track.

Her eyes were blazing, her breathing heavy, a look of steely determination on her face.

'Dead?' he asked, glancing at the bloodied knife.

Sarah nodded.

Ronnie was neither surprised nor disappointed. He recognized the pain in her face; he'd felt that way ever since Harry had broken the news about Tara.

'Did he tell you where the girl is?'

'Yes,' she replied, her breath white in the chill of the tunnel.

'How does it feel?' he asked, stooping to pick up the knife.

'Empty,' she said truthfully.

'Just empty? No . . . satisfaction?'

'I would have needed to kill him a hundred times, a hundred different ways to feel that.'

'Might have been more use to us alive, in case he was lying about the—'

'He wasn't,' she snapped.

Ronnie searched his pockets and handed Sarah a tissue. 'Blood on your face,' he said softly. She wiped the evidence of Billy's death away and threw the tissue on the floor.

'So where are we headed?'

'I'll tell you on the way.'

'You'll tell me now,' said Ronnie, his grip on the knife tightening.

'I've got a condition,' said Sarah, ignoring the blade as it glinted in the darkness. When Ronnie didn't reply, she added, 'I'm the only one who can tell you where you'll find her murderer.'

'What is it?'

'You and I go alone.'

Ronnie raised his eyebrows.

'No Harry,' Sarah said.

'Why?'

'He doesn't want revenge like we do.'

Ronnie was silent.

'He wants cuffs and trials,' she said. 'That won't end this, for either of us.'

Ronnie tossed the knife into the darkness of the tunnel.

'First kill?' he asked, slipping one hand inside his pocket and grasping the handle of a gun.

She nodded.

'You see, my problem here,' said Ronnie, stepping closer and revealing the weapon, 'is that when you lie, I can't help but think you're trying to play with us.' He pressed the tip of the gun to her forehead.

'Play with you?' She hadn't flinched.

Dripping water from the roof of the tunnel landed on her face, droplets running down her cheeks like tears.

'A first-timer doesn't act the way you do.'

'I've thought about it for years.'

'So, how did you do it?'

'I stabbed him.'

'Where?'

'What?'

'Where did you stab him? Chest? Head? Balls?'

Sarah realized her mistake. 'Does it matter?'

'To me it does.'

She hesitated, glancing at the gun.

'His throat,' she said reluctantly.

'You slit his throat?'

'Yes.'

'An amateur doesn't slit someone's throat.'

'I saw it in a movie.'

Ronnie rolled his eyes and repositioned the gun between her eyes. 'Watch this,' he said, and pulled the trigger.

Sarah didn't flinch. The click of the empty chamber echoed loud in the tunnel.

'Most people would have reacted, even if it wasn't loaded,' Ronnie said, lowering the gun.

'I lived in a nightmare for years. I don't scare easily.'

'So you say.'

'Why would I lie?'

'You tell me.'

Ronnie checked his watch.

'Half six. Maybe we'll stay here until this thing's over. Let Olivia go. I don't really give a shit about her anyway.'

'You want Ali. If the deal completes, you'll lose him, he'll disappear underground tonight,' she replied. She looked calm but there was a definite edge to her voice.

'I'll find him. There are other ways.'

'I'm leaving,' said Sarah, and turned to go.

'Only one way out,' said Ronnie, jangling keys at her.

She looked back at him.

'The truth,' he said.

Ronnie was bluffing and she knew it. He hadn't come this far to stop now.

'There's nothing I'm not telling you.'

Ronnie's anger flared. 'My brother and I work together. You wanting to cut him out makes me suspicious.'

'He told me everything,' Sarah said, unperturbed. 'I thought he was a bent cop, but he's not. He'll try and stop us doing what we've come to do. And after everything that's gone down,' she gestured down the tunnel towards Billy, 'I'm not willing to risk it.'

She could see Ronnie softening.

'Harry told me about a green door he can't knock on,' she continued. 'The house where the parents of that boy he killed live. He said what he put them through keeps him awake at night. You think he's gonna let us win?'

Ronnie's hands went to his hair. She had him, she knew it.

'I want the man who ruined my life. I want the boss of this gang to beg me not to kill him. Is what you want so different? Or are you more like Harry than you thought?'

'OK, you've given me your condition. Now you can hear mine.'

Sarah nodded.

'I'm calling in back-up. My partner, Enzo – he's got no problem with what we want.'

She nodded again. 'One more thing.'

'Christ, what now?' said Ronnie impatiently.

'Give me your phone. Harry's going to call and I don't want you torn.'

'I just told you—'

'No distractions,' she said, putting out her hand. 'I've waited too long for this to let brotherly loyalty confuse you.'

Ronnie found his phone, turned it off and slapped it into her hands. 'We don't have time for this, little girl,' he whispered.

'Don't call me that. Little girls don't play with knives,' said Sarah, and headed towards the entrance.

FIFTY

HARRY HAD PARKED ON Leeds Road. Google Maps showed him an alleyway at the back of Mughal's restaurant that looked like it led to a row of terraced houses.

Ronnie's location was still showing as Queensbury Tunnel. The plan to break Billy clearly still underway.

What now?

The alleyway was dark, the ground beneath him uneven.

Ten houses, five either side of the path. His attention instinctively fell on the house at the end. Two external locks, peeling paint and, instead of curtains, it looked as though dark sheets had been pinned across the windows. Glancing at neighbouring houses, Harry saw open windows, clothes lines, the usual signs of life.

The house on the end might as well have had a big *fuck off* banner across the door.

Broken guttering.

Internal security bars across cracked downstairs windows.

Harry opened the gate and walked to the front door.

No doorbell.

He hammered his fist on it, leaning closer to listen for any movement inside.

Nothing.

This was Ali's place; Harry could sense it.

Harry hurried down the neighbour's path where windows were open, the scent of garlic and frying onions.

He tapped on the door and an elderly Asian woman wearing a dark headscarf appeared at the window. Harry held his badge to it, leaned closer and said, 'Police.'

She glanced at the badge blankly, then turned away. Harry rapped on the door again, then impatiently on the window.

The woman shook her head. 'Come back six o'clock,' she said in broken English.

Harry sighed, repeated, 'Police,' again and tapped on the window with more urgency. She didn't move so he got on his knees and opened the letter box, speaking in Punjabi, hoping she understood.

Hesitantly, the elderly woman opened the door. Harry remained on his knees, making her feel tall and in control. He called her 'Bibi', a respectful term for someone his grandmother's age.

Asian gestures; overly dramatic but perfectly weighted.

He asked whether he could come inside, pushing his police badge into her hands. She looked at it blankly, Harry guessed she couldn't read, but the gesture seemed to work. She invited him in.

He apologized for the disturbance and asked her about the area, the neighbours. Finally, he asked her about next door.

She shook her head and scowled.

'No good?' he said.

The old woman told him a boy lived there – at least, she thought it was a boy. She seldom saw him and when she did, he always had a hood pulled over his face. She didn't think he lived there because she saw so little of him. She was always at home in the day but he only seemed to come out at night.

Ali.

All she knew of him were the noises she could hear from the cellar – loud banging noises like building work.

*

Harry opened the gate to Ali's house and walked to the front door.

No doorbell.

He hammered his fist against the wood, leaning closer to listen for any movement inside.

Nothing.

This was Ali's place. It had to be. Harry's skin was prickling with adrenaline.

He hammered on the door again.

Silence.

From an upstairs bedroom window, Ali held his breath and watched DI Virdee as he hammered on the door and turned to look around in the front yard.

Ali had thought about making a run for it, out the back and through the neighbours' gardens. But he'd made it this far. Olivia was here, in his house. He wasn't going to give up so easily.

The hammering on the front door started up again. It felt like it was thundering through Ali's body.

He moved to run downstairs and grab a knife from the kitchen.

If he stabbed him on the front step, would the dark protect him from witnesses?

He's a police officer.

Ali couldn't think straight.

Escape seemed like his only option, but he couldn't run. He couldn't leave Olivia.

No choice, he thought, hurrying across the room to the landing. At the top of the stairs he stooped to pick up a glass fragment, then held his breath as he prepared to defend his home.

On his knees peering through the letter box, Harry was certain that even in the darkness he had seen a shadow appear at the top of the stairs. He shouted, shining his torch through the letter box, the light reflected back at him by rows of shattered mirrors decorating the hallway wall.

Harry set off down the side of the house to the back door where he found iron bars across all the downstairs windows, just like the front. He tried the back door, surprised when it gave way.

An accident? Or a trap?

He pushed it open as far as it would go and immediately backed off a step, shining his torch into the kitchen.

His mouth dropped open and the hand holding the torch trembled.

There was a naked body on the floor.

With fireworks booming nearby, Harry stepped inside the kitchen, rushing to the body.

A mannequin.

A goddamn white plastic mannequin with the word 'Gori' carved into its forehead.

Harry looked into the empty corridor outside the kitchen.

An empty shithole.

He looked for a weapon but there was nothing.

He raised the torch high above his head; he could use it as a club if he needed to.

He checked his watch: 19:00.

Then he checked his phone to see if Ronnie was still at Queensbury Tunnel. They could end this here. Now. The app tracking Ronnie's location didn't load. Glancing nervously into the empty corridor, Harry tried to phone Ronnie but the call didn't connect.

No time to wait.

He put his phone away and tried the light switch.

Dead.

He could make out two doors in the corridor. One looked like access to under-stairs storage, the other was presumably a living room. On the wall were dozens of shattered mirrors, the floor covered in hundreds of pieces of jagged glass.

Harry kept his torch raised as he moved down the empty corridor.

The first door had three robust bolts across it.

So not a cupboard, a cellar.

Harry shivered involuntarily.

He tried to avoid crunching the sea of glass but it was everywhere. Harry stopped beside a square mirror, switched the torch to his other hand and pulled away a large V-shaped piece, nicking his hands on a serrated edge and cursing silently.

He crept into the living room. Dozens of white plastic bottles were scattered across the floor.

Harry picked one up.

Cosmetic skin bleach.

The small print was in a foreign language; Russian, he thought. He placed it back on the floor.

What is this place?

He heard a floorboard creak.

Upstairs.

His heart hammered loud.

He looked at the piece of glass in his hand. A poor weapon, just as likely to slice his own hand if he were forced to use it.

At the bottom of the staircase, Harry shone the torch into the upstairs landing space. The mirrors continued on the first floor too.

He crept up the stairs, grimacing at each creak of the floor. He turned off the torch, plunging the house into darkness, then waited a few moments for his eyes to adjust.

The sudden boom of a nearby firework startled him.

At the top of the stairs, Harry found three closed doors. He backed into the corner by a window and paused.

Which one?

The first door, Harry guessed, was a bathroom. He grabbed the handle, set his teeth and pushed the door open. Remaining on the landing, he shone his torch inside.

Empty.

The light showed the bathtub, full of a yellowy liquid. The nauseating smell of bleach stung Harry's nostrils.

Who is this guy?

Before Harry could enter the bathroom, the question was answered by the second door suddenly opening as a hooded figure leapt forward, crouched low to the ground. He sliced at Harry's ankles with a knife before rolling away into the landing.

Harry fell to his knees, screaming in pain. He dropped the torch but kept a firm hold on the fragment of glass. As he tried to stand, Harry moved back from the figure and lost his balance, teetering precariously at the top of the stairs. The hooded figure saw the peril and lunged forward. Harry had no choice but to allow himself to collapse down the staircase in three thunderous rolls. As he hit the bottom, the shard of glass he held caught in the floor. Somehow Harry's shoulder sank firmly over it. He screamed and the world wobbled hazily in front of his eyes as he saw the hooded figure charge down the stairs.

Ali leapt just as Harry raised his leg, catching him in mid-air. He landed with a thump; Harry heard the air as it was forced from his lungs. Ali crumpled back into the staircase, gasping theatrically as Harry writhed in pain on the floor. His vision wouldn't refocus but he could hear Ali starting to recover his breath.

Harry turned his head but failed to avoid the vicious kick to his face. One more to his stomach and he felt a choke-hold wrapping around his neck.

He felt the floor start to move beneath him as he was dragged down the corridor towards the cellar door. Glass cut through his clothes, the pain excruciating.

Then the blackness took over.

FIFTY-ONE

THE COW AND CALF Rocks were nothing more than two enormous black silhouettes against the starry sky. The rain clouds had cleared and in their wake the cold of a cloudless night was setting in.

Ronnie parked high in the car park, underneath the rocks so the vehicle would be invisible from the main road. In the far distance, fireworks exploded into the sky, Bradford in the full swing of Bonfire Night. He pictured Harry arriving back at Queensbury Tunnel to find it locked and deserted. He wasn't comfortable with Sarah's insistence to cut Harry out, but his focus had to be on ending this.

'We're on foot from here, I take it?' Enzo said to Ronnie. 'I need to get a look at this place. Would've been a damn sight easier if we'd got the location earlier. I don't like being blind.'

Ronnie checked his watch. 'Seven forty,' he said. He turned to Sarah, who was in the back seat, staring out of the window. 'Let's hope you're right about all this.'

Outside, Enzo opened the boot and pulled out two bulletproof vests.

'Give her one too,' Ronnie said.

Enzo threw one at Sarah.

She slipped it over the top of her burka.

Enzo handed Ronnie a gun, taking two for himself.

'I could—' started Sarah.

'Not a chance,' Enzo cut her short. He pointed towards the rocks. 'After you. Let's see what we're dealing with.'

Sarah didn't move.

Enzo and Ronnie exchanged a glance.

'Clock's ticking,' said Ronnie. 'You want to finish this or not?'

'Torch,' said Sarah.

Enzo handed her one. 'Now move.'

The three of them hurried forward, Sarah in the lead, trying to look as though she was uncertain of the terrain. She crested the smaller rock formation breathing heavily. At the base of the larger rock, Sarah stopped and shone the light up the steep sandstone incline.

'I'll wait till you're up,' said Enzo, shining the light on it. 'Makes it easier.'

Sarah slipped her torch into her pocket.

She started the climb.

'She's quick,' said Ronnie.

'Almost like she's done it before,' replied Enzo.

'You don't trust her?' asked Ronnie.

'Do you?'

'She's tricky. No doubt.'

Enzo nodded slowly, eyes never leaving Sarah.

'I don't trust anyone,' Ronnie said finally. 'Go,' he said, nodding at the rock as Sarah disappeared over the top.

As soon as Sarah reached the summit, she veered to her left and hurriedly uncovered the small rocks which, two hours earlier, Victor had used to conceal the black bag. Sarah had calculated that, in the darkness and with an uncertain ascent, it would take someone at least four minutes to reach the top.

Plenty of time.

She removed the bulletproof vest, then her burka, and used one of the rocks to carefully weight them to the ground before unzipping the bag. This was it; no margin for error.

By the time Enzo reached her, she needed to look exactly like before.

Once Sarah disappeared over the top, Enzo began his ascent. Ronnie waited till there was a gap of a dozen metres before he started.

At the top, they were brutally exposed to the elements, a gale ripping into them. Moving cautiously to the edge of the rock, they glanced at the ground below, but it was the distant view of Bradford that held their attention. Fireworks broke up dark skies with colourful bursts of light.

'Where?' Ronnie broke the spell, handing Sarah a pair of night-vision binoculars. She slipped them over her head, Enzo followed suit, both of them analysing the terrain ahead.

'There,' said Sarah, pointing just off to the left. 'You see it?'

'Got it,' said Enzo. 'Quarter mile. Farmhouse. Lights are on. One car outside, Mercedes.'

'You're sure that's the place?' Ronnie asked tentatively.

'That's it,' said Sarah.

'How can you be so certain?'

'Has to be. Billy said so.'

'If you'd kept him alive,' Ronnie couldn't help saying, 'this is the moment he'd have proved useful.'

'That's the place,' said Sarah, handing Ronnie the goggles.

'Down!' Enzo hissed, suddenly crouching low, stretching his legs out to lie flat on the rock, urging them to follow. 'Company,' he said, pointing to the east.

They dropped to the hard stone as an SUV drove close, past the rocks and on down the country lane.

Ronnie and Enzo watched intently as it slowed near the farm-house, before turning up the gravel driveway. The barbed-wire fencing was clear through their lenses.

The SUV manoeuvred around the Mercedes, and parked facing

the entrance. A powerful floodlight came on automatically, a spotlight on the car.

'Audi Q8, blacked-out windows,' Enzo recited. 'This is good, we'll get a visual on the driver.'

'Can I?' asked Sarah reaching for the binoculars.

'Not ye—' Enzo started. 'Boss?' his voice rose sharply.

'What?' said Ronnie, removing his goggles to look at Enzo's face. His neck was strained as he crept towards the edge of the rock.

'You've got to be kidding,' Enzo whispered.

'What is it?' asked Ronnie, puzzled by the unmistakable edge of panic in Enzo's voice.

Ronnie put his goggles back on but couldn't see anything new.

Sarah held her breath, ready.

'The licence plate,' said Enzo. 'Look at the fucking licence plate!'

Ronnie focused on it and when he realized what he was looking at, felt his heartbeat thud with a burning rage.

He lowered the binoculars and looked across at Sarah.

Her eyes were narrowed, her jaw set.

'You knew,' he said. '*You fucking well knew.*'

FIFTY-TWO

'SHIT!' SCREAMED ALI, SLAPPING his hands on the steering wheel. 'Shit! Shit! *Shit!*'

Everything was going to hell.

A whole year of planning and now, at the very last minute, Ali needed to come up with an alternative.

He drove recklessly towards the farmhouse.

Riz and the boss would be there by now.

Fucking Riz, nothing but a glorified accountant. Laundering dirty money through the boss's cab firm, safe behind his desk. He had no fucking idea how the real world worked.

Ali screamed; long, loud, pained.

Ruined.

He tried to calm himself. He'd got away with murder before. He didn't need to panic.

Why did you curse my house?

'Not now!' he shouted into the night.

Think, Ali, think.

The cellar was locked, both of them bound and gagged.

Ali braked suddenly.

Virdee.

What if Virdee found Olivia and wanted her for himself?

He shook his head, thoughts merging chaotically, considered a U-turn but decided against it. The farmhouse was only a mile away. He drove on.

The revolver on the passenger seat was a calming presence as Ali drove that final mile.

Soon, he would be leaving this town behind him. No longer would he live on the fringes of society.

He'd be rich after taking the boss's money, but most importantly Olivia would be his.

FIFTY-THREE

PERCY PULLED UP OUTSIDE Ronnie Virdee's cash-and-carry.

This was the heart of it.

The warehouse was closed, deserted. Virdee's employees would have left an hour before, and a calming darkness surrounded the depot. The silence was broken only by the intermittent fireworks in the clear sky.

Percy took the old packet of Capstan Full Strength cigarettes from his bag. He took a moment to admire the packaging: dull orange with a regal gold strip, with bold writing on the front that read 'Navy Cut Cigarettes'. The real deal. He held the last cigarette between his lips and lit it, taking a deep drag. He felt the familiar burning in his lungs.

He stared at the warehouse; it looked innocuous, just another place of business. But that was a lie. This was a breeding ground for misery.

He'd lost so much to this.

It was time for his own revenge. Percy was going to end Ronnie's toxic grip on the city.

His family had been ruined by the narcotics that Ronnie Virdee flooded the city with. If it hadn't been for the drugs, that gang who'd taken his granddaughter and others like her would never have stood a chance. Those young girls who had lost so much might still be safe in their homes.

Tonight Percy was going to cut them off at the source.

The truck screamed forward, its colossal weight crashing through locked metal entrance gates.

He backed up to the main shutter, positioning the truck centrally, leaving it in reverse.

There was a crescendo of metal buckling as forty-four tonnes of machinery smashed through the shuttered entrance of the cash-and-carry. Metal and glass rained down around him, the deafening noise of destruction as he forced the truck into the warehouse.

Something fell towards the windscreen. Percy threw himself to the side as a steel rod smashed through the glass, sending fragments showering around his body. He felt a sudden sharp shock in his right leg. The rear of the truck slammed against a steel girder and it came to an abrupt halt, juddering violently.

Alarms were sounding; a deafening wailing that made it hard to think straight.

Percy took a moment before he sat up again. His leg was bleeding badly.

So much blood.

He wasn't afraid of dying, but he wasn't ready to die just yet.

Percy opened the door of the truck, the security alarms shrill and threatening in the warehouse. He stumbled down the ladder, hitting the floor harder than he'd expected.

An animal noise escaped from his mouth.

A steel column had collapsed, splitting the truck in two, and petrol was pouring from the tank like water released from a dam. Percy was relieved. He'd intended to manually release the fuel but now all he had to do was light a match. He stared back into the cabin through the open driver's door where his cigarette had fallen to the floor, smoke rising from where it lay.

A final tribute to the greatest packet of cigarettes ever made.

The fumes were toxic, stinging his eyes, making it difficult to breathe. Percy staggered towards the cabin, using every last ounce of energy he had to climb back into the truck.

Inside, he lay across the front seat, reached for the cigarette with a shaky hand.

Time for one last drag.

He pulled the cigarette from his mouth, whispered a prayer asking for Sarah to finish what they had started, then threw the cigarette out into the warehouse. Just before the darkness took him, Percy saw the flames that would send everything Ronnie Virdee had ever worked for straight to hell.

FIFTY-FOUR

HARRY OPENED HIS EYES.

His mouth was coated with the metallic taste of blood and he felt a spasm of pain in his shoulder.

He struggled to breathe.

Saima.

Aaron.

Tara.

He glanced around the room. Everything was pink: the walls, the wardrobe and even the dressing table.

In the corner, bound and gagged on a child's bed, he saw the unconscious body of a little blonde girl.

Where the fuck am I?

He recalled the hooded figure, the fight. He must have found Ali.

Harry tried to move but his legs were taped together with thick brown parcel tape. So were his hands.

He closed his eyes, took a deep breath and forced himself to sit upright, trying to ignore the agonizing pain in his shoulder.

Sweat pouring down his face, his mind went into overdrive.

Ali's basement.

The bastard had created a prison cell for a very specific type of captive.

A dungeon for a princess.

Harry looked down. The tape around his hands had a little give, but he wasn't about to heroically break free. Just above the tape, he could see his watch: 19:40.

Get moving.

Somehow he had to let Ronnie know he had found Tara's murderer.

Defying the pain, he shuffled towards the sink in the corner. The blood from his slashed ankles must have saturated the tape wrapped around them; he could feel it loosening with each move.

He turned on the tap, hoping the hot water actually worked. When it started to flow, Harry put his bound hands underneath it. Even as the water scalded his skin, he kept his arms in place, rubbing his wrists together. The heat rendered the glue useless.

Less than a minute later, Harry's hands were free and he pulled the tape from his ankles, relieved the wounds looked superficial.

Harry could see the shard of glass embedded in his shoulder. It had closed the wound and limited his blood loss. It might just have to stay there for now.

He undid the little girl's restraints and tried to rouse her but she didn't respond.

After checking her vital signs, he returned to the sink, cupping cold water in his hands and splashing it on her cheeks, physically relieved when she started to stir.

He lifted a plastic cup from beside the sink, filled it with water and unceremoniously poured it over the little girl's face. She opened her eyes dramatically, looking at Harry with anger and then terror.

'It's OK,' said Harry, raising his hands passively, 'I'm the police.'

She saw the wound in his shoulder and screamed. The noise sent shock waves through Harry as he clamped his hand over her mouth. Her eyes widened with panic and she shuffled back against the wall, trying to break free.

'I'm a policeman,' he told her. 'I promise I am not going to hurt you.'

He relaxed his hand over her mouth but didn't let go.

'Is your name Olivia?' he asked.

She nodded, staring at him, terrified.

'I'm here to take you home, Olivia, to your mum, Lexi? That right?'

She nodded again and very slowly, Harry removed his hand and leaned back, putting his hands up passively.

'We need to get out of here, Olivia. So that I can get you home safely. Can you stay calm and trust me?'

She shook her head, staring in bewilderment around the room. Her breathing was laboured and Harry was afraid she would start hyperventilating if he didn't find a way to calm her soon.

He reached into his pocket for his ID, but it was missing. Son of a bitch upstairs must have taken it. It probably wouldn't have worked on a child anyway.

'I'm a detective.' He pointed to the glass in his shoulder. 'This happened when I was trying to save you.'

'I want my mummy,' she said in a soft whimper. 'There's a bad man in here! He said he was going to keep me! Please, I want my mummy.'

'I'm going to take you to her,' said Harry, smiling at her. 'Can you stand up?'

She shook her head.

Harry took a step away from her and lowered himself painfully to his knees, making himself as small and as unthreatening as possible. 'Bad people did this to you, Olivia. I'm going to arrest them, but first I need you to be brave for me. Can you do that?'

Slowly, she nodded her head then cautiously inched her way towards the edge of the bed and put her feet on the ground.

'Your . . . your . . . shoulder,' she said quietly.

Harry shook his head. 'It's OK.'

She stood up.

'Brilliant,' said Harry. 'Shall we get out of here?'

She nodded. A little more spark in her eyes now.

'Who did that to you?' she asked, taking a couple of steps towards him.

'A bad man. But don't worry, Olivia, I'm going to keep you safe. I think the door upstairs is locked, so I'm going to have to break it.'

She immediately shrank away from him, looking frantically around the room.

'I want to go home,' she said. 'I want to see my mum and Big Bee.'

He tugged the duvet off the bed with his good arm. 'Here,' he said, handing it to her. 'Wrap this around yourself.'

Harry watched as she did as she was told.

'Big Bee?' he asked.

'Uncle Billy. We were supposed to be moving to London.'

'What happened?'

'I don't remember.'

'What's the last thing you remember, Olivia? It's really important.'

As Olivia told Harry what little she could recall about the farmhouse and what had happened to her, Harry grabbed a small towel that he'd seen by the sink. He was going to have to get this glass out of his shoulder. If Ali was still in the house, he'd need to be able to fight back.

He glanced over his shoulder to make sure Olivia couldn't see what he was doing, then wrapped the towel around his right hand and grabbed the glass in his shoulder.

'What else, Olivia?' he asked, trying to keep his voice relaxed. 'Tell me everything you can remember.'

While she told him about the iPhone Big Bee had bought her and the toys and DVDs, Harry gritted his teeth and slowly, agonizingly, pulled the glass free, forcing the air from his lungs in a long and controlled breath.

'I . . . I . . . don't remember anything else,' said Olivia.

Harry reached for the pillow and removed the pillowcase, using it to make a clumsy tourniquet around his shoulder. He tied it off with one hand and his teeth. It wasn't ideal, but it would have to do.

'Good girl, you're being very brave. Now I need you to wait here a moment.'

He crept up the wooden staircase. In two brutal kicks, the locks smashed and Harry braced himself for confrontation.

No sign of movement. He let the silence linger while he stared into the dark corridor, listening.

Then he turned and waved for Olivia to join him. Reluctantly, taking agonizingly slow steps, she started to climb.

As she reached the top, Harry put his finger across his lips. She was crying quietly and, in spite of the duvet wrapped around her body, shivering.

Harry crouched and whispered, 'Olivia, do you want me to carry you?'

In the car, Harry tried to reassure her, but it was clear the only thing that would calm Olivia now was being reunited with her mother. He reached for his phone, but that too was missing.

He started the car.

'Olivia,' he asked, 'can you tell me anything else about where you were?'

Wrapped in the duvet on the passenger seat next to him, the little girl huddled against the door, sobbing for her mother.

'Olivia,' he said, more sternly than he'd intended, 'your mummy's in danger. I am going to rescue her, but I need your help. Please, tell me anything you remember about the house you were in. Had you been there before? Did you know the place? When you looked out of the window, what could you see?'

'It's a big place,' she said through broken sobs. 'Like *really* big. There's no other houses for miles and miles.'

'Good, keep going.'

'There . . . there . . . were big rocks,' said Olivia. 'I could see them from my bedroom.'

'Rocks?'

She nodded. 'When Big Bee drove us there, he told me what they were called, but I can't remember.'

'How big were they?'

'Really big – even bigger than the house. Big Bee said they were famous, that people climb them.'

Harry sighed. It didn't exactly narrow the options down in Yorkshire.

As he entered the city centre, heading for the hospital, Harry pulled the car over. In the boot, he found his iPad and hurried back to the driver's seat. He opened Google Images and typed in 'Yorkshire famous rocks'.

'Here,' he said, passing Olivia the iPad. 'Any of these look familiar?'

She looked down at the screen, shaking her head.

'Brimham? Cow and Calf?' Harry urged.

'That one!' she said, looking up at him triumphantly. 'The Cow! I remember, there was a pub we passed and that was its name. I thought it was funny!'

'The Cow and Calf Inn?'

'Yes!' she said.

'You, Olivia Goodwin, are a very clever little girl,' Harry told her.

FIFTY-FIVE

RONNIE LOOKED AT THE diplomatic licence plates in disbelief.

'Who the fuck is it?' he asked Sarah, lowering his night-vision goggles. 'Who've you kept hidden from us?'

'It's Faisal Abdul Shah, the Pakistani foreign minister, and his bodyguard, Qaseem, head of the ISI, the Pakistani Secret Service.'

'Christ! What are we supposed to do now?'

She shrugged. 'Nothing's changed.'

Enzo and Ronnie both sighed.

'It's only two men,' Sarah pressed on. 'Surely you can make them disappear.'

'They're fucking untouchables,' said Ronnie. 'They're diplomats – they disappear, there's going to be a massive investigation.'

'Are you really that stupid?' said Enzo, sidling up next to his boss.

'She is,' said Ronnie, scowling at her. 'She really is. You should have told us.'

'You would have backed off.'

'You're damn right. I'm here for Ali. Not some diplomatic shit-storm,' said Ronnie.

'They're all connected to the same thing,' said Sarah.

'For you, maybe.'

'I didn't come this far to quit.' Sarah looked him in the eye; she had to get this right. 'Because of them, your daughter is dead. You remember your daughter, don't you?'

'You talk to me like that again, little girl, and I'll throw you off this fucking rock.'

'Tara was in this with me. You want to avenge her death? We take them all out.'

Ronnie spread his hands flat on the rock. He turned to Enzo. 'Can it be done?'

'Are you serious?'

'Can. It. Be. Done?'

Ronnie was stony-faced.

'Yes,' replied Enzo. 'Doing it isn't the issue, it's the clearing up.'

'We'll torch the place,' said Sarah. 'Then you make the cars disappear and take the bodies to that crematorium of yours.'

Ronnie was startled.

'Tara told me.'

'It's messy, boss,' said Enzo. 'Risky.'

Ronnie stood up and turned to face the farmhouse. 'Get eyes on that place,' he said.

'Two guys are getting out of the car,' Enzo began a muted commentary.

'Sarah, take these,' Ronnie said, handing her his night-vision binoculars, 'give me confirmation it's them.'

She looked through them. 'Yes.' She swallowed hard. 'They're approaching the house. Ringing the doorbell,' she said.

'Door's opening,' said Enzo. 'Can't see who's inside. They're in.'

'Another car coming,' said Sarah, 'from the opposite direction, down the hill.'

Ronnie took the goggles from her.

A battered Ford Focus pulled into the driveway, parked next to the Audi.

'Small guy. Hood,' said Enzo.

'Could be Ali,' said Sarah.

'Short? Stocky? Face covered,' said Ronnie.

'That's him,' she said, 'can I see?'

Ronnie stepped aside, handed her the goggles again.

'Definitely him,' she said.

'Give her a gun,' said Ronnie to Enzo.

'What?' replied Enzo, lowering his binoculars.

'It's a three-man takedown. Minimum. We're going in,' said Ronnie.

Enzo didn't look convinced. Ronnie glared at him.

'Fine,' said Enzo. 'When we get off this rock – not before. Does she even know how to use one?'

'She's more than capable,' Ronnie said, looking at Sarah. 'Aren't you?'

Sarah didn't reply.

The men disappeared down the rock, Enzo first, then Ronnie.

Standing alone, feeling like she was on top of the world, Sarah slipped her hand underneath her burka, carrying out her final checks.

'Time to end this,' she whispered. 'Time for you all to die.'

FIFTY-SIX

OLIVIA WAS SAFE IN A & E with Saima's colleagues.

Harry pulled into the Cow and Calf car park, saw Ronnie's Range Rover parked at the top and accelerated towards it.

What's he doing here?

He inspected the vehicle but it was empty, doors locked. Harry scoured the area, frantically looking for any sign of his brother.

Then in the distance, somewhere beyond the giant rocks, he heard the muffled sound of a gunshot.

Ronnie, Enzo and Sarah were by the side of the farmhouse, figuring out their strategy. Enzo was about to make his move when they heard the crack of gunfire from inside the farmhouse.

'Something's happening!' said Sarah.

Ronnie and Enzo looked at each other.

'Dissent in the ranks,' said Enzo.

Ronnie ran to the house, pressed his back to the wall underneath the window and froze as the security lighting triggered. He waited for a presence at the window and when it didn't arrive, he cautiously turned and peered over the window ledge.

Two men were on their knees. A smaller guy with his hood up

was pointing a gun at them. Nobody had noticed the security lighting come on outside because they were all focused on the spread-eagled body of what looked like the bodyguard, blood pooling from his head.

Ali was double-crossing the boss.

Ronnie hurried back.

'Perfect,' said Enzo. 'He wastes the other two and, on his way out, we take *him* down.'

'I want Faisal,' hissed Sarah.

'He's not my priority—' started Ronnie.

He'd thought Sarah was reaching out to remonstrate with him. Instead, she snatched his gun and took off running.

'Shit!' muttered Enzo, grabbing for her.

But she was gone before they could stop her.

Sarah shot the lock on the door, then aimed another bullet at the living room window, knowing the shattering glass would distract Ali from the first shot. She fired again as she charged in.

Without hesitation, Sarah shot at Ali, hitting him in the arm. The bullet sent his body spinning across the room. Riz and Faisal were face-down on the floor, hands over their heads. Sarah stooped to pick Ali's gun from the floor where he had dropped it before he fell.

One gun in each hand, she held the attention of the room.

Harry heard more shots and ran back to his car.

He sped down the dirt track towards the noise and saw a farmhouse on his right. Pulling his car off the road, he killed the engine and lowered his window, listening.

The house had lost a front window and the door was only partially closed. He rushed to his boot, grabbing everything that might be of use: the bulletproof vest, his taser and the fifty-shot firework.

Ronnie and Enzo were in the living room, weapons drawn. Their eyes were wide in the wake of Sarah's entrance.

'Impressive,' said Enzo, moving towards her.

Ronnie glared at Ali's body writhing on the ground. Tara's murderer. Nobody else in the room mattered.

Ali was groaning on the floor, clutching his shattered arm, the hoodie still covering his face.

Riz and Faisal remained motionless.

'Who are you?' Faisal asked, his eyes lingering on Sarah for a moment.

'Don't you recognize me with my fucking clothes on, bastard?'

Sarah spat on him, the gun shaking in her hands. The composure of her entry had given way to incandescent rage. The sight of her abuser brought back harrowing memories of the weight of him on top of her, being forced to parade around naked or scantily dressed for his perverse pleasure.

'Sarah—' Ronnie started. He cut himself off when Sarah stepped behind Enzo and cracked the base of her gun into his spine. Enzo's legs gave way underneath him and his gun flew out of his hand.

Sarah pressed one weapon into Enzo's neck, using him as a human shield, then trained the other on Ronnie.

'Drop your gun, Ronnie,' she said.

'What the fuck?' he replied.

'Drop it,' she said.

He shook his head in disbelief.

'Are you a good enough shot to miss him and hit me?' she said.

'No. But if the first hits him, the second one's yours.'

Faisal was starting to move on the floor, sensing a chance to escape.

'Starting to lose focus here, Sarah,' said Ronnie, nodding in Faisal's direction. 'You want to give these guys the upper hand?'

Sarah stepped away from Enzo as Ronnie tensed, preparing to fire.

Keeping hold of one weapon, she placed the other in her pocket. Using her free hand, she removed the bulletproof vest Ronnie had given her and lifted her burka to reveal what was concealed underneath.

Ronnie's mouth dropped open and a tremor shook his firing arm.

Sarah stared at him coldly. 'Put it the fuck down.'

Harry ran towards the farmhouse, stopping where his brother had stopped only moments before.

There were three cars outside the house and only now did Harry see the Pakistani diplomatic plates on the Audi. *Fuck.* The ground he was standing on suddenly seemed shaky and he placed the firework on the floor, trying to understand what the hell he was looking at.

The boss.

He thought about what Billy had said:

You've no idea how powerful an enemy you are taking on.

'Christ,' he hissed.

Harry could hear Ronnie's voice through the window and hurried towards it.

Ronnie was staring in disbelief at Sarah, who was wearing a suicide vest and holding a detonator. Where the hell had she got that from?

'Drop the gun,' said Sarah, 'or I'll trigger the vest.'

'You'll die as well.' Ronnie's eyes never left her trigger hand, his gun trained on her forehead.

'Haven't you realized that whether I live or die isn't important?'

She retreated to the back wall so she could see all of them – Faisal, Riz, Ali and Ronnie.

'Got you,' she said. 'Every last one.'

'Sarah?' Faisal interrupted them, rising to his knees.

'Yes, Faisal, it's me,' said Sarah, revelling in his shock. Revelling at seeing him on his knees at her mercy.

'It cannot be,' he said, shaking his head.

'You were double-crossed by your own men,' she said, and looked around the room.

Ali lay still, watching the scene from underneath his hoodie, tightly clutching his arm.

'You cannot kill me,' Faisal cried. 'I am a diplomat. I am protected!'

'Fuck you, Faisal. I was nothing but Girl Zero to you. A test slave, your first white girl. There are so many lives you've ruined since then and all because you got away with it the first time, with me. Well you're not getting away with it any more.'

Sarah shot him in the groin. No hesitation.

He collapsed, writhing in front of her, screaming in agony.

Sarah pressed the gun to the back of his head and pulled the trigger, sending brain and bone fragments across the room.

Riz started screaming like a child. Sarah shot him too, one in the groin and another in the head.

Ronnie was counting the bullets.

One for the door.

Two when she came in.

One for Ali.

Two each for Faisal and Riz.

She's out.

Sarah dropped the .357 Smith and Wesson revolver on the floor and switched to Ali's gun, keeping the detonator tight in her other hand.

'I was trained well,' she said, seeing the disappointment in Ronnie's face.

'Trained?' he replied.

Sarah ignored him, turning her focus and the gun on Ali. 'Take off that hood so I can see who I'm executing.'

'No,' said Ronnie, interrupting her. '*He's mine.* You've had your revenge. Even if you're going to kill me, at least let me have my revenge.'

'Revenge?' said Ali, struggling to his knees, still clutching his bleeding arm.

'You killed my daughter,' said Ronnie.
'I didn't,' said Ali.

Outside, Harry heard Ali's confusion.

He put the fifty-shot firework on the floor but the fuse was only a couple of inches long. He searched his pockets for something to lengthen it with.

'I know you did.'

'She was already dead when I got there,' said Ali.

'You're lying,' hissed Ronnie.

Ali shook his head.

'You're lying,' Ronnie said again, becoming increasingly agitated.

'No, he's not,' Sarah said, her gaze now fixed on Ronnie.

'This all started with drugs,' Sarah continued, gripping the detonator tight. 'For years you've flooded this city with heroin and other shit that gives people like Billy and Ali power over their victims. You think you're not involved?' she spat mockingly. 'It all starts with you.'

Ronnie shook his head. 'That's bullshit.'

'Says the man who doesn't realize it cost him his daughter.'

Ronnie opened his mouth to protest, then stopped.

'You?' he whispered.

She nodded.

'You used my daughter to get to me?' Ronnie gritted his teeth, fists clenched, anger rising.

'No – *you* used your daughter, buying her off so you could protect yourself.'

'I don't believe you,' he said.

'It was finding out who you were that was the hardest part. Tonight – your warehouse? Gone. Greatest bonfire the city has ever seen. Your family, broken. The empire you built, ruined.' Sarah nodded at the others in the room. 'I've taken out the whole chain.'

*

Harry listened to Sarah's confession, momentarily stunned. Somehow he needed to get inside, before she blew the place apart.

Saima's taweez.

Harry broke the necklace then put the scroll back in his pocket. Attaching the thread to the fuse should buy him the time he needed.

He lit it and headed for the front door.

'You kill us and Olivia dies,' Ali shouted in desperation.

'No,' said Harry. 'Olivia's safe.'

They all turned to see him standing in the doorway.

'Harry?' whispered Ronnie, but Harry didn't look at him. He just carried on walking slowly towards Sarah, his hands raised in a calming gesture.

'Stop,' she said, waving the detonator at him. Harry kept inching towards her, stopping when he reached her outstretched hand, still clutching the switch.

He had to get this right first time.

'Olivia was at Ali's house,' he said, glancing at the hooded figure. 'She's safe now. I dropped her in A & E.'

'You're lying!' shouted Ali, hope strangling his voice.

They ignored him.

'Just walk,' Harry said softly. 'That way you win. You got them all. Ronnie's my problem now.'

'You shouldn't have come,' she said angrily. 'You're not like him, I know that now. I tried to keep you away!'

'You did,' said Harry gently, 'because you're not a bad person.'

Harry was doing all he could to force the image of her killing Tara from his mind.

'Ronnie can't live,' said Sarah, shaking her head.

'You've already destroyed him. Everything he has is gone.'

'He'll start again.'

'He's under arrest,' replied Harry.

'You wouldn't.'

The firework exploded with a deafening boom directly outside the window. As Harry had hoped, Sarah's focus turned instantly toward the sound. In that moment, Harry snatched the trigger from her, while driving the elbow of his other arm into her face. The impact sent her crashing unconscious into the wall. She dropped the gun.

Ali got there first, seizing the weapon and shooting twice at Harry.

Ronnie was already on him, smashing the butt of his gun into the boy's face, breaking his nose. Ronnie fired a shot into Ali's hood, sending his body careering into the wall alongside Sarah.

As Harry hit the floor, both bullets thudding into his vest, the switch fell from his hand. He rolled on to his side, trying to get air back into his lungs, and watched helplessly as Ronnie removed Sarah's suicide vest from her unconscious body and dragged her out of the front door.

FIFTY-SEVEN

HARRY STRUGGLED TO HIS feet and removed his bulletproof vest, feeling for broken ribs.

He looked around at the carnage in the room.

'Shit,' he whispered, his breathing so ragged it was an effort to form the word.

Four dead bodies and an unconscious Enzo, blood everywhere . . .

A political nightmare waiting to get out.

But Harry couldn't worry about Faisal now; he needed to get to Ronnie. Sarah deserved to be punished for what she'd done, but not the way Ronnie had in mind.

Harry got in his car and drove recklessly up the hill. He parked next to Ronnie's Range Rover and almost fell out of the driver's side.

Harry scoured the area and saw torches flickering by the base of the Cow and Calf Rocks. He hurried towards them, the incline brutal on his lungs, the pain in his shoulder boiling like lava as he reached the summit of the smaller rock.

Sarah was on her knees.

Ronnie had a gun to her temple.

'Don't,' shouted Harry.

Ronnie didn't acknowledge him. His every ounce of focus was on Sarah.

'You killed Tara – for what? To get me? You want to come at me, you don't go through my baby!'

When Sarah replied, she looked at Harry, not Ronnie. 'You must really love him to do what you just did.'

'I didn't do it for Ronnie,' replied Harry. 'I did it for my mother.'

'He makes you weak,' Sarah said. 'But you already know that.'

'Hey!' Ronnie kicked her, sending Sarah sprawling across the ground, closer to the lip of the rock. 'You want to worry about yourself.'

'Ronnie—' started Harry.

The gun was suddenly turned on him. 'You'd best get walking,' Ronnie told him, his voice seething with rage.

Harry shook his head. 'You can't end it like this.'

'Are you *defending* her?'

'No. But she's right about one thing. This is your doing. This all started with you.'

'Can you hear yourself? She killed *Tara*! Harry, she fucking *killed my daughter*!' he screamed.

Harry flinched. He'd kill her himself if he were a different man.

'She'll answer for that,' replied Harry, taking tiny steps towards his brother. 'But with cuffs around her wrists, not a bullet in her head. You do this? I've got to take you in. I'm not bluffing, Ron. She's damaged, no doubt. But not like the rest of them,' he said, nodding back towards the farmhouse.

Ronnie opened the revolver, removing all the bullets except one.

'Karma. You obsess about it, don't you, Harry?'

He spun the barrel, dragging Sarah to her knees and placing the gun at her temple once more.

'Eight to one.'

Sarah raised her chin. 'After he puts a bullet in me, it's on you, Harry. Protect this city. Protect girls like me from monsters like him. Otherwise I'll be forced to curse you, and I'm going to be far worse than that door you can't knock on.'

Her eyes shifted to Ronnie. 'You might think you've won, but you're always losing. Every day you disrespect your daughter's death by doing what you do. She was innocent – that's something *I* have to live with.'

Ronnie pressed the gun to her head and pulled the trigger.

Sarah didn't flinch at the sound of an empty chamber.

'Ronnie!' Harry saw nothing but rage in his brother's face.

'You want the truth? Tara fucking hated you,' said Sarah, spitting on the ground. 'That's what you were to her.'

Ronnie fired again. Another empty chamber.

'Don't!' urged Harry. 'If you do—'

'You'll what?' Ronnie turned to face him. 'You risked your life to save me, just so you could kill me five minutes later?'

Harry shrugged.

'And Mum?' asked Ronnie.

'Ronnie? Put. The. Gun. Down.'

In that instant, Harry saw he would never win this argument.

He lunged, striking the gun from Ronnie's hand and taking him to ground.

The brothers scrambled in the dirt, adrenaline masking the pain in Harry's shoulder.

After everything they had been through, it all came down to this: who would get to his feet first?

Ronnie trapped Harry in a choke-hold, rolling them both to Sarah's feet.

While they were fighting, she'd gone for the gun.

'Don't,' said Harry to Sarah. Ronnie relaxed the choke-hold.

Sarah opened the barrel and put the lone bullet into the right slot. 'You going to move?' she said to Harry. 'I don't want to hit the wrong brother.'

Harry shook his head and stayed in front of Ronnie. 'Don't, Sarah.'

'After all this,' she said bitterly. 'You think I'm not going to finish the job?'

'Look at what you've done,' hissed Ronnie to Harry.

'I killed your niece,' said Sarah. 'And I did much worse than that in Pakistan to get here.' Sarah turned the gun and put it underneath her chin. 'If I miss Ronnie? You'll arrest me. If I hit Ronnie, you'll arrest me.' Sarah got on her knees.

'You don't get your revenge, Ronnie, not tonight.'

Harry followed Sarah's glance down to the tattoo on her hand. *GZ. Girl Zero.*

'You need to stop him, Harry,' said Sarah. 'If you don't?' She closed her eyes. 'This moment will haunt you far worse than that green door you can't knock on.' Then she tensed her jaw, and as the tears ran down her face she pulled the trigger.

FIFTY-EIGHT

HARRY TURNED AWAY FROM Sarah's body.

Ronnie remained by his side, arms folded, head bowed. Not out of respect for Sarah but because he knew tonight was the end.

'You're toxic,' whispered Harry. 'Everything about you. I'm always going to be in the firing line. *Always.*'

'Walk away,' replied Ronnie.

'Not like this.' Harry nodded down the hill towards the farmhouse. 'Four dead, Ronnie. What are you not seeing here?'

'Bradford won't miss them.'

Harry shook his head, exhaling deeply. Turning finally to look at Sarah.

'I never groomed her,' Ronnie protested.

'Come on.'

'If it hadn't been drugs, it would've been booze. If not booze, something else. You can't pin their evil on me.'

'Just let it go. You've got enough money.'

'It's not about money.'

'Then what?'

'Bradford. I'm changing this city.'

'Look at what's just happened. Are you fucking blind?'

305

Ronnie remained silent, stony-faced.

'We need to clean this up,' said Ronnie.

'Without you, there'd be nothing to clean.'

'I've told you before; you remove me and someone else rises to the top, someone you can't work with.'

'Does it look like we're working together?'

'Every business has a bad week.'

'*A bad week?* A bad fucking week? Is that what Tara's death is to you? Jesus Christ—'

'Hey!' Ronnie stepped in front of Harry so they were eye to eye. 'You lose a child? Then you get to talk about it. Until then, shut the fuck up.'

For the first time, Harry could see his father's rage and inability to back down in Ronnie's eyes. It made him step back.

'What have you become?' he whispered.

'By dawn, there'll be no trace.'

Harry looked at Sarah. 'And her?'

Ronnie gritted his teeth. 'I'll feed her to the fucking dogs.'

Harry's body tensed.

'You deal with her then,' Ronnie sighed. 'We're on the moors. You want a shovel?'

Harry pushed him. 'Don't you test me, Ronnie.'

'Why? What are you going to do about it? Shit, you can't get some teenage prick who burgled our store twenty years ago out of your head.'

'You can't hold that over me for ever.'

'I can. I will. It's put us here. You don't like it? Too fucking bad.'

'This has to stop,' said Harry. 'You're done.'

'I've got a mess to clean up. Don't make threats you can't see through.'

Harry lifted Sarah's body from the ground, cradling her in his arms. 'You see this?'

Ronnie stared into Harry's eyes.

'She's a child.'

'She could have taken the shot at me.' Ronnie stood his ground, returning Harry's glare. 'Go home, little brother. We're done here.'

Harry felt Sarah's blood dripping through his fingers. He was taken back twenty years. Blood soiling his karma.

He thought about her last words. How this moment would haunt him as much as 19 Belle Avenue. Harry replaced her body on the ground. He picked up the gun, covered in Sarah's blood, and handed it to Ronnie. 'You've got bullets in your pocket?'

Ronnie nodded.

'Right here, right now; I want you to remember I gave you a choice. If you don't want me to bring you down, this is your chance.'

Ronnie sniggered. 'You love this macho shit, don't you?'

'If you walk from this? If you choose that life? I'm coming for you, Ronnie. This city needs rid.'

Ronnie took the weapon from Harry, removed a bullet from his pocket and loaded it into the gun. He forced it back into Harry's hand, raising it to his own temple.

'How about I give *you* the choice, little brother?' Ronnie let go, leaving Harry with his finger on the trigger. 'You choose: your brother or your damn city.'

Harry tensed his hand, seeing more and more of his father in Ronnie. If one man had never changed, what hope was there for the other?

End this now.

Harry's jaw quivered. 'I want to,' he whispered. 'Believe me, I want to.'

Ronnie closed his eyes. 'Here. Is this better?'

'Shit!' screamed Harry, throwing the gun to the floor. 'Shit!'

'Go home. We're done.'

Harry turned away, lifting Sarah's body once more. He hated what she had done but couldn't leave her for Ronnie to throw to the dogs. With moonlight casting his shadow long across the moors, fireworks exploding in the distance and the Cow and Calf Rocks looming above him, he walked away from his brother, knowing their relationship was over.

Knowing Bradford had room for only one of them.

AUTHOR'S NOTE

Girl Zero is a work of fiction and, to that effect, the timings of Diwali and Ramadan within the book are not accurately reflected.

ACKNOWLEDGEMENTS

Thank you, once again, to my friend Vinod Lalji – I don't know what I would do without you! You're always there for crisis management and to help me create anarchy with the plot.

Darcy Nicholson – my stellar editor. For a writer to be unable to find the words to describe just how hard you have worked with me must be a first! Thank you for always offering solutions to problems and for keeping me on-point. Quite simply – you rock.

My publisher at Transworld, Bill Scott-Kerr, and my agent, Simon Trewin, for launching Harry Virdee into the mainstream. Guys, you started something far removed from 'ordinary' and I'm very grateful.

Thank you to every member of the team at Transworld for collectively working so hard on *Girl Zero* and for shaping it into the book it has become.

Thanks to former DCI Stephen Snow for allowing me to pester you even when you were working in a different continent! Any police errors in the book are strictly mine, but having your support has been invaluable.

The 'Crime and Publishment' team for weekly encouragement and help when it was needed. It is so important to have a network of peers who are never more than a social-media click away. I look forward to more 'word-count-Wednesday' competitiveness!

Morgen Bailey for an early analysis of the book and for your constant positivity.

To my family for allowing me to become (more) anti-social than usual, and for their unwavering support.

Final words, as always, for my wife. A famous author once said, '. . . *write for one special person . . .*'

And I do.

When I see you completely lost in the world I've created, it makes it all worthwhile. A sly smile, the widening of your eyes or the shedding of a tear – it is in those exclusive moments, when words become emotions, that 'team A. A. Dhand' wins.

So keep doing what you do – it makes me do what I do.

About the author

A. A. Dhand was raised in Bradford and spent his youth observing the city from behind the counter of a small convenience store. After qualifying as a pharmacist, he worked in London and travelled extensively before returning to Bradford to start his own business and begin writing. The history, diversity and darkness of the city have inspired his Harry Virdee novels.